CUT TO THE BONE

CUT TO THE BONE

A HOLLIS GRANT MYSTERY

JOAN BOSWELL

DUNDURN
TORONTO

Copyright © Joan Boswell, 2012

All rights reserved. No part of this publication may be reproduced, stored in a retrieval system, or transmitted in any form or by any means, electronic, mechanical, photocopying, recording, or otherwise (except for brief passages for purposes of review) without the prior permission of Dundurn Press. Permission to photocopy should be requested from Access Copyright.

Editor: Allister Thompson
Design: Jesse Hooper
Printer: Webcom

Library and Archives Canada Cataloguing in Publication

Boswell, Joan
 Cut to the bone : a Hollis Grant mystery / Joan Boswell.

Issued also in electronic formats.
ISBN 978-1-4597-0207-3

 I. Title.

PS8603.O88C8825 2012   C813'.6   C2012-901546-6

1 2 3 4 5   16 15 14 13 12

We acknowledge the support of the **Canada Council for the Arts** and the **Ontario Arts Council** for our publishing program. We also acknowledge the financial support of the **Government of Canada** through the **Canada Book Fund** and **Livres Canada Books**, and the **Government of Ontario** through the **Ontario Book Publishing Tax Credit** and the **Ontario Media Development Corporation**.

Care has been taken to trace the ownership of copyright material used in this book. The author and the publisher welcome any information enabling them to rectify any references or credits in subsequent editions.

J. Kirk Howard, President

Printed and bound in Canada.

VISIT US AT
Dundurn.com | Definingcanada.ca | @dundurnpress | Facebook.com/dundurnpress

Dundurn	Gazelle Book Services Limited	Dundurn
3 Church Street, Suite 500	White Cross Mills	2250 Military Road
Toronto, Ontario, Canada	High Town, Lancaster, England	Tonawanda, NY
M5E 1M2	LA1 4XS	U.S.A. 14150

For Nick, Katie, Francis, Trevor, Christy, Brendan, and Tyler

ACKNOWLEDGEMENTS

I would like to thank Allister Thompson and Sylvia McConnell at Dundurn for their support and editing as well as my writing group, Barbara Fradkin, Mary Jane Maffini, Sue Pike, and Linda Wiken, who carefully read the manuscript before it was submitted. Also thanks to my family for always being there for me.

ONE

HOLLIS Grant slumped in her uncomfortable office chair thinking that she hadn't expected her life to turn out this way. When she'd read the advertisement in the *Toronto Star*, it had seemed like the answer to a prayer.

"Immediate vacancy for mid-size apartment building superintendent. Salary and two bedroom apartment."

She'd rationalized that the job wouldn't be as time-consuming as being a community college professor, her former occupation. It would give her time to paint as well as providing a bedroom for her eleven-year-old foster daughter, Jay Brownelly. She'd grabbed the bait like a hungry trout and signed a year's contract without investigating further. That had been in February. Now, three months later in early May, she hoped she'd made the right decision.

The apartment building had surprised her. Four years earlier a developer had bought the elegant but aging eight-storey building and begun renovations working from the roof down. He'd completed work on the top four floors, where he'd ripped out walls to create large apartments and added upscale bathrooms, granite countertops, the best of the best. To match their luxury he'd upgraded the lobby, the gym, the party room, the guest apartment, the office, and the security system — all located on the first floor. But he'd gone broke before he reached the lower floors. The next owner sold the renovated apartments and charged high monthly maintenance fees.

Initially, all the building's balconies had been condemned as unsafe, and those on the top four floors had been refurbished. Now, scaffolding festooned the lower floors and a Dumpster squatted on the ground below a chute for the disposal of the disintegrating concrete.

Small rental apartments crowded floors two, three, and four. The super's apartment on the first floor across the hall from the spiffy office retained its original fixtures. The tenants, a mix of seniors, students, and middle-class single women, lived in cramped quarters and frequently needed tradespeople to attend to their decaying wiring and plumbing. Hollis found that responding to the tenants' demands took up more time than she had hoped.

The building reminded her of an aging movie star. The surgery, the Botox, and the hair extensions couldn't conceal the aged hands, the thickening waist and ankles.

Hollis hadn't envisaged being quite as busy as she was, and every day she rose hoping for a few hours to dedicate to painting. Sitting in her office she thought longingly of the half-finished painting on the easel in her apartment. Should she play hooky and ignore several phone messages from tenants? Not a good idea. Reluctantly, she left the office door open and anchored a baby gate in the apartment doorway to allow her two dogs, Barlow and MacTee, to see her.

She played the machine's messages, dealt with them, answered mail, called the plumber to arrange an appointment for a second-floor apartment's blocked toilet, and leaned back. She glanced at the wall clock and pushed herself away from her desk, a large, ostentatious chrome and mahogany job bought by the high-end renovator.

Eleven thirty. Could she spend time on the painting before she collected Jay? She ran her hands through her curly blonde hair and repositioned her red-framed glasses on her nose. More than three hours before she leashed her over-exuberant Flat-coated Retriever puppy, Barlow, and her Golden Retriever, MacTee, and walked to Jay's school. She believed the child was more than capable of walking home, but Jay's father, still playing a role in his daughter's life, insisted that she be accompanied to and from school. Hollis used the walk for her own and her dogs' exercise.

Barlow and Jay, both recent additions to her life, provided an equal measure of pain and pleasure. Given the constraints imposed by the job, the dogs, and the child, it seemed likely that the year she'd allotted to establish herself as a full-time artist might not be enough to provide a true test.

"Sorry to bother you," a voice said.

Both dogs barked.

Hollis looked up to see a slim, brown-eyed young woman clutching a green plastic shopping bag hovering in the doorway. Her long, shiny black hair framed an anxious face.

Ginny Wuttenee, a new tenant on the fifth floor, had dropped in several times before to talk to Hollis and ask for information about Toronto.

"No bother. What can I do for you?" Hollis asked.

Ginny caught her lower lip between her teeth and frowned. "I have a problem…."

"Tell me," Hollis said, hoping it would be a simple one. She might just get in an hour on the painting if nothing else intervened.

Ginny stepped into the room, leaned on the doorframe, and looked ready to bolt momentarily. "The painters are doing Sabrina's living room."

Sabrina. Hollis ran through the photo gallery of tenants she knew and fastened on a long-legged, blue-eyed brunette who also lived on the fifth. Sabrina Trepanier loved dogs and had dropped in several times to pat MacTee and Barlow.

"Yes, I know Sabrina."

"Her apartment is being painted. She's allergic, so she slept in my small bedroom last night. This morning when I got up I didn't hear her. I went out to buy croissants and groceries at Bruno's." She chewed on her lip. "I didn't take my key. I figured she'd be up by the time I got back, because we'd agreed to go shopping and have a late lunch at a Japanese restaurant, because I've never eaten sushi. Sabrina has been really nice to me since I moved in." She placed the bag at her feet. "I've rung the buzzer, phoned her cell phone, tried the land line, and I don't get an answer. I guess she must have gone out early, but I can't imagine why. Will you let me into my apartment?"

"Of course. And don't worry about bothering me. That's what I'm here for and you're not the first person to leave without taking a key." Hollis stood up, unlocked a wall cabinet, and removed a ring of keys, relieved that the problem was nothing more serious than a forgotten key.

"Maybe she's a heavy sleeper. Give her another call," she temporized.

Ginny whipped out her cell phone, tapped in the number and listened. She snapped it shut. "I get *not available, leave a message.*"

"Give me a minute to lock up."

"I'm really sorry to bother you," Ginny said, again shifting her bag from hand to hand. "It's probably nothing. Maybe Sabrina was up really late and took a sleeping pill. I do that sometimes. You have to sleep, and since they started work on the balconies there's banging and crashing all day. When will they finish?" She grinned ruefully. "The truth is I shouldn't complain because I hate absolute quiet. When I moved in it surprised me and made me happy that the builder wired every room for sound. I play CDs or leave an easy listening station on night and day."

"Why don't you like the quiet?" Hollis asked as she removed the baby gate and shut the dogs inside the apartment.

"I don't know. I guess I always listen to see if something or somebody is creeping up on me. I know it's weird, but I've been like that for a long time. I come from Saskatchewan and sometimes when the wind stops blowing, it's so quiet the silence hurts your ears."

"Lucky for you that you have the music. The balconies should be repaired by the end of July," Hollis said, leading the way to the elevator, where she pushed the button for five.

Ginny followed Hollis into the elevator and set the bag on the polished floor. "I really like Sabrina and we have fun. Since I moved in she's taken me shopping and we went to see George Clooney's last movie. She's been really, really nice," she said as if this explained something.

They exited at five and moved silently along the thickly carpeted hall. At Ginny's door Hollis rang the buzzer. Musical tones but no response. Hollis knocked and turned to Ginny.

"Probably you're right. She remembered something she had to do and didn't want to wake you," she suggested as she fitted the key in the lock and pushed open the door.

TWO

THE homicide office was stifling. Toronto was experiencing an early season, late April mini heat wave, and Rhona Simpson wished the department would turn on the air conditioning. Sweat dripped down her back, and she worried that the dye in her new black-and-white silk blouse would run.

She should be grateful for the weather bonus. But she wasn't grateful — she felt grumpy and unpleasant as she finished up the paperwork on her current case. Again, she and her partner, Ian Gilchrist, had fingered the perp, and she felt confident they'd lined up the evidence and would be a match for any overenthusiastic defence attorneys.

But it wasn't the heat or the tediousness of her task making her cross. Rather it was an article in the morning paper reporting that the Sisters in Spirit, a Native women's organization devoted to uncovering and drawing attention to the numbers of missing and murdered Aboriginal women, had published an update on their previous year's report. She'd gone online and read their 2009 report. The statistics shocked her. How could so many women, more than five hundred, have disappeared or been murdered without being found or their killers apprehended? The Sisters in Spirit charged that mainstream society regarded First Nations women as dispensable throwaways and the police devoted minimal time to finding the missing women or their killers. The Sisters in Spirit had amassed statistics clearly showing that the solution ratio for crimes involving Aboriginal women and non-Aboriginal was heavily skewed. They demanded that police forces take action.

If there was an upside, it was that Ontario had not figured largely in the report. Nevertheless, Rhona knew opposition members of the legislature would raise the issue and journalists would join them in demanding a provincial investigation. Although the Toronto Police maintained an upfront website where they identified and detailed both current and unsolved cold cases, Rhona didn't want to be paranoid but suspected that if her department launched an inquiry, she'd be front and centre. As a woman of colour, even if the colour was only one quarter inherited from her Cree grandmother, having her in charge of an investigation would look good.

Rhona believed she'd find cases where the police had paid perfunctory attention to an investigation. In her dealings with other officers she'd seen evidence that prejudice existed against Aboriginal women, prostitutes, and drug addicts. She had heard officers articulate their feelings that these men and women got what they deserved. No senior officer condoned this attitude, but it existed.

She asked herself if she shared the feeling that low-life wiping out low-life saved the taxpayers the cost of incarceration. She hoped not, but often she found it hard to defend First Nations and their problems. In fact, she avoided all such discussions, as she didn't want to become a "spokesperson" for Native affairs.

Partly she wondered if she felt both sad and guilty because in another life situation she could have turned out like these women. Again, in her heart, she thanked her loving grandmother who'd brought her up to be the strong woman she was.

Her feelings shamed her, particularly her refusal to proudly claim her Aboriginal heritage and her desire not to have genetics given as the reason for assigning her to any case. It was hard to acknowledge, even to herself, that she felt that way, but she did. She had to face the fact that she was prejudiced and move on.

Rhona stared at the computer. Her acknowledgement of her feelings shocked her. For years she'd half-heartedly considered volunteering in the Aboriginal community, thinking that she could be a role model, a woman who'd pursued an education and joined the police, but she hadn't done anything about it. Now she decided that the time had come. Moreover, contact with others in the community might help her deal with her issues.

Time to act.

She went online and found a health unit on Queen Street and a centre on Dundas where homeless First Nation people received help and counselling. She felt a faint shudder of distaste. Not the way to go. Her professional dealings with the down-and-out First Nation people had shown her that this wasn't the way to counteract her prejudice. Rather, she'd begin her search for a role in the community at the Native Friendship Centre. Located on Spadina Road north of Bloor Street in the heart of the Annex and the student ghetto, this meeting place pulled in students and newcomers in the city looking for other upwardly mobile Aboriginals. Perhaps she could act as a mentor, a support for bewildered young people making their way.

Ian Gilchrist, her partner, touched her shoulder and made her jump. He looked at her computer screen. "What's going on?" he asked.

Rhona held out the morning paper. She tapped the article about the Sisters in Spirit and their need to receive promised federal funding. "I think the boss is going to respond to this."

He scanned the article. "How so?"

"I read their report. Most of the missing and murdered women came from western Canada, but Ontario is not exempt."

"So?"

"There's sure to be an investigation. Sometimes our reports identify women by race, but I suspect the chief will want us squeaky clean as far as unsolved cases go. I bet he puts us on this right away, since I'm the token Aboriginal and a woman."

As Rhona spoke her phone buzzed. She picked it up. It was their superior, Frank Braithwaite.

"Frank wants to see us in his office. Boy, that didn't take long," Rhona said.

Ian shrugged. "Unless you're clairvoyant, we really don't know why he wants us."

"You'll see."

In his office Frank stood by his window lifting weights. He set them on the floor when the two officers entered.

"Getting the biceps in shape," he said. "Juno and I are going on a two-week wilderness canoe trip following old fur trade routes in the barren lands, and I need to toughen up."

Considering that he went to the gym as often as he could, rode his bike to work from his condo in the Distillery District, and watched his diet and weight obsessively, Rhona thought it must be an "extreme sport" trip.

"I didn't know you could take dogs on trips like that," Ian said.

"Juno isn't just *any* dog. I thought after my ex-wife hijacked Bailey that I'd never find another dog like him, but Juno is remarkable." He smiled. "I've cleared it with the tour leader. Even have a backpack for Juno so he can carry his own dehydrated food."

"Sounds great. When will this happen?" Rhona asked, thinking it would be absolutely horrible, and she couldn't even imagine the mosquitoes, the rain, the discomfort.

"July, but it takes a while to get really fit." Frank moved behind his desk and picked up the newspaper.

Rhona resisted the urge to give Ian an "I told you so" look.

"Did either of you read this article on the Sisters in Spirit report?" Braithwaite asked, waving the paper in the air.

"I did and told Ian about it," Rhona said.

Frank tried a "cute" or perhaps a "coy" smile, which he didn't do well. "So you figured out why I wanted to see you?"

Rhona played dumb. She didn't want this assignment. Sifting through files, following up on cold cases, talking to families who had lost hope, was not what she wanted to do. She shook her head. "No."

Wisely, Ian said nothing.

Frank waved the paper. "To follow up on each and every Toronto case which involved an Aboriginal woman and make sure we've done everything possible to find them or the perp that killed them." He slapped the paper on the edge of the desk. "According to this, there aren't many cases in Ontario, let alone Toronto, so it shouldn't take you long, especially with two of you working on it. I want to be able to tell the police commissioner and the mayor that we have a perfect record, that we do not neglect any of our citizens."

He must be hoping for a promotion or at least a commendation from the city.

THREE

"HELLO. Anybody home?" Hollis called after she opened the door.

No answer. Although easy listening music flooded the apartment, it felt empty.

"Come in with me," Ginny said.

Hollis felt sorry for Ginny and agreed. With Ginny, still clutching the grocery bag, following her like a puppy on a leash, Hollis flicked on the lights in the hall and then in the living room. Two black leather sofas with contrasting red suede cushions aligned at either end faced each other across a gleaming brass-and-glass coffee table. Black velvet drapes were drawn across the window and a white floktari carpet completed the décor, which looked as if it had just been delivered from Leon's furniture store. When Hollis turned on the kitchen pot lights, they reflected from a black granite countertop and highlighted stainless steel appliances. Only a coffee maker marred the pristine counter. It could have been an advertisement from Home Depot or IKEA. Perfectly appointed, sparkling clean, and empty.

"Everything is very new," Hollis said.

"It is. Fatima thought it needed new furniture."

"Fatima?"

"Yes. I rent the apartment from Fatima Nesrallah. You know that she owns all the apartments on the fifth, don't you?"

"Actually, I didn't. The fees go to the accountant."

Hollis knew Fatima and wouldn't have pegged her as an entrepreneur. People constantly surprised her.

"Why does it feel spooky?" Ginny whispered.

Hollis also lowered her voice as they moved down the hall to the two bedrooms. "Maybe because you left all the curtains and blinds shut," she said as she pushed a door open.

"This is the master bedroom," Ginny said.

An unmade king-size bed with a quilted red satin duvet pulled partly back, piles of silk and velvet pillows tossed on the white rug, along with discarded clothing reflected in the ceiling's mirrors.

Mirrors on the ceiling — she wondered if they featured in all the fifth floor apartments. She associated them with honeymoon hotels and bordellos.

Hollis backed out of the room, colliding with an anxious Ginny. "One to go," Hollis said.

Ginny hung on to the shopping bag as if it was a life raft. "I'm afraid," she whispered.

"I think it's contagious," Hollis confessed as she slowly turned the knob and gently pushed the second bedroom's door open.

Blood, urine, and feces — the smell assaulted them.

"Oh my god," Ginny whispered.

Sabrina lay on her back, her throat gaping. Blackened blood stained flowered white sheets, the bedside table, the adjacent wall, and her neatly folded clothes on a chair close to the bed. Blood had spattered her pink coat. Her blood-soaked Snoopy pyjamas added an extra element of pathos to the scene.

"Sabrina ..." Ginny exhaled the word.

Hollis stepped into the room and touched Sabrina's cold hand.

"She's dead, isn't she?" Ginny said.

"She is. We mustn't touch anything." Hollis breathed shallowly and stepped back. This wasn't the first time she'd seen a murder victim, but that didn't make it easier. She put her hand on Ginny's arm and turned them both toward the door. "Give me your cell phone to call the police."

Ginny placed the groceries on the floor before she dug into her shoulder bag and handed over a pink phone. Watching Hollis, she moaned, "Oh my god. She was nice. Why would anyone kill her?"

"The police will find her killer."

"The police won't give a fuck," Ginny said harshly.

"What?" Hollis stepped back in surprise.

"Get real. She was a call girl. Cops don't care about women like us. We're throwaways." Ginny bent to retrieve the groceries.

Call girls.

Hollis had had no idea. Fatima Nesrallah must be running an escort service. She had noticed that the women who lived on the fifth were an attractive lot, but she'd never suspected what trade they were practising.

Did the police consider sex trade workers throwaways? Hollis didn't want to believe it but suspected it was true.

"Bring the groceries with you," Hollis said before she punched in 911.

"This is Hollis Grant, superintendent of the Strathmore Apartments, 68 Delisle Street. A young woman," she paused. Sabrina's last name had disappeared from her mind.

"Yes," the male voice on the line prompted.

"A young woman has been murdered."

"Are you in danger?"

"No. She appears to have been dead for some time."

Ginny and Hollis rode the elevator in a deep silence, punctuated by Ginny's occasional sniffle. In Hollis's office

Ginny collapsed on one of the two armless leather upholstered visitor's chairs, covered her face with her hands, and cried.

"Ginny, the fire, police, ambulance, the whole response team will arrive in minutes. They'll talk to us after they've been upstairs. We've suffered a shock. My knees feel shaky and …"

Ginny dropped her hands and raised her head. "Me too. I'm all wobbly."

"No time for hot, sweet tea but I have orange juice and I'll get us both a glass. The sugar will help."

When the approaching siren screams shattered the morning calm, they gulped the juice and went to meet the police.

FOUR

ASSIGNED the task in late April, Rhona and Ian had laboured for more than a week examining files relating to the murder or disappearance of Aboriginal women. Rhona feared they'd find evidence of negligence but none surfaced. Now, on a cool May morning the two detectives faced each another in the homicide office, which hummed with activity.

"Enough of this," Ian said, holding up their summation. "We're finished."

Rhona tapped her pen on the desk and surveyed the office. "God knows everyone is busy. We need to do our bit and work on an active case." Her phone buzzed. "Right. Ian's here. We'll be right in," she said.

Ian raised an eyebrow.

"Looks like I got my wish. Frank has a case for us. Bring the report."

When they entered his office, Frank was leaning back with his feet propped on his desk's open bottom drawer.

"Sit down," he said, waving a hand at the two steel- and blue-plastic chairs parked in front of him like recalcitrant students appearing before the principal.

He lowered his feet before leaning forward. "So what did you discover?" he asked.

Ian handed him the document and summarized their findings.

A slight smile cracked Frank's lips. "Good practice for your new assignment," he said.

Good practice — what did that mean?

"In the last twenty-four hours a perp slit a call girl's throat. It's your case. Not an Aboriginal, but given the fuss about sex trade workers and the accusations that the police don't do enough ..." He waved the report. "Your research may come in handy. Take a car from the pool and get over to 68 Delisle Street. The superintendent, Hollis Grant, will wait for you in her office. She found the body."

"Did you say Hollis Grant?" Rhona said. A feeling of déjà vu swept over her. Not again. It couldn't be Hollis Grant?

"Should I spell it? H-o-l-l-i-s G-r-a-n-t, do you know her?"

"Yes, and so do you. She was involved in the Danson Lafleur case last October."

"The name didn't register. Now that you mention it, I do remember. Didn't she provide useful information?"

"She meddled, but, yes, you're right, she helped."

"Well, maybe she'll do it again," the chief said.

Rhona hoped Hollis would not play *any* part in the investigation.

"We don't want the mayor, the papers, or any of the city's do-gooders making an issue of the case. Do I make myself clear?" Frank said.

"Perfectly. We're on our way," Rhona said.

Outside the chief's office, Ian muttered, "If I remember correctly, she was a pain in the ass."

"She was, but without her leads the case could have turned out much worse. She's a loose cannon and I hope her only involvement is finding the victim," Rhona said.

At 68 Delisle, Hollis had left Ginny in her office and dealt with the initial onslaught of emergency responders arriving in the lobby. The police, once they knew what had happened, requested that residents arriving or leaving wait there for an interview. The lobby rapidly filled with tenants, along with the crew working on the exterior repairs to the balconies, who used the opportunity to flop on the grey marble floor and chow down on whatever food remained in their lunch buckets.

Hollis circled the area and briefly spoke to those she knew before nipping into her apartment, leashing Barlow and returning to the office with the puppy. She dug out the dog biscuits she kept in her desk drawer.

"Help me practice his dog training homework?" she said to Ginny, who was huddled on the visitor's chair gripping her second glass of orange juice and staring into space.

Ginny frowned. "How can you talk about dog training when Sabrina's been murdered?" she asked. "All I can think about is what we saw up there."

"Me too, but practising the exercises with Barlow will distract us," Hollis said.

Hearing his name, Barlow squeezed close to Hollis, waiting for her to scratch his bony back. Instead, she stood and fished a treat from her pocket, which energized the dog and focused his attention. Barlow performed *sit* and *down* with no problems, but when Hollis ordered him down and then told him to stay, he refused to co-operate, repeatedly leaping to his feet and lunging for the treat.

Hollis, for the fifth time, held her hand aloft and again commanded the dog to stay. With eyes locked on the puppy, she backed toward the door. A voice behind her said. "A puppy and a new job as apartment super. You've been busy since I saw you last."

It couldn't be. Hollis dropped her hand and turned. Barlow, tail wagging like a metronome on speed, leapt toward Rhona Simpson, who stepped back and crashed into Ian.

"Rhona Simpson. I can't believe it," Hollis said. She grabbed the puppy's blue collar with her left hand and held out her right to Rhona.

Rhona, her equilibrium restored, shook the proffered hand. "You remember my partner, Detective Gilchrist?"

Hollis acknowledged Ian and waved her free hand toward Ginny. "This is Ginny Wuttenee. Sabrina Trepanier was sleeping in her spare room when she was murdered."

"What a shock you've had," Rhona said to Ginny.

Ginny, wide-eyed, said nothing.

"There's a crowd up there already," Hollis said.

"And the coroner is on his way along with the rest of our team. Tell me about the victim."

"Let me put this monster back in my apartment. It's right across the hall."

With the reluctant puppy stuffed away, Hollis moved to the cabinet and removed Fatima Nesrallah's file.

"The murdered woman, Sabrina Trepanier, was staying in Ginny's apartment, 504, while her own living room was painted. Sabrina was allergic to paint. All the apartments on the fifth are owned by one woman. I don't have individual renters' files." She passed Fatima's file to Rhona.

Rhona glanced at it. "She lists her occupation as personal assistant but doesn't mention a company."

"Fatima tells everyone to put that down on their income tax forms," Ginny said. "Personal assistant is a joke. We're escorts."

"I suppose personal assistant isn't exactly a lie, it's another way to describe what you do," Rhona said. "Were you good friends with Ms. Trepanier?"

The question upset Ginny, whose chin quivered before she burst into tears. Through her sobs she said, "Yes. She was so nice. Why would anyone do this?"

"That's what we'll find out. Hollis, did you know the victim? Why were you in her apartment?"

"When Ginny woke she popped over to Bruno's to buy food and didn't take her key, because she thought Sabrina would be up and would let her in when she returned. When she couldn't get her on the phone, she worried that something had happened and asked me to open the door."

"Did you know the dead girl?" Rhona asked.

"I've only worked here a couple of months. The job keeps me busy but I did chat with her on several occasions, never about anything important. The dogs attracted her. In fact, one day when she patted MacTee, she cried and told me how much she missed her family's Golden."

Rhona made a move toward the door. "I'll be back later to talk to you about the other tenants."

Hollis glanced at the clock. "At three thirty I pick up my foster child at her school."

"Foster child?" Rhona's eyebrows skyrocketed. "Have you had a mid-life crisis? You've changed everything."

Hollis nodded. "Not everything. I'm painting. That's why I took this job — to give me time to paint and have an apartment with room for Jay and the dogs."

"One more question. Did the victim seem afraid? Did she ever talk to you about anything that was bothering her?" Rhona addressed the question to both Ginny and Hollis.

"Not to me," Hollis said and looked at Ginny.

Ginny shook her head.

Rhona glanced at the bank of security monitors. "The info from those should help. We'll take all the stored info. We'll talk more later."

Hollis was left wondering how to tell Jay and her friend, Crystal, about the murder without terrifying them.

FIVE

RHONA and Ian divided responsibilities and assigned officers to control the waiting group in the lobby until they could interview them.

As they contemplated the crowd, the forensics team and the coroner, a tall, thin black man, arrived. The two detectives accompanied them to the murder scene, where all donned protective footwear and gloves.

Inside the small, bloody bedroom, Rhona looked at the figure on the bed and sighed. Death was never easy to contemplate and this murder had been a gruesome one. It was hard to know for sure, but the woman appeared to have been young and beautiful. What a waste.

The coroner made his preliminary exam before the body was removed to the morgue.

"What can you tell us?" Ian said.

The man shrugged. "Because the window was open and the room was cool, I'd estimate she was murdered sometime after midnight. As we see, the assailant slashed her throat with what must have been considerable force and a sharp knife. She was lying on her back. Because of her position I'd say the attacker stood on the left side of the bed and used his right hand or both hands. She doesn't appear to have resisted nor does she seem to have been raped. I believe she died almost instantly. I'll tell you more after the autopsy."

"Thanks. Now we'll ask the residents where they were and

what they were doing last night," Rhona said.

"Most will say they lived alone, were in bed, and had no one to vouch for them," Ian grumbled.

"Too true. I'll talk to the women on this floor. Ian, get Ms. Grant to provide you with a copy of the building's plans and a list of the residents. We will also need former tenants' names, ones who had lived in the building as long as Ms. Trepanier. As Ms. Grant hasn't worked here for long, when we interview those in the lobby we'll make sure to note their apartment's location and the length of time that they've lived here."

Upstairs, the other women living on the fifth were at home. Rhona had sent a uniform along to ask each to remain inside and wait for the interview. She began with the tenants living adjacent to Ginny.

The door directly across the hall opened as she raised her hand to press the buzzer. A quick glimpse at the door revealed a peephole — a good idea for any door and not one that Rhona had in her own building.

"Come in." A plump woman with enormous black eyes heavily fringed with what had to be false eyelashes stepped back to allow Rhona inside.

The woman was shorter than Rhona. Addicted to high-heeled cowboy boots to increase her height, Rhona always measured herself against others. She'd done it since childhood. As a police officer she'd found it helpful because it allowed her to position herself so that interviewees or perps seldom towered over her. She always insisted tall interviewees sit down, and she herself never chose low, squashy chairs or sofas.

"Fatima Nesrallah," the woman said, extending a tiny, ring-encrusted hand with scarlet fingernails topped with gold dust. A musky scent surrounded her.

Rhona shook the woman's hand and followed her into a living room airlifted from a north African souk, with oriental carpets, leather ottomans, silk-draped lamps, and lots and lots of polished metal. Several brass trays rested on black lacquered bases and acted as end tables and a coffee table. Brass bowls abounded, some filled with rose petals, others with nuts and dates. Brass candle holders held fat white candles.

"Please, sit down. May I offer you Turkish coffee?" Fatima asked.

Rhona anticipated that Fatima Nesrallah would make a superior brew. Although Rhona realized coffee would keep her awake, it wouldn't matter, for in all likelihood she wouldn't see her bed until very late. "I would," she said.

While they waited she took in the room. Everything in it would conspire to make a man feel adventurous, as if he'd ventured deep into the Kasbah and was about to experience whatever went on behind the closed doors of that exotic setting.

Fatima returned with coffee and baklava. "I don't make it. I buy it from Artez, a wonderful Lebanese bakery on Eglinton," she said.

In her head Rhona repeated the name, determined to visit the bakery at a later date. After she sipped the dark, aromatic coffee, she complimented Fatima before she said, "Time for questions. I understand you own all the apartments on this floor and rent them to women."

"I do. I did well in the market and invested in real estate," Fatima said.

"You run an escort agency for them."

"For some I do the booking and check out the clients," Fatima said.

"Online advertising?"

"Indeed. It's made for businesswomen."

Rhona could have pushed further, but she wanted to catch a killer, not an entrepreneur.

"Did you know Ms. Trepanier well?"

The woman sipped and considered the question. "Not well. None of the women who live on this floor are close. When we meet we talk only about non-important things."

"How long have you been here?"

"Four years. Since they created these lovely apartments."

"I am not interested in the details of your lives except as they relate to Ms. Trepanier. Has she ever spoken of being afraid?"

Fatima laughed without conveying any sense of mirth. "Afraid? When you do what we do you're always a little bit afraid. We didn't have much in common. I'm from Lebanon, a Middle Eastern woman, and she was a classic American cheerleader type. I can tell you she was kind. Ginny's new to Toronto and Sabrina made a point of taking her under her wing."

"Did Sabrina have friends or family in the city?"

"I don't ask personal questions or note who goes in or out of any of my apartments, but I'd say not."

"How do men find you?" Rhona asked.

"We advertise. We're officially 'escorts.' All legal," Fatima said, watching Rhona to see how she'd react.

"Directly, or do you have someone who vets the callers?"

Fatima broke off a morsel of baklava and chewed slowly. Rhona figured the woman was giving herself time. "The young women pay me rent and some ask me to check out new callers. As I'm sure you know, a bad apple registry exists. If any of the women have trouble with a client, we add his name to that list. Otherwise they have regulars and don't consult me."

"Do you keep records?"

Fatima smiled but said nothing.

Rhona realized she wasn't going to answer and changed the topic. "Do you have your own list of unwelcome customers?"

"We all use the websites for that." Fatima smiled. "There are enough lovely men who appreciate bright, pretty women they can take to events, to hotels, or visit here. We don't need the weirdos."

"We'd like the names of men who gave you or the other women trouble, particularly if they were Ms. Trepanier's or Ms. Wuttenee's clients."

"Ms. Wuttenee's?"

"The attack occurred in her apartment. Perhaps the killer intended to murder her," Rhona said.

Fatima considered their request.

"Give us the leads and we'll do the rest," Rhona assured her.

SIX

JAY and her eleven-year-old friend, Crystal Montour, backpacks bouncing, bounded through the Deer Park schoolyard. Jay hugged Barlow and MacTee before greeting Hollis. Crystal trotted after Jay and contented herself with patting the two dogs.

Hollis waited until the crowd of children, nannies, and parents thinned before she stopped.

"Girls, I have something terrible to tell you. I wish I could soften the impact of what I'm about to say."

Both children waited.

"Sabrina Trepanier, who lived on the fifth floor of our building, was murdered last night," Hollis said.

Neither child said anything for a moment while they processed the information.

Jay recovered first. "Do we know her?" she said.

When she heard Sabrina's name, Crystal's hands had flown to her mouth. "Oh, that's awful. Awful, awful." Her eyes filled with tears. "Sabrina is friends with Ginny who also lives on the fifth floor. Is Ginny okay?" Her eyes fixed on Hollis. She lowered her hands. "Ginny's my friend. She's an Indian like me and she's beautiful."

"She is beautiful, and she's fine," Hollis said. "Ginny often stops in the office to play with Barlow." Hollis didn't tell them that Ginny had discovered the body or that Sabrina had been killed in Ginny's apartment.

"My aunt knows Ginny too," Crystal volunteered.

"What about Sabrina Trepanier? Did you or your aunt know her?"

"She's the pretty one with the long dark hair. She always looks great and she always says hello. One day she had a box of Tim Hortons Timbits and gave them to me. She said if she kept them she'd eat them all and that wouldn't be good."

Jay chimed in. "She likes dogs. Barlow jumped up once and he had muddy paws and made marks on her coat and she laughed and said dogs did that. If it had been me I might have been mad but she wasn't."

Crystal nodded. "I don't think my aunt ever talked to her. She doesn't have much to do with the people in the building."

When they turned onto Delisle, they saw TV trucks and a cluster of people in front of their building.

"Are they there because of the murder?" Jay asked.

"They are. The police will be here for at least twenty-four hours, and they've strung yellow tape to keep onlookers away. They will interview everyone in the building."

"My aunt won't like that," Crystal said.

"Most people won't. But if you and your aunt and everybody else tell the police every little thing you can remember about Sabrina and Ginny and anyone or anything different that you saw, it could help them. They need as much information as they can get if they're going to track down her killer."

"Ginny's related to Poundmaker, he was a famous chief," Crystal said. Her brow furrowed. "Is she in danger? Are we?"

"I don't think so but we'll be extra careful."

Crystal peered at her shoes and mumbled, "Maybe whoever did it meant to kill Ginny. People don't like us. They wish we'd disappear."

Jay bent like a pretzel until she stared up at Crystal's face. "*I* don't feel like that. Hollis doesn't either."

Crystal lifted her head. "Some people do and have for a long, long time."

"That's really sad," Jay said and seemed at a loss about what she could say to make Crystal feel better.

Barlow and MacTee tugged on their leashes.

"We'd better go in. Because I manage the building, the police will have more questions for me."

As they moved along, Hollis tried to remember her Canadian history. Poundmaker had been involved in the second Riel Rebellion in Saskatchewan. He must have been a Cree. Poor Crystal, feeling that everyone disliked her because she was an Indian. How awful and how hard to imagine if you didn't belong to a minority.

On Tuesdays, Crystal's aunt, Mary Montour, worked a split shift as a waitress, breakfast and dinner with a break for lunch. Not wanting the child spending time in an empty apartment, Hollis had taken to inviting Crystal to have supper and go with them to Barlow's obedience class. Tonight of all nights she didn't want the child alone.

"Jay, you and Crystal do your homework while I talk to the police. I'll make sure it's okay for us to take Barlow to his class. It will be good to get away from the building," Hollis said.

At the apartment they found Ginny curled up asleep on the sofa, looking very young and vulnerable. Hollis realized that Ginny couldn't return to her own apartment. It was a crime scene, as was Sabrina's.

Ginny stirred when dogs and kids crowded into the apartment. Hollis waited until she saw that Ginny was truly awake.

"Ginny, do you have anywhere to stay?"

"Oh my God. I won't be able to go back to my place." Ginny shuddered. "I don't know if I ever will, but maybe Fatima will rent me Sabrina's place."

"Not until the police finish," Hollis said.

Barlow, tired of being ignored, jumped on the sofa and settled down next to Ginny, who stroked him absentmindedly.

"I guess I don't have anywhere to go," Ginny said.

"Why can't Ginny stay with us? I have a trundle bed," Jay said.

"So you do. If Ginny wants to do that, she can."

Ginny's eyes widened. Clearly the invitation surprised her. "Thanks. That's nice of you, but now that I think about it, I know that Fatima will take me in," she said.

A buzz at the door. Hollis answered and found Rhona outside.

"I'd like to talk to Ms. Wuttenee again. May I use your office for the interview?" she asked in a tone that indicated she was merely being polite.

Hollis nodded. "Of course. Tonight is my puppy's obedience class. Is it okay if we go?"

Rhona considered. "Leave me your cell phone number. We have your records, the security tapes, and are interviewing the tenants. If I need any more information it'll wait until you get back."

Rhona led Ginny into Hollis's office.

"I can't get Sabrina out of my mind," Ginny wailed as she settled on one of Hollis's office chairs. "Who would have killed her? She was only twenty-two. Why? Why would anyone do that? What about me? Will I be next?" Her voice rose after every question until it was a shrill scream. Abruptly she buried her face in her hands.

"Ms. Wuttenee, if we're going to catch Sabrina's killer, we need your help."

Ginny lowered her hands but her downcast eyes, drooping

head, and projecting lower lip combined to create a picture of despair. She remained quiet.

"I want you to think back to *every* conversation you ever had with Sabrina and tell me what you talked about."

"That won't help you. We talked about Brad Pitt and Angelina Jolie and everyone else in Hollywood. We both liked *In Style* magazine and fashion. Sabrina told me where the best places to shop were. And ..." She stopped.

"Work? Clients? Drugs?" Rhona said.

Ginny stared at the floor.

"I'm not trying to trap you. I'm looking for links to the person who killed Ms. Trepanier. Could it have had anything to do with your —" Rhona hesitated "— landlady? Did you share information about a really bad client? Do you have a source for drugs and could Ms. Trepanier have been in trouble with that person?" She leaned forward and tapped the desk. "That is the kind of information that will help us."

Ginny continued to stare at the floor?

"Do you want us to find Ms. Trepanier's killer?" Rhona asked.

Ginny's head snapped up. Rhona read fear and doubt in her eyes. "Of course, but I'm afraid."

"Of the killer or of me?" Rhona asked.

"Both," Ginny admitted.

Rhona leaned back and steepled her fingers as she considered the young woman's reply.

"I do want to help," Ginny said.

"Okay. I'm not recording this conversation. It's strictly off the record. Why don't I ask questions and you answer? If you volunteer more information, that will be great."

Ginny fidgeted and glanced at the door as if she'd like to escape. "Okay."

"Did Sabrina have any trouble with Ms. Nesrallah?"

"No."

"Did she have clients who treated her badly or frightened her?"

Silence.

Rhona repeated the question.

"Yes, we both had one guy who scared us."

"Did he tell you his name?"

Ginny pursed her lips. "He said to call him John, and he thought that was very funny."

"What was it that frightened you? Something he said or something he did?"

"He brought handcuffs with him and promised me extra money if I'd wear them. Sabrina and Fatima had both warned me that that kind of kinky stuff, bondage it's called, could be dangerous, could get out of hand, but I agreed. As soon as the handcuffs were on he smashed me really hard. His eyes were crazy. I screamed before he could stop me, and that put him off. He was a very scary guy."

"Do you keep any kind of diary or appointment book? Could you tell me when you saw him?"

Ginny shook her head. "It wasn't long ago. I don't keep anything like that, but Sabrina does. It has a pink cover with a photo of a quilt on the front and she keeps it in the kitchen drawer. She writes all kinds of info in it — computer passwords, addresses, and every day she puts in the name or the initials of the clients and what they like."

Rhona felt a flush of optimism. They'd get this guy. "Why does she do that?"

Ginny shrugged. "If guys like you, they leave a big tip. Sabrina made sure to record what they asked her to do 'cause she wanted to make money. She was saving for something big."

"What was that?"

"She wanted to start her own business, and she figured this was the best way to get enough money."

"Anything about friends, family, where she went to school, why she decided to come to Toronto?"

"I never asked."

"I understand, but did she ever volunteer any information."

Ginny shook her head. "I've only been here for a little while, and we didn't talk that much." She leaned forward and whispered, "Do you think the killer is after all of us? Is someone punishing us because of what we do?"

SEVEN

AFTER Ginny left with Rhona, Hollis looked longingly at the studio end of the living room, where a commissioned, half-completed four-foot-high papier-mâché giraffe stood waiting for her attention. Right after the Second World War, her client's father had brought him or sent him a large plush giraffe named Louis Phillipe from France. Now the man wanted a facsimile to put among the palms and ferns in his solarium.

Not the time to work on it or on her current painting, an abstraction of her Canadian series. Until the police solved the murder she'd have her hands full keeping Jay on even keel and her tenants placated. She could only guess how the over-protective Calum Brownelly would react when he learned that his daughter lived in a building where a woman in the sex trade had been killed.

Dealing with those issues lay in the future. Tonight they'd scarf down a quick supper before obedience class at seven.

Jay and Crystal joined her in the kitchen. Hollis asked them to chop peppers for a stir fry. That task completed and rice steaming in the cooker, Hollis poured herself a glass of wine.

"I think I'll watch the news. See what they say about what's happened here. Want to do that?" she asked the girls.

"No. I want you to give me an answer," Jay said, moving to face Hollis and block her retreat to the living room.

Hollis sighed. She'd hoped to avoid the topic she knew Jay wanted to talk about.

At moments like this she questioned her decision to foster. Had she made a mistake? Was she capable of dealing with a complicated eleven-year-old toting a trunkload of emotional baggage, not to mention a mysterious father?

Wrong, wrong, wrong. She shook her head to expel doubt, as if the idea were water trapped in her ears.

Bringing Jay into her life had been *exactly* the right thing to do. But at this moment when Jay, arms akimbo and chin thrust out, stood eyeball-to-eyeball, she faced the fact that this might be a bigger test than she'd anticipated. She knew a lot about dogs but not much about girls other than what she'd learned from her own experience. And most of that experience probably didn't apply.

She'd realized from early childhood as she grew into an almost six-foot-tall, big-boned young woman, that her tiny, perfect mother had expected a carbon copy of herself. After years of dressing Hollis in pink dresses trimmed with lace, her mother finally conceded that the feminine frills she loved looked ridiculous on her daughter.

No, she didn't want to emulate her mother and she didn't have any other role models. She'd read the *how to* books on bringing up children, talked to her friends, and listened to her heart, the best teacher of all, and she prayed that would be enough.

From the moment she'd met Jay, Hollis loved the enthusiastic, wiry, dark-eyed child with the mass of curly brown hair. When Jay was happy, her wide mouth curved into a big smile that made everyone around her respond positively.

Hollis loved Jay's spirit but, applying dog theory, knew she must establish herself as the alpha dog, the pack leader, the woman who provided love and guidance in equal measure. She had to be up to the task and not allow herself to fail — Jay could not be moved to another foster home.

Standing toe-to-toe, Hollis waited for Jay to tell her why she had her hands on her hips, her chin thrust forward, and her entire body expressing her outrage.

"You don't trust me," Jay stormed.

The age-old accusation. If she said she did, she'd be lying. If she said she didn't, it would confirm Jay's belief.

"We don't know each other well enough for me to know whether I do or I don't," Hollis said.

"That's crap. You don't," Jay said.

"Tell me why I should?" Hollis answered.

That stopped Jay, but only for a second. "Because I'm a foster kid and no one trusts foster kids. You think we're all the same. That somebody gave us up because we're rotten kids and we lie all the time."

"Do you?"

Jay retracted her chin. A tiny smile curved her lips. "Maybe." She shrugged. "Maybe not."

"I'd like, no make that I'd love to trust you, but you've only been here for a few weeks. I'm responsible for you. I can't let you get in trouble."

Hollis wished this was a private conversation. Heaven knew what Crystal thought as Hollis and Jay battled.

"I only want to go to the Eaton Centre Thursday night to meet my dad. All you have to do is walk me to the subway. That isn't a big deal," Jay whined.

Barlow, the puppy, raced into the kitchen dragging a fuchsia woollen hoodie.

Jay grabbed for it as Barlow shot toward the front hall.

Crisis averted for the time being.

Jay reappeared hugging the hoodie to her chest, then extended it and examined it carefully. She thrust it in Hollis's face.

"The asshole ripped it," she said.

Hollis ignored the language. She'd pick her battles, and for the moment language wouldn't be one of them. "Where was the hoodie?"

"In my room."

"Where in your room?"

"I don't know."

"If it had been hanging in the closet or folded in a drawer, he couldn't have got it. I'm guessing it was on the bedroom floor."

Jay said nothing as she picked at the hole in the cuff.

Each time the puppy chewed a shoe or clothing, they had this conversation. Cupboard doors had to be shut and clothes put away to prevent Barlow from conducting the search-and-destroy missions he loved.

"I'll mend it," Hollis offered and reached for the garment.

"I *have* to go to the Eaton Centre," Jay said, extending the hoodie.

The crisis had not been averted.

Hollis checked her watch. "We'll resolve this issue later. Right now it's time to haul Barlow off to his dog-training class."

"Good thing Crystal comes with us. You love our dogs, don't you, Crystal?" Jay said.

Crystal nodded but added nothing to the conversation

Our dogs. That seemed a good indicator that Jay was settling in and accepting her new situation.

"Let's hope we all learn a lot tonight. I'll take Barlow for a quick walk before we go." For a few minutes Hollis had almost forgotten she was living in the midst of a murder investigation, but in the lobby where residents waited to be interviewed, the crowd jolted her back to reality. She glanced through the large lobby windows and saw parked TV trucks making passage along the narrow street almost impossible. She should have anticipated that the murder would attract journalists and the curious public. After speaking to the policeman at the door, she walked down the drive and ducked under the tape. A mike was pushed into her face.

"Was it a hooker? How was she killed?" A shower of questions rained down on at her.

"No comment," she muttered and dragged a now reluctant Barlow through the crowd toward Avenue Road. On her return, she again refused to answer questions and sped into the building.

Jay and Crystal sat in the kitchen.

"Ready?" Hollis said, packing quantities of dog treats into her pockets. Time to hustle the girls away and involve them in the obedience class chaos.

EIGHT

AFTER Rhona interviewed the women on the fifth floor she moved to Hollis's office, where Ian showed her the list of tenants.

"I'm running all names through our files to see if any of them have a record," he said.

"The lobby is full — the uniforms are keeping everyone there." He handed Rhona a piece of paper. "I thought we'd check off the apartments as we talk to the tenants."

"We mustn't forget to ask if any of the residents have guests or other family members in the apartment," Rhona said, waving the paper. "None of that information will be here."

Coming into the office, Rhona had noted the number of people congregating in the marble-floored sunken lobby. They crowded together on leather sofas arranged on three sides of an oversized square, smoked-glass table that rested on an ornate carved stone base. Others occupied a host of black-and-chrome folding chairs. A few tenants leaned against the walls or sat on the floor.

"Time to get out there and start bringing them in for interviews," Rhona said, digging into her bag for her notebook and tape recorder, although in this preliminary go-through she didn't think she'd need the latter. In the interview rooms at the station, video cameras recorded the interviewees' facial and body reactions as well as their speech.

"For our interviews there's this office, a fitness centre, a party room, a visitor's apartment, the laundry room, and a sauna on this floor. If you want to use the office I'll use the party room," Ian said. He nodded at the crowd. "They removed all the folding chairs to use in the lobby but left the sofas and upholstered chairs."

"Good idea. I'll stay here," Rhona said.

When they entered the lobby the conversational buzz diminished. All eyes were on them when they stopped at the top of the four marble steps leading up from the sunken lobby to the first floor. Together they moved sideways behind the wrought iron railing. It was a natural podium. Rhona rapped on the metal with her pen.

Talk ceased.

"Good afternoon. Let me introduce myself and my partner. I'm Detective Rhona Simpson and this is Detective Ian Gilchrist. You will be interviewed by one of us. If there is anyone who has medical issues and needs to be first in line, please come forward. Otherwise, please sort yourselves out and follow one another."

An elderly woman sitting on a walker stood up, positioned herself between the handles, and creaked forward. She carefully manoeuvred her squeaky machine up the first step without dropping her white plastic handbag. Ian stepped down and offered a hand, but she shook him off. It seemed as if everyone in the lobby held their breath until she reached Rhona. She spoke in a clear, carrying voice. "I'm Agnes Johnson. I should take my heart medicine in fifteen minutes."

They progressed slowly to the office.

Rhona motioned to the visitor's chair but the woman braked the walker and perched on its seat. "What would you like to know?"

"Did you know Sabrina Trepanier?"

"The murdered woman?"

Rhona wondered who else Ms. Johnson thought she'd be asking about but contented herself with a nod.

"She was one of *those* women on the fifth floor, wasn't she?" Ms. Johnson said, leaning forward and narrowing her eyes as she enunciated *those*.

Again Rhona nodded.

"I didn't know them but I watched them. I don't sleep much and from my living room window I see the entrance. I like to keep track of who comes in and out." A rueful smile. "They might be no better than they should be, but my they have nice clothes. The men with them always walk as if they're happy." She tilted her head and frowned. "I didn't mean to sound critical when I said *those*."

"I'm sure you didn't."

Ms. Johnson cocked her head to one side and grinned. The smile and the twinkle in her eyes made her look younger and hinted at how pretty she must once have been. "If people make other people happy it can't be all bad, can it?"

"No." Rhona smiled at her. "Can you see faces from your window?"

"I'm on the fourth and that's too far up to see them, but I do notice how people walk and what they wear. I worked as a security guard at the Royal Ontario Museum. It's a boring job and I amused myself watching people and guessing about their lives. Now that I'm retired I go to court to see the trials. It's interesting and it's free." She shook her head. "But you know all about that. Imagine me telling a detective how much fun court is."

"It is interesting," Rhona agreed, thinking that Ms. Johnson might be very helpful. Many people she interviewed had poor observation skills and proved useless as witnesses. "Did you see anything odd last night after midnight?"

Ms. Johnson scrunched her eyes shut for several seconds before she opened them. "Lots of coming and going last night. Surprising because it was a Monday night, but the Ottawa

Senators were playing the Leafs." She grimaced. "They didn't make the playoffs again and the game doesn't mean anything, but Toronto fans turn up no matter what. I think there was a rock concert somewhere too. On *Q* yesterday morning, they interviewed the band. They looked weird but sounded surprisingly normal. I suppose people go out to eat or drink after a game or a show." She chewed on her lower lip. "I think Ms. Trepanier came in about midnight."

Rhona hid her surprise. "How did you know it was her?"

"She often wears a pink coat. It's very pretty and easy to recognize."

"Was she alone?"

"No. I can't tell you anything about the man she was with." She shook her head. "Sorry, but it was the pink coat I noticed."

"Anything else?"

"No."

"Have you lived here long?"

"Twenty years."

"I'll talk to you again when the investigation is further along. You've been helpful." As she accompanied Ms. Johnson to the elevator, Rhona thought that the security cameras would have recorded Sabrina and her escort.

"I don't give a fuck who got killed. It had nothing to do with me and I've got a plane to catch." A stocky, unshaven man swung a sports bag and narrowly avoided cracking an officer who had extended his arm to detain the man.

Rhona couldn't hear what was said but the man, his body tense and radiating anger, followed the officer's finger and headed toward Rhona. Lucky her.

"Sir, please come into the office."

Inside, he refused to sit and Rhona too continued to stand. She didn't intend to allow this man to tower over her.

"Barney Cartwright. I live on the sixth."

"Did you know the deceased, Sabrina Trepanier?"

"I knew what they did," Cartwright replied.

Rhona sensed he was lying. "That wasn't what I asked. Let me be straightforward. Have you ever been a client of any woman on the fifth floor?"

Cartwright shifted from one large black unpolished shoe to the other.

"You did understand the question?" She'd bluff. "You do know they keep records and it's not in their interest to keep secrets."

"Once or twice," he said, chin jutting forward. "So what?"

"Once or twice. Who did you see?"

"Fatima."

"And?"

"Sabrina."

"When was that?"

Cartwright grunted, "I don't know. I've been away. Before that."

How to phrase her next question. "When you visited Ms. Trepanier, did you ever talk about anything personal?"

"I might have. She didn't. I wasn't paying her for chit-chat about herself," he said. His brows drew together. "I have a plane to catch."

"Where were you last night?"

"My place. I watched TV and went to bed." He stared at Rhona. "I hope you're not going to say what I think you're going to say."

"Can anyone verify that?"

"What the fuck do you think? Of course not."

Rhona knew he wouldn't react well to her next statement. "I'm sorry, but you're not going anywhere."

She ducked out of the office before the boiler blew and motioned a thin, unprepossessing young man to join her.

Rhona watched him approach. Nothing distinctive about him. Middle height, average weight, short, light brown hair — an unremarkable man in his thirties.

"Tim, Tim O'Toole, I work a four-to-twelve shift, so I thought I'd better be one of the ones who talked to you first."

He stretched out his hand. His grip was minimal. It reminded Rhona of holding wet, cold pasta, slimy and sticky simultaneously.

"Did you know Ms. Trepanier?"

"Sabrina. Oh yes, a beautiful woman." His lips curved into a smile that revealed uneven teeth. "Oh, yes."

"Did you ever talk to her?"

"Oh, no. Woman like that don't talk to men like me." His smile faded into an apologetic grimace. "The women who talk to me are the ones in grocery stores, women who *have* to speak to me."

What young man would say something like that? He wasn't movie star handsome, but there was nothing wrong with his looks.

"Where were you last night?"

A quick glance to either side. "Oh, I go out," he said in a voice so low Rhona strained to hear. "I don't get home from work until almost one and I can't sleep, so I walk the streets at night." He produced a rueful smile. "Ever since I worked as a watchman, I got used to being awake at night." He produced a tiny smile. "You couldn't call it a *night* life, but it's definitely a *nocturnal* life."

"Where do you work?"

"At Sobey's supermarket. I stock the shelves." He shrugged. "Not a great job, but if you don't want to work in the daytime, there isn't a huge choice."

A second nocturnal witness was a plus. She hoped he was as observant as Agnes Johnson.

"Did you see anything unusual last night?"

He appeared to be running a mental video. "Oh, not here. All sorts of people coming and going, though. The fifth floor women are busy, busy women."

"Have you ever used their services?" Rhona asked.

His small, pale blue eyes widened, showing yellow, bloodstreaked whites. "Oh, not me. Never." He bent forward, releasing an enveloping cloud of pungent aftershave. "Oh, I'd like to, but I don't imagine I could afford to."

Rhona felt an urge to laugh. It wasn't the answer she'd expected. Maybe she should suggest he save up and give himself a treat.

"Perhaps when we run the tapes to see who came and went last night, you could help identify people."

He leaned even farther forward, overwhelming her with his aftershave. "Oh, I'd like to *help* the police. Just let me know."

When he'd gone, she checked how many were waiting and rendezvoused with Ian, whose most recent interviewee had walked down the hall.

"How's it going?" she said.

"It'll take us a while to sift through this mob and find out who might have had cause. Nobody so far lit up the red buttons. How about you?"

"Two residents who are up at night. One, Agnes Johnson, sits at her window and doesn't seem to miss anything. The other didn't offer any information. Also spoke to one angry man who admitted using our murder victim's services. Not bad for starters."

"Next I'm talking to the construction workers repairing the balconies. Ms. Trepanier's window was open, and scaling the scaffolding the extra few feet to reach it would have been a cinch for any of those guys."

That could be promising.

NINE

CHAOS reigned in the hangar-like room where ten dog owners, supporters, and puppies awaited their lesson. Hollis, Jay, and Crystal fought to control the overexcited Barlow, who lunged forward, barking and whining to be allowed to socialize with each and every dog.

Previously, Hollis had taken him to young puppy training, where his one claim to fame was being the only puppy not to pee on the floor. Hollis had spent hours trying to train him to walk on a loose leash, rather than hauling her along in his wake. She'd become a devotee of Cesar Millan, the National Geographic channel's dog guru, and adopted his ideas of dog psychology. Most of the time Barlow accepted her as the alpha dog and, except on occasions like this, even eleven-year-old Jay could control him.

Waves of ammonia-laden air forced Hollis to breathe shallowly, but she'd signed what she suspected was a legal agreement with the breeder committing her to enroll Barlow in dog training classes. She'd vowed to herself that she'd turn the willful, headstrong puppy into a well-behaved dog.

Chris, the rotund instructor, who wore a too-small purple T-shirt with "City Dog" blazoned across her ample chest, bellowed over the cacophony of barking. "Please take a seat and listen."

Metal folding chairs scraped on the concrete floor as dogs and owners settled down. It wasn't quiet, but the decibel level had dropped. Hollis, anchoring Barlow close to her with a short leash and an iron grip, invited Crystal and Jay to sit on either side, knowing their barricading presence would prevent Barlow from launching himself at any dog parked next to him. Sitting in the third and last row of chairs, she observed the crowd.

Mabel, the adorable low-energy St. Bernard, leaned on her owner, a pretty, petite blonde woman. MiMi, the impossibly tiny teacup Chihuahua, was huddled under her owner's chair, tail tucked between her legs. Hollis thought that if she was that small in a surging mass of half-grown dogs, she'd hide too. Three rescue dogs of indeterminate parentage along with a chocolate Lab, a labradoodle, a Wheaton, and a Jack Russell that bounced with the elasticity of an Indian rubber ball completed the roll. It was a diverse group of dogs, and the owners or handlers were equally varied.

"I see that a number of dogs have brought several people with them," Chris said. "You will remember from previous classes that we have only one person with a dog. You may take turns, as we will do each exercise at least three times." She smiled toothily, with little warmth. "Take positions around the room. We will do a long down and stay," she instructed.

Chairs scraped.

"I'll go first, then Jay and then Crystal," Hollis said, tightening her grip on Barlow.

Despite his afternoon failure to obey this command, when there was an audience he could do it pretty well, and she'd brought a pocketful of liver treats to keep him focused.

At the hour's end, Hollis felt exhausted but Barlow resisted being led out.

"He did really good, didn't he?" Jay said. "Crystal and I did too."

"You certainly did, you'll be dog trainers before you know it," Hollis said.

"I'd like to be a vet," Crystal said as she walked beside Hollis. "It could never happen. It would cost way too much."

Hollis turned to look at Crystal. It surprised her when preteens expressed long-term goals. "There are always scholarships," she said and was about to add a cliched comment about working hard when it occurred to her that she knew nothing about Crystal and shouldn't make facile remarks.

"I don't want to be a vet," Jay said, jumping over the cracks in the sidewalk. "I'll be a detective like Nancy Drew."

This ambition didn't surprise Hollis, but she smiled to herself thinking how surprised Jay would be if she knew how much detecting her foster mother had done. Maybe someday she'd tell her. They'd reached the second-hand Mazda van Hollis had bought to replace her much-loved truck. She'd purchased it when the CAS's notification that they'd accepted her foster parent application arrived on the same day as an email saying that the Flat-coat breeder had a puppy for her. There was no way to squeeze two dogs, Jay, and herself into the truck, let alone bring along Jay's friends.

"How about a mug of hot chocolate when we get home," Hollis said.

"I'll go up and tell my aunt," Crystal said.

Hollis dealt with the police officer stationed at the entrance to the underground parking garage, manipulated the van into her allotted space, and shepherded her pack to the elevators.

"I'll be down in a minute," Crystal promised as Jay, Hollis, and Barlow got out on the first floor.

Inside the apartment Hollis flicked on the lights, said hello to MacTee, and headed for the kitchen, where she filled and plugged in the kettle. She spooned powdered hot chocolate into three mugs, pulled a package of oatmeal raisin cookies from the cupboard, and was arranging them on a blue-and-white plate when the apartment door banged and Crystal raced into the kitchen.

"She's gone," she shouted. "She didn't wait, didn't take me. She's gone. Aunt Mary's gone. The door was unlocked. She's gone. She left me behind. I went down to the garage. Her car's gone."

Crystal's angry eyes, white face, and shivering told Hollis that the child was both furious and frightened.

Time to take charge.

"There's probably an explanation? Sit down while we figure out what it might be."

Crystal didn't move. "I knew it. I just knew it. Now what will happen to me?" she wailed.

"Right now what will happen to you is drinking something sweet to make you feel better. I'll make the hot chocolate and we'll talk about what *could* have happened."

Jay took her friend's hand. "It'll be okay." She pulled a chair away from the table for Crystal, who allowed herself to be moved like a piece of furniture.

Hollis poured the boiling water on top of the chocolate powder in each blue mug and stirred thoroughly before setting them on the table.

Crystal stared at the drink but made no move to raise it to her lips.

Jay picked up her friend's cup. "You need this, Crystal. I read that a big slurp of sugar helps you get over shock. If you think your aunt has left you, you've had a big one, so drink."

Her words penetrated. Crystal obediently sipped.

Hollis marshalled what little she knew about Crystal, who lived with her Aunt Mary, a woman Hollis pegged as an Aboriginal without any concrete evidence to support her assumption. The accountant had Hollis check up on tardy tenants, and Mary's name never appeared on his list, so she must pay her rent on time. Whenever Hollis met Mary in the lobby, the woman responded minimally to Hollis's attempts to chat.

Not much to go on. She tried to think if anything in the files would help. A few months earlier at the start of the job, she'd read through all the lease agreements and found out as much as she could about the building's tenants. For some she made notes to help her remember their idiosyncrasies and obsessions, but she had none for Mary.

Hollis sat down. She'd probably get more information if she didn't loom over the child. Being almost six feet tall, she knew she could be intimidating.

"Couldn't your aunt have gone out and forgotten to lock the door?" Hollis asked.

Crystal reached for a cookie, swallowed a mouthful of hot chocolate, and shook her head. "No way. Whether she's home or out she never, never leaves it unlocked. She has three locks and she's super careful to always lock the door."

"There are other people living with you, aren't there. Are they gone?"

Crystal shrugged. "They're not there."

"How many people live with you?"

"Sometimes one, sometimes two or three."

"Family? Friends?"

Crystal eyed her warily and shrugged.

"I suppose they're your aunt's friends. Maybe she left you a note to tell you where she's gone," Hollis said.

Crystal tipped her mug and finished her drink before she replied. "I doubt it. Aunt Mary took me because my mother's dead and my grandmother's sick. She didn't want me but there was no one else." The bitterness in Crystal's voice shocked Hollis.

What had happened to the child's mother? Why didn't Crystal think Mary would leave her a note if she'd unexpectedly gone out? Clearly, Crystal didn't want to tell her anything about her aunt. Maybe the apartment would reveal more.

"When you finish your drink we'll go upstairs and search for clues to tell us where your aunt went."

Jay, jiggling from one foot to the other as she followed their conversation, took the matter in hand. "Hey, just like Nancy Drew. Maybe we should wear gloves and take a magnifying glass." She looked at Hollis. "Have you got stuff like that?"

Hollis shook her head. "I have, but we haven't reached that stage." She registered that the puppy had inserted his nose into the pocket of the jean jacket Crystal had hung on the back of the chair. Hollis pointed to the jacket. "Don't leave anything where Barlow can get it," she said as she did every time they left the dog alone.

Crystal grabbed the jacket, shrugged into it, foraged in the pockets of her blue jeans, and yanked out three keys on a grubby blue satin ribbon. "I didn't need these. I didn't lock the door when I left in case my aunt came back." She frowned at Hollis. "We should lock it after you see that there's no way to tell where she's gone. You could write a note telling her I'm here and stick it to the door. I don't know why you don't believe me, but if it makes you happy we'll look." She picked up her cup and carried it to the sink before she headed out.

Jay left her mug on the table and scrambled to join Crystal. Hollis sighed as she followed the girls. She suspected Crystal was right and they wouldn't learn anything about Mary's whereabouts.

Upstairs, the three hesitated outside the apartment before Hollis led them into a small foyer that opened directly into an apartment that was the mirror image of Hollis's. The door might have been open when Crystal came home, but nothing untoward appeared to have happened in the hall. The pictures hung on the wall, the rug lay on the floor, and a bowl of keys sat on a demi-lune table. Only rhinestone-encrusted sunglasses lying on the floor were out of place.

The three stopped.

There was no evidence that Mary's departure had been involuntary. And how would her kidnapper have evaded the police, who had checked everyone entering and leaving the building and garage since Hollis reported Sabrina's murder?

Crystal had told them Mary's vehicle was gone. But there was no law against leaving the garage. Perhaps a very cool customer could have risked forcing a woman into her own car and driving out, but Hollis had trouble visualizing a man hustling Mary out of the building into the garage, hitting her on the head, and sticking her in the trunk.

The security tapes recorded activities in the garage. The police possessed them. Surely they would have noticed? And what of the unidentified tenants? Who and where were they?

"Nancy Drew would see if anything suspicious has happened in the rest of the apartment," Jay said, barging ahead of them.

"Jay, wait. Let me go first. We don't know what happened here," Hollis said and again led the way.

First they forged into the combined living and dining room. A sectional dark green velour sofa, wood-and-glass coffee table, two folding chairs, two standard lamps, and a large old-fashioned TV on a stand were undisturbed. On the wall over the sofa a large poster that reproduced a classic photo of an American 1930s woman sharecropper standing in a doorway added a depressing note. On the opposite wall another poster of an Indian chief in full regalia dominated the room. Venetian blinds covered the windows. A utilitarian room with nothing to indicate a struggle.

In the dining area a bridge table with four folding chairs pulled up to it, a brown laminate china cabinet, a white particle board bookcase stuffed with books, and a treadmill filled the space.

Hollis didn't know what signs to look for, but it wouldn't hurt to learn more about Mary. She squatted in front of the bookcase. Many books on Aboriginal history and law. A neatly alphabetized section on addictions. A few novels and cookbooks. An eclectic mix. A worn book with a soft green cover lay horizontally on top of the others. Hollis removed it. *The Song My Paddle Sings*, a well-thumbed collection of Pauline Johnson's poetry. Interesting. If she had time she'd come back and look through the volumes to see if Mary had annotated or folded and inserted relevant articles between the pages.

The adjoining kitchen's tidiness impressed her.

Crystal grabbed her sleeve. "Never mind the kitchen. *Our* stuff, Aunt Mary's and mine, is in there." She pointed down the hall to a closed door. Heavy-footed, she stomped down the hall and flung the door open.

Hollis and Jay traipsed into the bedroom, where two neatly made single beds, one with a bedraggled toy monkey on the pillow, shared a small chest of drawers with a two-armed gooseneck lamp.

Two unmatched white DIY bureaus crowded together, as did two desks and a tall grey filing cabinet. The contents of a bulletin board over one desk, along with a collection of bobble-headed dolls lined up in front of a computer, clearly belonged to Crystal. The second desktop with its mug of pens and computer must be Mary's. A navy backpack tucked under the desk attracted Hollis's attention.

"Okay if I take a look in this?" Hollis said to Crystal, who stared sadly around the room.

"It's Aunt Mary's. Go ahead."

Opening zipper after zipper, Hollis found nothing and was about to replace it when she poked into a small side pocket and found a notebook. She looked at Crystal, who shrugged. "She always kept that with her. *Really* weird that she doesn't have it. Maybe it'll tell you where she is."

"I'll return it," Hollis said as she stuffed it in her pocket. She waved a hand at the room across the hall. "Whose bedroom is that?"

"Different people's," Crystal said, not meeting Hollis's gaze.

"Let's have a look."

Hollis opened the second bedroom door. Two bunk beds, one with bottom and top neatly made, contrasted dramatically with the tangle of bedding and clothing on the other. It was as if an invisible line divided the room. Order versus chaos. Hollis imagined how difficult it must be for the neatnik to live with her absolute opposite.

Hollis turned back to the girls who hovered in the hall. She pointed to the cyclonic confusion. "Crystal, is this half of the room always like this?"

"I don't know. I never come in. They keep the door closed."

"Who lives here with you?" That was the first thing to determine. Then she'd find out what they'd been doing.

Crystal allowed her short-bobbed black hair to swing forward and partially hide her face as she scuffed her shoe and fixed her gaze on the floor. "Different people," she muttered.

"That doesn't tell me much. Why did they live here?"

"Aunt Mary never said. I asked once and she told me it was better if I didn't know."

Crystal's obstinate refusal to provide meaningful information irritated Hollis. "You must have wondered. Didn't you talk to them? Didn't you ask their names?"

Crystal shook her head. "Mary didn't want me to know and I stopped asking. I didn't want her to send me away."

Send her away? What had gone on in this room? "I don't think we're going to find out anything here," Hollis said, although she longed to search the drawers, lift mattresses, read clothing labels, and go through pockets. She might be the building's custodian, but until she had a few more answers, she'd be abusing her job if she succumbed to the urge

Stepping out of the room, she gently put her hand under Crystal's chin and raised her head until the girl finally looked at her. "Did your aunt have enemies?"

Crystal shook her head. "I don't know."

"I don't understand any of this and you're not helping," Hollis said.

The angry lines around Crystal's mouth and eyes disappeared. Her brown eyes filled with tears. "I'll never see her again," she sobbed.

Not the time to give the child the third degree. Hollis pulled her close and hugged her. "I'm sure you will, but you must help me if we're going to find her. Let's have another look in your room and see if we can figure something out." She released Crystal. With shoulders bowed like a prisoner facing execution, the child walked directly to the cupboard in her room, where she clutched a blue velour robe hanging on the back of the door, buried her face in the robe's soft folds, pulled it from its hook, and sank to the floor.

Jay squatted beside her, wrapped her arms around her friend, and rocked her. "You don't know she's gone for good. Hollis will find her. She's really smart and her boyfriend's smart too. Don't worry, we'll get her back."

Tears filled Hollis's eyes. Given that Jay had lost her own mother when she was a young child and her longtime foster mother only months earlier, it was clear that she related to Crystal's pain. Maybe, if they could find Crystal's aunt, in some small way it might compensate Jay for her losses.

"I'll speak to the police at the door...." Her voice trailed away. What would she say? If there had been an abduction, how had the abductor managed to get a grown woman out of the apartment and the building without attracting attention? It seemed like an impossible task. Furthermore, unless there were clear indications of foul play, the police counseled waiting twenty-four hours before filing a missing persons report.

Crystal dropped the dressing gown, stopped crying, and stared wide-eyed at Hollis. "No. No police. Never. No police." A shuddering sob. "No. Don't do that."

Crystal might not know or admit that she knew whatever it was that her aunt was involved with, but she knew the police mustn't be called.

Whether she liked it or not, Hollis had a job: finding Mary Montour.

TEN

RHONA and Ian finished the tenant interviews at seven thirty.

"What have we got?" Ian asked as he swept the relevant documents into a pile on Hollis's desk.

"Not much. Those first interviews told us the most."

"No one knew anything about Ms. Trepanier or her background. That has to be a priority. Her appointment book and her laptop may provide useful connections," Ian said.

"First we need to eat. Let's walk over to Yonge Street and pick up a burger," Rhona said, thinking that junk food was the police officer's secret enemy.

"Good idea. While we're there I'll tell you about the construction workers. One knew more about the fifth floor residents than he should have."

Leaving officers to monitor, to take the names of any tenants to whom they hadn't spoken, and to caution them not to leave the area, the two detectives walked to Yonge Street and crossed to a pub.

Inside the door a sound wave smacked them. The place was hopping and the decibel level approached the auditory danger mark.

"We can't talk here. There's a Tim Hortons down the block, but it isn't conducive to quiet chatting. I wonder where else we can get a quick bite?" Rhona shouted.

"A friend of mine lives near here. We often eat at Terroni. Good Italian food. It's a block south of St. Clair."

A friend? Male or female? Rhona longed to ask, but Ian would sniff disdainfully and ask her why she wanted to know.

Pedestrians thronged Yonge Street. People exited from the St. Clair Centre coming from the subway stop in the basement or from a thriving Goodlife Fitness Studio. Terroni proved quieter than the pub and they followed the hostess to a table that promised privacy.

Rhona informed the server that they were in a hurry. After taking a minute to survey the large menus, they chose the day's special, penne with a rose vodka sauce, and Verde salads. While they waited Rhona gave in to temptation and enjoyed the warm bread that she dipped in olive oil and balsamic vinegar.

Ian refused the bread. As Rhona worked her way through the contents of the bread basket he said nothing, but she took his silence and raised eyebrows to reveal his contempt for her obvious lack of willpower.

Munching happily, she chose to ignore his attitude. Instead she said, "What about the construction workers?"

Ian sipped his water. "Most had no idea who lived in the building and only cared about doing the job." He folded his hands in his lap. "But one young guy with dark hair and dark skin, maybe East Asian or Aboriginal, said he always looked in the apartments when they worked on the balconies. Didn't seem the slightest bit embarrassed either."

"Did he admit that he knew any women on the fifth? According to Hollis, the owners replaced their balconies when they renovated the building a couple of years ago."

"Said his boss worked on them but that was years before he was around."

"Get any background on him?" Rhona asked as she reached in her bag to make sure she'd switched on her cell phone.

"He'd only been here a couple of weeks. When I asked him what he did before this job, he said he'd worked on high steel construction."

The server delivered their meals. Both opted for freshly ground parmesan, and after the initial taste, agreed they'd chosen well and ate in silence for several minutes.

Rhona took the opportunity to study Ian. Although they'd now worked together on several cases, she wasn't any closer to knowing more than a few facts about him. Reticent didn't begin to describe her partner. To herself she acknowledged how appealing she found him, but he'd given no indication that he was attracted to her. Probably just as well. The department frowned on romances between detectives.

"Why are you staring at me?" Ian said.

"Sorry, I was thinking about what you said. Often Newfoundlanders and Iroquois work on high steel. They built half the skyscrapers in Manhattan and are famous for their ability and skill, and most of all for their lack of fear when cavorting around forty floors above the ground." She popped the last morsel of bread in her mouth. "Was he an Aboriginal?"

"Could have been. Would that be important?"

"Might be. We don't know for sure that Ms. Trepanier was the real target. After all, Ginny Wuttenee usually occupied that bed, and Ginny's a Saskatchewan Cree. Could be a coincidence, but we'll follow up on this guy. What's his name?"

Ian pulled his notebook from his pocket and consulted it. "Donald Hill," he said.

While Ian and Rhona waited for the bill, Rhona said, "Have you settled into the department?"

Ian eyed her as if measuring the reason for the question. "Pretty much."

"You found a good place to live?" Rhona said.

"Twenty questions?" Ian replied.

"When you have a partner, it's good to know more about him than name and badge number. You certainly aren't the most forthcoming partner I've ever had."

"I'm forty-two, unmarried, don't have any pets or plants, and like my job."

Rhona sighed, "Okay, I get the picture. You want your life to be private. I accept but ..."

Ian produced a grin, revealing very white teeth, lighting up his face and making him more attractive than ever. He pushed the shock of black hair off his forehead. "You feel that if one day a decision I make may determine whether you live or die, you'd be happier if you had background information."

Rhona accepted the cheques from the server and nodded at Ian. "Something like that."

"I love horses and horse racing but not enough to belong to Gamblers Anonymous. If I had time, I'd buy a horse but I don't. I like Thai and Indian food, hate KFC, and give the Swiss Chalet chicken an A rating. I like clothes, especially shoes, expensive shoes. I've furnished my apartment with antiques and I have a home gym,"

"Antiques?" Rhona repeated. She would have pegged him for a minimalist who loved modern.

Ian continued to grin. "Surprise, surprise. Early Canadian. I own a pine sideboard from the Eastern Townships, probably made around 1830, two corner cupboards, a spool bed in my guest room, and a settle in my living room."

"A settle. What's that?"

"A day bed. Farmhouse kitchens had one so the farmer could have a lie down after the big noon meal, or anyone who was sick could recuperate in the warm kitchen."

"I am surprised," Rhona said as they stood and moved to the door. She wasn't going to find out anything else. Time to move on. "To change the subject, whoever killed Ms. Trepanier must have realized it wasn't Ms. Wuttenee, but maybe he was too out of control to stop or he was afraid if she woke and saw him he'd be caught. How much information about Ms. Wuttenee's background did you get from your interview?"

They'd reached the door. Ian held it open for Rhona. "Sorry. I know all about equality, but opening doors for women is a hard habit to break. About Ms. Wuttenee, I agree she may have been the intended victim. It's not too late to talk to her again. Why don't we tell her to come down to Ms. Grant's office and speak to us after we check out Ms. Trepanier's apartment? If we have time after that, we could go through Ms. Trepanier's appointment book."

"Good plan. If the killer got the wrong girl, Ginny Wuttenee may be in danger, and the sooner we pin down her life story, the more likely we are to know whether or not she needs protection."

"Ginny Wuttenee is staying with Ms. Nesrallah. We'll stop and tell her to meet us downstairs in the party room in an hour when we've finished in Sabrina's apartment," Rhona said.

"Not Ms. Grant's office?"

"No. We've interfered enough in their lives. The party room will be fine."

"We should have it to ourselves. No one will be partying right now," Ian said.

Before entering Sabrina's apartment, they pulled on gloves and protective covers for their shoes.

"If we turn up anything significant, we won't have contaminated the site," Rhona said.

The apartment reeked of paint.

"I thought the new paints didn't smell," Ian said.

"Latex is better. They've used oil in here," Rhona said, flicking on the hall light to reveal deep amber walls, the colour intensified by the amber shade on the overhead light. The effect was strange but attractive. From the hall they moved to the living room.

"Charcoal. Isn't it smashing," Ian said. "The white woodwork, the ebony furniture — absolutely smashing."

Rhona wasn't quite so taken with it, but it was a stunning room.

"I never considered charcoal. My pine furniture would stand out against it. I see a project coming on."

Rhona reflected that if Ian had made that statement with any of his male colleagues, he would have been mocked, if not to his face then behind his back. Maybe the fact that he revealed so little about himself was a careful cover-up because he realized how he'd be perceived. Interesting. Maybe he wasn't the metrosexual she'd pegged him for. Maybe ... but what did that have to do with anything.

"Nothing personal here. It could be a hotel," Rhona said.

They continued to the master bedroom, also painted charcoal with a black iron bedframe and white linens. A well-stocked bar cart and the same mirrored ceiling they'd seen in Ginny's bedroom as well as a white floktari rug on the black-stained floor made a dramatic but impersonal impression.

Ian slid open the drawer of one bedside table.

"Anything?" Rhona asked.

"A selection of condoms," he said and bent to open the cupboard underneath. "Sex toys to please almost anyone."

"See what's in the one on the other side," Rhona instructed.

Ian walked around the bed and checked. "Same kind of stuff, but there's more sadomasochistic things — a whip, handcuffs." He probed further. "Leather masks and other things," he said and shut the door.

"Tools of the trade, I suppose. Could be relevant — too soon to tell. We need to know more about her, who she is, and where she came from. Let's try the other bedroom. She must stash personal belongings somewhere. This room reveals nothing about her personality other than her dramatic taste in furnishings and colour and her willingness to do whatever her clients asked."

She opened the door of the second bedroom and stopped to absorb the total contrast to the rest of the apartment. Soft rose walls, a white wooden single bed with a beautiful quilt. Four more beautiful antique quilts hung on the walls. On the white desk an open, ready-to-go, state-of-the-art sewing machine and a closed Apple laptop took up the space. Two tall white bookcases filled with rectangular white baskets and a series of black binders, a chest of drawers with a wall-mounted flat-screen TV, and an armchair slip-covered in cream cotton with a footstool upholstered in rose-patterned chintz completed the furnishings. A multi-coloured rag rug on the floor added to the room's welcoming coziness.

"The *real* Sabrina Trepanier lived here," Ian said.

"No photos, which may or may not mean she's totally alienated from her family. Some people don't like having photos around."

"Because they think a photographer steals their soul? I remember learning in introductory anthropology that some tribes in the South Pacific believe that and won't have their pictures taken," Ian said.

"Maybe that's their reason, but I think I've read that for some people photos remind them constantly of happier times, of the speed with which life is passing, of people they've loved who've died, and of their own mortality," Rhona said.

"Interesting explanation. I'll think about that, because I don't display photos in my apartment. I have some stashed away but not on display."

Rhona, who'd been about to open the top bureau drawer, smiled at Ian. "At last we have something in common. I feel the same way. Photos make me sad, and you won't find any in my apartment either. I do have photo albums. It's funny, people who visit always comment and their remarks always sound critical."

Ian grinned back. "What do you know, something in common." He turned to the desk, where he pushed the sewing machine to one side, opened the computer, and booted it up.

Rhona found a tidy selection of underwear in the top drawer of the bureau. On the left it was black, filmy, and sexy, and on the right utilitarian and unexciting. This woman certainly had compartmentalized her life.

"The computer doesn't require a password, which is not usually a good thing for us," Ian said over his shoulder. "The user either has nothing to hide or doesn't think anyone else will ever look at it." He folded himself onto the white wooden desk chair, which had a grey Obus cushion attached to its back, and began clicking away. "Speaking of family, I'll check the address book."

A minute later he said, "No Trepaniers here. Now I'll pull up her emails."

Rhona continued with the drawers. She felt underneath each pile of T shirts, sweaters, workout clothes, but found nothing. She then removed the drawers to check their undersides and the back interior of the bureau. Again she found nothing.

"We need to know if her real name is Sabrina Trepanier and if she has any family contacts. You may have to scan subject headings to figure that out," Rhona said.

"I'm ahead of you. I've done a brief run-through. Most correspondence is with quilters, suppliers of fabric, and other people connected to sewing. Now I'm looking in her folders. None labelled family. One for friends in Toronto, one for passwords, one for Aeroplan."

"Aeroplan. Check that one. If she ever travelled she had to have a passport, and it will have her birth certificate name."

"Got it. Claire Sabrina Trepanier."

"Mystery solved."

"Now to find her family. I'll check filed information and the sent emails. Usually that list is shorter than received."

"Is there a heading for clients? I thought that was how escort services operated," Rhona said.

"Nothing."

Rhona, finished with the bureau and moved to the bookcase. Sabrina had not been a reader. A pile of *People, US, In Style,* and quilting magazines did not count as literature. The baskets held fabric and sewing equipment. Rhona glanced at the bed. She thought the carefully pieced pattern was called double wedding ring. She didn't know where the information had come from — crafts and sewing had never interested her. In one basket, completed blocks in pinks, creams, and mauves almost filled the space. They were beautiful and she felt a momentary sadness that Sabrina's quilt would never be finished. She opened another covered basket and found neatly organized files. Thumbing through, she discovered that Sabrina had taken a small business course at George Brown College. She had documented her progress towards the establishment of a quilt- and latch-hooking business. A file on possible properties, another on sourcing, on quilt shows and competitions. On a piece of paper she'd written possible names for the store.

"She was a quilter, not a reader, and she was in the final stage of preparing to open a business," Rhona said, reaching for the first of the black binders.

In a minute or two Ian looked up. "What's in the books?" he asked.

"The first one contains dozens of erotic photos, very explicit pictures that Sabrina probably used for escort publicity.

The second one has the traditional shots photographers take for models preparing portfolios. The second album may have been made before she got into the escort business. The photos are the kind a model presents to an agency," Rhona said. She carefully extracted one that showed smiling Sabrina modelling a plaid shirt and jeans that might have come from an L.L. Bean catalogue. She recorded the removal in her notebook. "We'll make copies of this for the white board and to show to any family we find."

"Maybe she intended to take the first route and either didn't get the bookings or learned that the escort business was more lucrative," Ian said.

"That would be my guess," Rhona agreed. "She seems to have been an organized woman who had a goal and was prepared to do whatever it took to get there."

"I agree. I just checked her trash. She used the computer to make dates and dragged the info into the trash so there wouldn't be a record. Presumably she did that in case her apartment was raided and her computer was seized. Fortunately for us, she hasn't emptied the trash in quite a while, so we'll retrieve the information."

Rhona moved to the cupboard. "Still no family."

"No, only friends and not many of those. We could contact them and ask about her background," Ian said and he leaned over. "Wait a minute. I've moved to the desk drawers. In the bottom one she has files, and one contains personal documents."

Rhona left the cupboard and moved to stand beside him.

He flipped open a purple folder with inside pockets and extricated a birth certificate, a will, and other legal documents.

"This copy of her will is two weeks old. Why so recent?" Ian said.

"Because she was afraid and wanted to tidy up her life in case anything happened to her," Rhona said as she bent to read over Ian's shoulder. "Aside from two special bequests, she leaves everything to the Toronto Children's Aid Society. Her collection of antique quilts is to go to her mother, Marie France Trepanier, of Oakville, with a thank-you to her and to her grandmother, Marie Claire Arsenault, if she's alive, for teaching her to sew. All other clothes and personal possessions go to Virginia Wuttenee, currently living at 68 Delisle Street. Now all we have to do is locate her mother. Trepanier can't be that common a name in the Oakville area."

Ian picked up a file of monthly bank statements. "She has money, most of it in GICs. She must have been cautious, 'cause they don't pay much." He looked over at Rhona, who had opened the cupboard. "Seems she thought of being an escort as a business and a way to accumulate as much capital as she could."

"I wonder why we didn't find her purse in Ms. Wuttenee's place. Perhaps the killer took it to cover his tracks or make it look as if the crime was a robbery gone bad," Rhona said before they moved downstairs. She phoned the investigating team and emphasized how important it was to intensify the search for the missing purse.

When Rhona and Ian entered the party room, Ginny, long hair shining, face scrubbed clean, wearing blue jeans and a cavernous maroon sweatshirt with "Toronto" emblazoned on the front, stood staring into the large fish tank, one of the room's distinguishing features.

"Ms. Wuttenee, we're here," Rhona announced and waved the young woman to a soft, upholstered chair while she chose a firmer one for herself. "Have you remembered anything more that could help us?"

"No. I can't imagine why anyone in the whole world would kill Sabrina. She was nice, really, really nice. You asked about clients. If she didn't make a client happy he wouldn't come back, but why would he kill her? Maybe somebody from her past. She never talked about the past." She rubbed her eyes. "I've tried and tried and tried but I can't think of a single thing to tell you that might help. I wish I could."

"Thanks. If anything does come to you, phone us immediately. Now tell us about yourself, about your background. Give us a picture of yourself," Rhona said.

Ginny glanced quickly at the door as if weighing her options for escape. "You mean a photo?" She looked puzzled.

"Sorry, I didn't mean an actual picture. I meant that we want to learn about you, where you come from, who you know in the city, if you and Ms. Trepanier had any friends in common. That sort of thing." Rhona smiled as encouragingly as she could. She sensed that any previous encounters Ginny had had with the police had been unpleasant, so she did her best to put the young woman at ease. "Take your time and don't worry about deciding what might or might not be important. We'll do that."

Ginny looked from one to the other. Clearly she felt uncomfortable. She shrugged. "Nothing much to tell. As you can see I'm an Indian. I'm a status Indian and grew up on the Red Pheasant reserve. When I was," she paused, "eighteen I came to Toronto."

"How old are you now and where is Red Pheasant?" Ian asked.

"I'm still eighteen. It's in Saskatchewan."

"Then you haven't been here long."

"No. Four months."

"Is Red Pheasant where you went to school?"

"Clifford Wuttenee to grade nine."

"A relative?" Rhona asked.

"Lots of Wuttenees." She shrugged. "I think he was the guy who signed Treaty 6. No relation."

"After grade nine?" Rhona said.

Ginny shifted as if sharp nails covered her chair. "Battleford. North Battleford Comprehensive. My grandmother didn't want me to go to Sakawen. She thought you could fight whites better if you went to their schools."

"What's Sakawen?" Ian asked.

"An Aboriginal high school. They've got two of them now. I had to go to the white school. Believe it or not I stuck it out to graduate because my grandmother really cared. She wanted me to be proud to be Cree, to be strong. She didn't want me to end up like my mother." Unexpectedly, her eyes brimmed and she wiped them with the back of her hand, drawing attention to her bitten nails and cuticles.

"My grandmother insisted that I be proud of who I was and where I came from too," Rhona said. "It makes a difference in your life if someone who loves you believes in you, doesn't it?"

Ginny didn't say anything but she considered Rhona's remarks. "I don't think it's the same when you're an Indian," she said.

"I am and it did," Rhona said.

This time Ginny stared at Rhona as if she could check out her DNA. "*You're* an Indian?"

"My grandmother was born on Poundmaker's reserve. She took me back there in the summers when I was a little girl."

"But she didn't live there?"

"No. After she left residential school she worked as a maid in Battleford and married a young Methodist minister. You won't remember, but until they changed the Indian Act, an Indian woman who married a white man lost her status and couldn't live on the reserve. We visited family but we couldn't stay. "

Ginny smiled. "Wow. And now you're a cop. Pretty good for an Indian kid."

"Thanks, but we need to get back to you." Rhona glanced at Ian and knew by his raised eyebrow and quizzical smile that he thought she'd been out of line. He probably considered it a tactic to persuade Ginny to reveal whatever she was hiding. It wasn't true. Rhona hadn't intended to reveal as much. She was still reacting to the Spirit Report and her own acknowledgment of the shame about her past that she sometimes felt.

"What happened to your mother?" Ian probed.

"She died," Ginny snapped without looking at him.

"People do. What did she die from?" Ian said.

"This has fuck-all to do with anything, but for your satisfaction, my father killed her and he's in the Prince Albert pen."

"I'm sorry." Ian did look as if he wished he hadn't been quite so abrupt. "How old were you?"

"Four."

Rhona closed her eyes. How horrible and traumatic. Probably another example of a man who felt undervalued and inferior using alcohol to deaden the pain, and when that didn't work, turning his self-hatred and rage against those closest to him. She opened her eyes and met Ginny's steady gaze.

"There's nothing I can say except I'm sorry."

"Thanks," Ginny said.

"What happened after you graduated?" Ian asked.

Pause. Rhona felt Ginny was considering whether to tell them something else. From experience she knew they should sit back and wait. But there was no way to communicate her belief to Ian, who plowed on.

"Well, what did you do?"

"Came to Toronto. Got picked up at the bus station. Worked the street until Fatima found me and here I am."

"Your pimp must have been angry. Did he come after you?"

"Probably, but he didn't find me, and now I'm always careful where I go."

Time for Rhona to issue a warning. "I'm glad to hear that, because we believe you, not Ms. Trepanier, may have been the target. Sabrina was in your bed and the killer may have been after you. That's why we wanted to know your background, to see if you could think of anyone who might have reason to kill you. Tell us about your pimp."

A clearly shocked Ginny pulled back as if Rhona had menaced her with a hot poker. "My god," she said, looking from one detective to the other. "Do you really think so?"

"Your pimp?" Ian persisted.

"Jigs, I never knew his last name. A guy from Nova Scotia. Treated me real good at first but ended up beating me."

"Drugs?"

Ginny shook her head. "He wanted me to. My older sister, Loraine, got caught in that mess. She died from an overdose and I didn't want that to happen to me. I just wanted to make money and have nice clothes. Fatima saved my life." A flash of fear on her face. "If you find him don't tell him I told you, or tell him where I am. If he could, I think he *would* kill me."

"We won't," he assured her. "Now tell us about Ms. Trepanier. You were good friends?"

Rhona watched the tension drain from Ginny. Her shoulders, which had been bunched around her ears, resumed their normal position, her hands which had been clenched in her lap, opened and her lips, which had been pressed into a straight line, softened.

"Yes. It surprised me that Sabrina wanted to be friends, because she was so smart." Her eyes lit up and the corners of her mouth lifted. "Did you find out that she planned to open her own business?" Ginny didn't wait for an answer but rushed on. "She said that when she did I could live with her and help her in the store. She was teaching me all about fabric and quilts and stuff. My grandmother used to do quill and beadwork and sew. She taught me the old-time stuff when I was a little girl and said I had a gift for it. I guess maybe Sabrina thought so too." Ginny stretched her fingers as if to prove that these were hands that could make things.

"Sabrina took me downtown to Queen Street to the most beautiful fabric stores. She knew the people who worked there and they all liked her. No one there knew what we did. I never said much but she was always telling me stuff about how important it was to use the right thread and buy fabric that was suited for quilt-making." Ginny looked as if she was reviewing a lesson. "Not all quilts are made of cotton. Only the ones used on beds. The ones that hang on walls can have all kinds of stuff on them. You can print photos on fabric and sew lace and buttons and make them so they stick out. I've forgotten the name for that, but you use cord and a special foot on the sewing machine. I had fun."

"I'm sure you did and you'll miss her," Rhona said.

The smile disappeared and Ginny stared hopelessly at them. "Now it will never happen. Poor Sabrina."

"Did you and Ms. Trepanier have friends other than the women on the fifth floor?" Rhona asked.

"I didn't. I don't know about Sabrina."

"Have you identified any clients who threatened or frightened you?"

"Only a couple. I told you already that Sabrina kept records and wouldn't have had a man like that again. She was so beautiful and elegant that men took her places when they needed a date. Did you look in her cupboard?"

Rhona nodded.

"Didn't she have gorgeous clothes? She dressed like a lady and she talked like one too. I didn't know her for long but I loved her," Ginny said in a small voice.

The feeling must have been mutual, Rhona thought, because Sabrina's will made Ginny her beneficiary. "I'm sure you did. If you think of anyone who might have wanted to hurt her or any client who threatened her, please call either one of us." Rhona handed Ginny a card. "That's my cell phone number on the bottom, and you may call at any hour if you think of anything."

"I'll think hard. I want you to catch the guy. He took away the most important person in my life, and I'll do anything I can to help you," Ginny said with her chin thrust forward.

This was a different woman than the one who'd begun the interview a few minutes earlier. The change had come about not because they'd discussed Ginny's background but because talking about Sabrina had motivated Ginny to do everything she could to help find the killer.

Ginny returned to the security of Fatima's apartment. Once she'd gone Rhona looked at Ian with raised eyebrows. "Could Ginny's pimp have killed Sabrina thinking it was Ginny?"

"Not too likely. Sabrina slept on her back. In even the dimmest light he would have realized the difference," Ian said. "One of the women on the stroll will identify Jigs. We'll talk to them about him. He's sure to have a sheet and that'll help."

"The pimp lost a meal ticket, which must have pissed him off and could have stirred up his other women. We both know a pimp will beat up a girl to keep the rest of his crew in line, but I can't see what he'd get out of killing her except a jail sentence. And how did he get in? He had to come through the window. I can't imagine the pimps we see on the street doing that," Rhona said.

"Not in those white suits and flashy clothes they fancy. Until we know more about Sabrina's life, we won't know if the perp targeted Ginny and got the wrong woman. I'd put my money on a client, and Sabrina's book should help us identify him," Ian said.

"On the other hand, Ginny may be hiding something. I felt she was. If the perp was after her she may have an idea of who it is, but for some reason she isn't telling. We need to consider whether to provide protection," Rhona asked.

"Not yet. The killer won't attack again with the police and security here."

Rhona reached for the bagged diary they'd removed from Sabrina's apartment. "Let's have a look at this and see what we can figure out." She chose a couch that wasn't too deep. Ian joined her.

The diary began in January and Rhona paged through to the day of the murder. Sabrina had noted an afternoon appointment with ST, and beside it she'd added an S in brackets. Opera was listed for the evening and in brackets a circle.

"The security footage will show the time she departed and returned and if her escort came in," Rhona said. "Those security cameras will help, but in this case Agnes Johnson, the woman I interviewed earlier, said she recognized the pink coat and saw them come back."

"Suppose the circle is a zero and it means the guy didn't want anything but an escort?"

"Could be. We'll ask Fatima to match initials to names but not tonight."

"Should be simple to figure out the meaning of her notations. We can check anything that puzzles us with Fatima," Ian said.

Once they'd decided to call it quits, exhaustion wrapped itself around Rhona like a heavy woollen blanket. She couldn't wait to get home for a vodka martini and a tête-à-tête with Opie, the world's largest and most demanding cat.

"I'll be in early," she said to Ian as they parted in the underground parking lot. "Finding and informing Ms. Trepanier's next of kin will be first on the list. Then an analysis of her diary, a review of the security tapes, and more interviews. I still wonder if we should have offered Ms. Wuttenee protection?"

Ian nodded. "The department's resources are stretched. If the killer plans to try again, he won't return until the 'scene' is a little quieter. She should be okay."

As they stood in the dark echoing garage, Rhona couldn't resist one more question. "You off for a drink or home to your petless, plantless condo?"

"Twenty questions again. Here's another item to add to your file folder. Something I thought you would have noticed by now. I seldom drink."

Rhona clapped her hands over her mouth. "Not a drinker! I'm surprised they allowed you on the force. I suppose if I say, 'how come,' you'll regard that as nosiness."

Ian, swinging his keys, shook his head. "You never stop. I'll leave it to you to imagine the worst," he said, turning on his heel to walk away.

No alcohol. Maybe he was an alcoholic. She shouted, "Maybe you'd like to go for herbal tea and talk about the case."

As her words boomed through the cavernous garage, two homicide detectives who had given her a hard time when she joined the Toronto force emerged from the elevator.

"Harassment is illegal. You could be charged," one of them said, only half joking.

Rhona felt colour flood her cheeks. "Right," she said and stepped smartly towards her own vehicle.

At home, work clothes dropped in a pile on her bedroom floor, martini in hand, she flopped on the sofa and flicked on the TV to see what kind of coverage the murder was receiving. On the way to work in the morning she'd pick up *The Sun*, Toronto's best source of information on crime and criminals.

Amazingly, the news reader only reported that a woman had been stabbed. The police spokesperson said the investigation was underway, that they wouldn't be releasing the victim's name until her next of kin had been notified, and that they didn't believe this was a serial killer.

Serial killer indeed. The public and novelists thrilled to the idea. Certainly such killers existed but not in great numbers. Thank god for that. One Robert Pickton was enough. That thought led to second one. The police and the Crown had blown an early charge against Pickton when he'd been accused of attempted murder. The case had been dismissed because the chief witness, a prostitute who'd barely escaped with her life, had been considered unreliable, although all the evidence supported her allegations. Now most police forces realized that prejudice against such testimony must not happen again.

On the off chance that this had been one of a series of killings, in the morning she would feed the details into the computer, searching for similar unsolved cases and watch for new ones that could be related. What thread would tie them together? Prostitution? Robert Pickton killed sex trade workers, as did several other noted serial killers. Sometimes victims physically resembled one another. Brunettes or redheads or blondes of a certain age. Sometimes the killer apparently chose his victims randomly, but closer investigation usually revealed he had known each of the women and none would have been alarmed by his initial contact.

Opie, who'd received a special fishy treat to make up for Rhona's late arrival, finished his snack. Reeking of fish, he jumped on her lap, kneaded her legs, and settled down to watch TV with her.

ELEVEN

HOLLIS needed information. "Crystal, I understand how upset you are, but to find Mary I need you to level with me, to tell me more about your aunt and the women who live here."

Crystal stood up, still clutching her aunt's robe. She shook her head from side to side but said nothing. Her mouth set in a straight line, she continued to shake her head.

Loyalty or fear? Each would require Hollis to take a different approach. Maybe a little of both. Careful wording required.

"Crystal, please help."

She paused. If she promised not to go to the police, Crystal might talk, but that wasn't something she could do. What if Crystal's aunt was involved in drug dealing, murder, human trafficking — Hollis couldn't be part of that. How about a specific question.

"Crystal, can you think of a reason your aunt might leave suddenly?"

Crystal again buried her face in the robe's folds. When she looked up her face had a bleak, grey midwinter look of despair. "Not really," she said.

"What does 'not really' mean?" Hollis asked. Time was important. "Can you *guess* why she might have gone?"

Another head shake and a shrug. No co-operation from Crystal.

Hollis sighed. "Okay, girls. Time to go downstairs and get ready for bed. When I've settled you down I'll plug in the baby monitor and take the receiver with me so I can hear what's happening in our apartment when I come back here to see if I can figure anything out."

Neither Crystal nor Jay objected. Pale and wide-eyed, they needed to sleep to ready themselves for school and the questions they would get from their peers.

When the CAS had okayed Hollis's application to foster, she'd searched Toronto until she found a white trundle bed for her foster child's bedroom. She'd remembered fun-filled sleepovers from her childhood and intended to give her foster child the same pleasure. Crystal had spent several overnights with them, so their routine was familiar.

"Crystal, grab your pjs and toothbrush. Bring clean underwear and whatever you want to wear to school tomorrow."

Crystal followed instructions and scooped up her bedraggled stuffed monkey, Caspar, originally designed as a pyjama holder. She couldn't sleep without it and always brought it with her.

In the elevator it occurred to Hollis that the one thing she probably should do immediately was phone the police and tell them she had Crystal. She shook her head. She wouldn't do that, at least not right away. She knew the drill. A female officer would come and they'd remove Crystal and place her in foster care. Well, *she* was foster care, and she would keep the child, at least for now.

Downstairs the two dogs rushed to greet them as if they'd been absent for months. MacTee presented one of his toys and Barlow dropped one of Hollis's favourite Nine West shoes at her feet. Apprehensive, she picked it up and discovered the black foam platforms sported dozens of tooth marks.

She eyeballed the puppy, whose tail slowly stopped wagging. "Barlow," she said, extending the shoe toward him. His tail dropped and he avoided her eyes. "Barlow," she repeated. He turned and slunk away.

The girls giggled, despite their tension and fatigue.

Maybe it was worth a mutilated shoe to provide a lighter moment.

"We have our work to do training him," she said. "Off you go. Call me when you're ready for bed and I'll come in to say goodnight."

In the kitchen the phone's message light blinked. Willem Andronovich, her, what was the current phrase? Her significant other, much better than boyfriend, had promised to drop in after his University of Toronto evening lecture ended at nine. She hoped he hadn't changed his mind: all day she'd looked forward to his visit. With everything that had happened, it would be good to get his take on events.

She pressed play.

After telling her she had one message that had come while they were in Crystal's apartment, it began.

First there was background noise. "Keep Crystal until I come back. Keep her safe." The message was over.

If she hadn't believed it when she saw the despair on Crystal's face, she believed it now. Something serious was happening to Crystal's aunt. Hollis turned away from the phone to see Crystal standing in the doorway, her eyes wide and her small hand covering her mouth.

"She's okay," she breathed.

"She is and I'm sure she'll return soon," Hollis said, although the abruptness of the message created deep unease. "Now off you go to bed."

Hollis retrieved the notebook she'd found in Mary's backpack. Mentally she crossed her fingers as she picked up the small black book and flipped it open to the first page.

She thumbed through it. *Everything* was in code. A string of letters and numbers with no separations to provide clues. Unlocking the code would require work. Later, she'd google alphabetical codes and try various options. This coded notebook showed that Mary intended this book for her eyes alone. Hollis thought of several reasons why this might be so, but until she broke the code, they'd remain guesses.

Hollis took the baby monitor's receiver across to her office. She plugged it in before she opened her office files searching for more information. Mary had signed her lease two years ago, long before Hollis took over the building's management. Because of Crystal, Hollis knew Mary worked as a waitress. Now she learned the name and location of the restaurant — the Golden Goose on Jarvis Street.

Hollis considered the Aboriginal clan system where custom obliged you to welcome any relative to your home. For upwardly mobile Aboriginals who chose to live off the reserve, this presented problems. If they allowed multitudes to stay with them, it not only depleted their resources, it enraged other tenants in the building, particularly if late-night parties were part of the package. This explanation didn't explain Mary's tenants. Crystal would have known and named aunts, uncles, or cousins.

Perhaps Mary was involved in some other situation that necessitated a code and had nothing to do with the women who passed through her home? Maybe another search upstairs would provide answers.

With the girls tucked in, the dogs on guard, and the monitor plugged in, Hollis pocketed Crystal's keys. If anyone needed her, they had the after-hours emergency number.

Upstairs, she rapped, and after a suitable wait inserted the key and opened the door. Nothing had changed. No one had returned.

What should she be looking for? She examined the door. Three top-notch expensive locks, registered and impossible to duplicate. Mary intended to protect herself and whoever lived with her. Was she expecting trouble, or had her life experience trained her to be extra careful?

Hollis went to the kitchen. The phone on the counter showed four missed messages. She clicked on the first one.

Message one was a hang-up, as was message two.

Message three came four minutes later. "I know what you're doing and I'll stop you." It was a deep, menacing male voice.

Message four. "It's Bridget again. The scary dude who asked about you came in again and threatened the boss. I think the asshole gave him your address. If you haven't left, leave now. Be careful. Call me."

Mary hadn't been at home or hadn't picked up these messages, but she must have got the earlier one from Bridget. Time to find out more about Mary and her tenants.

A quick survey of the cupboards and refrigerator revealed that Mary fed everyone well. A closer look and she discovered several bottles of medication in the meat keeper.

Methadone.

Someone in the apartment used drugs or had used them. Methadone presented an escape. She ran through what she knew about the drug.

In the dark ages of her past, a druggie rock band boyfriend had kicked the habit taking the methadone route. Addicts depended on it to get them off illegal drugs and prevent them from falling back, but methadone required a prescription and monitoring. She remembered that for the first months a user was required to turn up daily at a clinic or doctor's office for a mandatory urine test before his methadone dose. Only after the addict proved his commitment and reliability was he allowed a weekly supply. Whoever lived in this apartment had reached stage two. Could this interesting discovery have something to do with Mary's flight? On the other hand, whoever took the methadone had left without it, and this would pose a problem, because the drug was taken daily.

She poked half-heartedly through the garbage, but nothing ratcheted her up to high alert.

Bathrooms often revealed more than kitchens. If she found anything in the apartment's only one, she would have no way of knowing to whom it belonged. There was no need for concern, as the cabinet revealed the usual collection of painkillers, nail polish remover, tampons, dental floss — nothing out of the ordinary in a house full of women.

In Mary and Crystal's shared bedroom she paid little attention to Crystal's belongings. Like Jay, Crystal owned the same brand name T-shirts, CDs, DVDs. Both girls loved the Jonas Brothers and found vampires fascinating. None of this would tell her where Mary had gone. She looked at Crystal's computer but didn't start it up.

The bedroom and the rest of the apartment led her to speculate about Mary's life and personality. The large poster in the living room might reveal a sympathy for the downtrodden, an appreciation of the artistic merit of the photo, or both. On the other hand a former tenant could have left it behind. But if Mary belonged to a First Nation, her awareness of the long-term plight of her people might have motivated her to hang it as a constant reminder. The same reasoning could be applied to the chief's poster and the collection of scholarly and popular books dealing with Aboriginal life and issues. If this was the case, what was she doing that she needed these reminders?

The lack of a personal stamp could have no significance. Perhaps Mary wasn't into decorating or refused to spend or didn't have the money for anything but the essentials. If she'd always worked as a waitress, money would be tight. Did the treadmill mean she was a fitness fanatic or had she bought it after making a January resolution? Hollis had not considered Mary to be fat, thin, tall, or short. Rather, she'd seemed ordinary.

The computer required a password. Given the coded notebook, Hollis had expected this but it disappointed her. She opened the single desk drawer. A neat array of stamps, name stickers, paper clips, and elastic-bound used chequebooks met her eye. At this point she felt like a voyeur and didn't remove the elastic to see who and what Mary had paid.

Instead she moved to the file cabinet. Locked. Again, no surprise. Mary didn't want anyone trolling through her computer or her files. Was she hiding something or simply acting like a person who treasured privacy? If she harboured an ever-changing series of women, these precautions might be designed to prevent them from snooping in her private business.

The cupboard, like the rest of the room, revealed little. Mary owned few clothes. An assortment of jeans, none of them high-end, four pairs of black slacks, a number of white cotton shirts, one black skirt, three jackets, two black hoodies, several pairs of shoes, and four purses — not a large wardrobe.

Without much hope of finding anything, Hollis combed through each handbag checking all the compartments but, as she'd expected, found nothing. Conclusion: Mary Montour, a private person with low-key clothing, kept all personal information stored safely away.

This expedition marked the fourth time she'd riffled through an apartment looking for clues to lead her to a missing person or to provide insight into a life. The worst had been her search in her murdered husband's files, where shocking surprises had awaited her. Investigating a home always made her feel sneaky and somehow guilty. As she had in the past, she reassured herself that she'd taken a useful first step.

Time to move to the second bedroom with its bunks and scattering of brilliant, tawdry clothing. Only a paperback book, splayed open and spine up, lying beside the bed, spoiled the military neatness of half the room. When she picked it up, she realized it was one of thousands of self-help books offering to guide readers along the path to self-actualization.

This woman was working on her self-image. In absentia Hollis wished her well.

The other side gave the impression that an out-of-control, over-the-top person lived there. Copies of *People* and *US* along with a pile of comic books lay on and under the bed, along with chocolate bar and gum wrappers, empty diet soda cans and chip bags. Amid a tangle of bedding, vivid nylon, spandex, and microfibre clothes added intense colour. The occupant had tossed a black lace bra atop the brilliant mountain. Hollis edged over to the bed and gingerly plucked it from the debris. It was 38DD — this buxom woman with her peacock clothes always would have been noticed. Spike-heeled shoes with run-over heels or platform soles were everywhere. If she had to guess she'd say this was a hooker's wardrobe. Unlikely that she had worked as a civil servant or a receptionist in a staid law firm. The idea made Hollis smile.

Chests of drawers next.

Nothing cluttered the surface of the tidy bureau, and all its drawers were tightly closed. Hollis opened the top drawer. Beside neatly folded serviceable white underwear she saw an arresting, well-thumbed purple pamphlet with red lettering: *Methadone Maintenance Treatment — client handbook*. Either it was second-hand or its condition revealed how frequently its owner had referred to it. The methadone in the fridge belonged to Miss Tidy.

Lowering herself to a bunk, Hollis thumbed through the Canadian Mental Health Association booklet. Well-written, frank, easily understood. If only all manuals were like this. As she read through it she stopped on various pages and learned that like her long ago boyfriend, individuals testified that they'd used the drug for decades and lived productive, normal lives. Apparently methadone users carried cards that allowed them to receive treatment if they could not get to the regular clinics. Hollis stopped worrying about the missing woman, because this information, along with the absence of a purse, reassured her that wherever the unknown woman had gone, she most likely had the card she needed to continue her treatment.

The other bureau with its half-open drawers spilling gaudy clothes couldn't have been more different. A clutter of spilled makeup, open jars, lipsticks along with necklaces, bracelets, and earrings covered the surface. Hollis spotted a gold necklace that spelled out a name — *Veronica* — new information to feed into the mix.

In one drawer she viewed a mishmash of lace and nylon underwear, mostly black or red, jostling for space with two blonde wigs. In another several pairs of white jeans, none too clean, were stacked in the bottom drawer along with leotards, v-necked sweaters, and long scarves.

A look in the cupboard revealed that the bird of brilliant plumage did not respect boundaries. Miss Tidy's clothes, a navy blazer, grey sweater coat, navy suit, and two pairs of navy slacks huddled on one side, pushed there by a bizarre collection of short skirts, leather jackets, and dresses.

Hollis sat back. Who were the women who lived with Mary? What role did Mary play in their lives?

She glanced at her watch. Nine thirty. Willem would arrive in a few minutes. Time to hike downstairs, because search or no search, she wanted to change from her washable dog training outfit into something more alluring.

The dogs again welcomed her as if she'd been away for months, which surprised her, as they usually retired at nine.

After they settled she checked on the girls. Jay had kicked off the covers and lay on her stomach, her face buried in the pillow. Hollis tucked her in, although she knew that the girl would throw off the covers again. Her souped-up metabolism kept her warm even on chilly nights with the window open. Crystal had curled into a ball and clutched her monkey close to her chest. Contemplating the vulnerable child, Hollis again vowed to find Mary.

In her own room Hollis peered into her cupboard. She loved bright colours and luxurious fabrics, but they had to pass the comfort test. Tonight she opted for red denim jeans. She pulled on a long-sleeved black sweater which provided the perfect background for a chunky chain that, had it not been silver, would work as a bicycle lock. In the bathroom she cleaned her teeth and was wondering if she needed fresh makeup when the buzzer sounded.

Too late.

She zoomed lipstick on her mouth and raced to press the button to allow Willem through the lobby door.

He enveloped her in a hug, tilted her face up for a kiss, and then stepped back. "What's happened in the building? I had to undergo the third degree before the officer allowed me in."

"I gather you've been out of touch with radio and TV. It's been on the news," Hollis said.

"You're right. I closeted myself in my office for most of the day and took the subway here. What's this all about?"

"You should have read those screens that hang from the ceiling on the platforms. They carry the latest breaking news stories," Hollis said before she remembered Willem's contempt for sixty-second sound bites.

As she told him what had been happening, she admired him. She never tired of looking at his tall, well-built body. Willem was a study in warm brown. Hair, eyes, beard all reminded her of a cuddly teddy bear, one you could take to bed and be happy. She continued to marvel that he seemed to feel the same admiration and desire for her.

Willem considered her, his expression serious. "Maybe it's you. Something about your karma draws you to violence. Maybe you're murder-prone," he said, his lips curling upwards and his eyes sparkling.

"The murder had *nothing* to do with me, but something *has* happened that involves and worries me," she said.

As she spoke she wondered if Mary's disappearance was related to the murder. Perhaps the two events tied together in some way. It hadn't occurred to her until now, but if that was the case, maybe she should give up searching for Mary and pass the problem to Rhona.

Willem shrugged off his caramel leather bomber jacket. "It may be May but it's cold out there tonight. I'm afraid to ask what else has happened. From your expression when you mentioned it, I don't think I'm going to like whatever you tell me."

They moved into the living room. While Hollis, wrestling with the idea that there might be a connection, marshalled her thoughts and decided how to present her conundrum, she pointed to the end of the room. "I'm still working on the giraffe and I'm pleased with him." She was marking time. She had to tell him about Crystal and Mary.

"Is he winking? He's very appealing. But this isn't the time to consider him. It's true confession time. Tell me everything." Willem stood, feet slightly apart and body braced as if he expected a blow. He would have looked at home on a sailing ship facing into the wind as he dealt with a storm.

"I have a small problem, and I thought you might have an idea how I should deal with it," Hollis said.

Willem scrutinized her face. "I'm nervous when you talk about a *small* problem. I have vivid and painful memories of the last time we worked on one of your *small* problems." He folded his arms over his chest and maintained his stance. "Shoot."

Hollis longed to sit down, snuggle close to him, and tell her story without looking at him. Instead she too remained standing.

"Do you remember meeting Crystal Montour, Jay's friend who lives upstairs on the second floor?"

Willem nodded. "Pretty girl. Aboriginal, I think."

"Right. Well, she lives with her aunt, Mary Montour, who has disappeared."

"Disappeared? Is this connected to the murder? When did it happen?"

"I'm pretty sure it's a coincidence. Crystal was with us after school. We had dinner and all went to dog training. When we got back her apartment door was unlocked and her aunt was gone. Two women who live with them weren't there either. When I calmed Crystal down, we went up. There was no indication that anything untoward had happened."

Willem frowned.

"When we came downstairs Mary had left a short phone message asking me to care for Crystal until she came back."

"This story has a déjà vu ring to it," Willem said. "Why would she do that? Do you have halfway reasonable explanation? This makes me nervous. You have a talent for mixing yourself up in heavy stuff."

Hollis nodded. "I know. I wish I wasn't involved but I have to find Mary for Crystal's sake. If I report this the authorities won't allow Crystal to stay with me. Who knows where they'll place her. The really odd thing is that although Crystal is terribly upset, she won't give me the information I need in order to help."

Willem took her hand and pulled her toward the sofa. "Let's sit down."

Hollis shifted away from him and perched at the end of the sofa. She couldn't allow herself to cuddle, to be distracted before she described the situation. She wanted his opinion.

"What do you mean? What won't Crystal tell you?"

Hollis frowned. She needed a minute to decide how to tell her story. "I'm not being much of a hostess. Did I offer you a beer? I'd like a glass of wine." She shifted forward ready to stand up.

Willem unfolded himself. "I'll do the honours. But be aware that I *know* this is a diversionary time-buying tactic."

"There are cashews in the cupboard next to the stove. They're unsalted, so eating them won't make us feel guilty."

"Since you know my fondness for cashews and always stock my favourite beer, I suspect this could be a prelude to giving me reasons why I should become involved." Willem grinned. "You are not noted for your subtlety."

Hollis returned his smile. "That *could* be true, but the fact is I need a drink. A murdered tenant, a battle with Jay, a dog training session where Barlow was as intractable as ever, and Mary's disappearance add up to stress times four."

While Willem collected the drinks, Hollis planned her strategy.

Beer in hand, Willem cocked his head to one side. "Okay, give me the details. What do you want me to do?"

"Nothing right now. Just listen as I explore my options for dealing with Crystal and Jay."

"What's the problem with Jay?"

"She desperately wants to meet her father at the Eaton Centre on Thursday night, and I'm not prepared to let her go alone."

Willem turned to her. His eyebrows rose and his eyes widened. "*Alone?*"

"Yes. She says Mrs. Cooper took her to the subway and her father met her when she got off in the Queen Street station. Have I told you the situation with her father?"

"Only that he's still in the picture and makes infrequent appearances." Willem reached forward and tipped cashews into his hand.

Hollis sipped her wine before she began. "When I met him, before Jay came to live with me, he gave me the third degree." She thought back to the meeting. When she arrived at the CAS offices she was ushered into an interview room.

A burly, muscular man dressed in pressed grey flannels and a forest green polo shirt stood up when she entered the room. He held papers in his hand. After the social worker introduced Calum Brownelly, they sat at a pale wood table.

"I'm sorry, but I didn't have time to read these papers before you arrived," Brownelly said.

Hollis waited while Brownelly skimmed the documents.

While he read Hollis examined him. She noticed that his nails were clean, that he wore no rings, and that his watch was a garden variety Timex. She guessed he was in his early forties, although his leathery skin and the silver hair escaping from the neck of his shirt as well as the streaks in his full head of curly brown hair made her wonder if he was older. He would look much the same at sixty as he did now.

Brownelly laid the papers on the table and sat back. He allowed a minute or two to elapse before he spoke. "A working artist, a building custodian, a dog owner — will you have time to look after my girl?" He had a smoker's raspy voice.

Hollis checked his hands but didn't see the tell-tale nicotine yellow. He hadn't smiled, so she didn't see his teeth. Perhaps it was simply his voice. Why did she feel so defensive?

She removed her trademark red-framed glasses and tapped them on the table as she met his gaze. "My studio is part of the apartment. I have a large living room/dining room combination and use the dining room for painting and creating papier-mâché animals. Working at home means I *am* at home and will be there for Jay."

Brownelly tipped his head to one side. "Did they tell you I want Jay walked to and from school? I looked up your address. She would have to cross Yonge Street and walk several blocks, and I don't want her doing that alone."

No one had mentioned this. Hollis had assumed that Jay would walk to school just as Hollis had done when she was eleven. She'd forgotten how protective parents had become and quickly made an adjustment.

"As I'm sure the CAS has told you, I have a Golden Retriever and a Flat-coated Retriever puppy. I plan to combine the walk to and from school with a trip to a nearby off-leash park."

Brownelly's hooded eyes opened slightly wider, giving him the appearance of a surprised reptile. "And what about your job as building custodian? How will you combine that with caring for Jay?"

Hollis settled her glasses back on her nose. "Mostly I make sure the cleaners, snow plowers, window washers, and other regular workers do their jobs. If a tenant has a problem I arrange for the tradespeople to come and repair whatever is broken. If I have to see to a tenant's problem, I've purchased a baby monitor that I can plug in and take the receiver with me. I'll know what's going on in the apartment and my dogs will also alert me if I'm needed."

"As a single woman you have no experience with children. Mrs. Cooper's sudden death shocked Jay. She lived with her since she was very young and she's suffering. You need to deal with her loss. In addition my daughter will challenge you because she's strong-willed. She needs a firm hand. How do you feel about dealing with those issues?"

Hollis felt as if she was applying for citizenship. Who knew the child's father had the right to question her as if she was in custody for a heinous crime? But she had to be positive, had to assume it meant he cared. As she had since the social worker told her how he'd asked for Jay to be placed in a foster home, she wondered what kind of life he led if he couldn't care for an eleven-year-old. She understood a man feeling unable to look after a baby but, by eleven, after school programs, good sitters, and other caregivers made single parenting possible. An odd situation. Maybe Jay or the social worker would provide more information to help her to understand.

For the moment she needed to respond honestly to Brownelly's interrogation, to be proactive and establish the ground rules.

"I've read books since I applied to be a foster parent. I particularly like the approach of Alyson Schafer, a Toronto psychotherapist. She's a parenting expert and wrote, *Honey I Wrecked the Kids*."

"Stupid title. I don't want you applying nutty psycho ideas to *my* daughter."

Neanderthal, Hollis thought, but decided not to challenge him.

"You should read the book. Very sensible ideas. For me the truth is, and you may strongly disagree, that the same concepts that apply to dogs apply to children. You have to establish yourself as the alpha dog, the leader. You are not their friend, not their equal, you are in charge. If you take this approach a child will be relieved to know there are boundaries and she doesn't have to constantly push to see when you will finally say *no*."

Hollis caught a smile flickering across the social worker's face.

Brownelly's bushy eyebrows rose and drew together like sparring caterpillars as he frowned and snapped. "My Jay is not a dog."

"I'm aware of that. I'm giving you the philosophy I've learned from training dogs." As she said this Hollis envisioned Barlow tearing through the apartment dragging various items of clothing, of the food he stole, of his refusal to come when she called him.

Brownelly leaned back, steepled his fingers and stared at her. "We should try this on a trial basis."

The social worker spoke up. "Nothing is ever permanent. People and circumstances change. We want our charges in happy homes and we believe stability is important, but sometimes things don't work out. We will be keeping an eye on Jay and assessing her situation."

Now Willem reached over and tapped her knee. "Come back, come back, wherever you are."

Hollis shook her head. "Sorry, I was thinking about Jay's dad. He made me uneasy. They're supposed to have supervised visits at the CAS offices."

Willem rubbed his chin and regarded Hollis. Then he held up his hands and used one finger to tick the fingers on his other hand.

"First, you want to keep Jay safe. Second, you're not comfortable about her father." He tilted his head to one side as if listening to a speaker Hollis couldn't hear. "He *is* her father, so he has the right to see her. We don't know why the CAS wants them to meet in their offices. And, unless the CAS knows something they haven't told you, I'm assuming he could take her back at any time." He tapped a third finger. "There are predators who hang out in the Eaton Centre." He placed his hands in his lap. "There is no way you or anyone else should allow an eleven-year-old to go there alone."

"Thanks. That's what I think too, but I'll park that problem until I figure out what to do about Crystal and Mary. How can I persuade Crystal to talk about her aunt?"

"If she doesn't want to she won't, but we have to wonder why. What secret is she hiding?"

He'd said *we*. He'd bought into the problem.

"Where does Mary work?" Willem asked.

"A restaurant on Jarvis Street where she's been for years. If she's a good waitress I wonder why she hasn't applied to a more upscale place where she'd make more money and get better tips."

"Interesting question. If she ever comes back you should ask. Which First Nation does she belong to?"

"There's a huge poster of an Indian chief in her apartment, but I don't know who he is or where he comes from. Maybe Crystal knows."

Willem got up and refilled Hollis's glass. Hollis looked surprised. "Boy, I swilled that down, didn't I? Better slow down or I won't be able to talk, let alone think."

"Should Crystal stay with you? What did her aunt say?"

"I'll play it for you. Come out to the kitchen."

After they heard the short message, Willem, fresh beer in hand, said, "I agree. You must keep her for a few days. As a man about to attend law school, I'd hazard a guess that the message protects you for a while. It gives you breathing room."

"Thanks. That's what I thought. Enough about me and my problems. On Sunday you planned to tell your family about your decision to turn your life around and become a lawyer. Tell me how they reacted."

Willem poured cashews from the container into his hand. He shook his head. "I can't resist these. How do you think they reacted? They're Eastern Europeans and extremely proud of their son, Herr Doktor Professor. They can't accept that I believe I can do more good as a lawyer. My mother cries and my father says nothing."

"Do you still believe it's the right decision?"

"I do. Let's sit down."

This time they didn't talk. Safe in his embrace, Hollis felt the day's tension slip away. She'd worry about Mary later.

Hollis and Willem moved from the couch to Hollis's bedroom, where they jettisoned their clothes before collapsing into bed.

"You're beautiful," Willem murmured as his hands explored her body.

A scream from the second bedroom stopped all action. They jumped apart.

"What the heck?" Hollis said.

A second scream ripped the night's silence.

Hollis slipped out of bed, reached in the cupboard for her terrycloth bathrobe, and hurried from the room.

In the girls' room she flipped on the light and found Jay hugging Crystal, who sobbed uncontrollably. Jay looked up when the light went on.

"She's scared," she said.

Hollis lowered herself to the trundle and gathered the girls into her arms. The three of them rocked and Hollis patted their backs for several minutes until Crystal's sobs slowed. Hollis released them and sat back.

"I had a terrible dream," Crystal said.

"Do you want to tell us about it?" Hollis asked.

"I don't think so. It will make it seem even more real."

"Or not so real," Jay said.

Crystal shook her head. "No. It was awful." Her face crumpled and she hugged herself as tears flowed down her cheeks. "I saw my mother." She couldn't say more.

Hollis rocked the two girls until Crystal's sobbing turned into hiccups. "Maybe we should go in the kitchen and see if a mug of hot milk would help," Hollis suggested.

Crystal nodded. "I'm afraid to go to sleep, afraid I'll see it happen again."

Happen again! What had the poor child seen? Her mother was dead. Could she have seen her die? Hollis didn't want to press, didn't want to stir up any more memories.

"Let's go. Nothing like a midnight snack to drive away bad dreams."

"Is Willem still here?" Jay asked.

As she spoke Willem appeared in the doorway, fully dressed. "I am and I'm on my way home."

"Join us for a glass of warm milk," Hollis said.

Willem made a face. "Not my drink of choice, and it's time I headed home anyway. Big day tomorrow." He stepped into the room, bent down, kissed Hollis, patted the girls' shoulders and left.

So much for their romantic evening. Hollis hadn't factored in what having an eleven-year-old living with her would do to her sex life. When she and Willem decided he wouldn't ever stay overnight, because if he did Hollis wouldn't be a good role model for Jay, Hollis hadn't considered the price. The decision was one thing but the reality was another. Hollis hated having him depart after they'd made love and missed overnights at his apartment. She was going to have to work something out, but now was not the time to solve the problem.

By midnight the girls were back in bed. Hollis didn't feel like sleeping and wished she could return to Mary's apartment, but, like all the dogs she'd ever owned, MacTee and Barlow went off duty at nine. Even had she turned on the monitor and the dogs took on guard duty, she couldn't leave the girls when Crystal's nightmare might return.

She curled up on the couch and planned the next day's activities. After she walked the girls to school she'd visit the restaurant to see if Bridget, the woman who'd left the warning message on the answering machine, worked there. She crossed her fingers, because if Bridget wasn't there, she couldn't imagine how to find her. If Bridget couldn't tell her anything useful she'd trek to the Anishnawbe Health Centre looking for information. Her best source would have been Crystal, but unless the situation changed, Hollis wouldn't get anything from her.

A light flashed in her brain. She hadn't closely examined the methadone container, which had to have the user's name on it. Once she looked at it she'd float the name past the women working in the restaurant and at the Native Friendship centre.

Someone had to know something.

TWELVE

OPIE'S snoring woke Rhona at six. She opened her eyes to see Opie's head inches from hers on the pillow. She pushed the cat to the floor and clambered out of bed. He stalked off, back high and tail swishing.

Showered, dressed, and makeup applied, with a travel mug of high-test coffee in hand, she headed for the office. When she turned up at seven expecting to have the homicide office to herself, she found Ian at his desk and several other detectives also there.

Ian waved as she crossed the room.

"Any leads?" Rhona asked.

"I've contacted the RCMP in North Battleford to ask for any information they have on Ginny Wuttenee and Donald Hill. It's earlier out there, so I don't expect anything for several hours. Should know if any of the apartment tenants have a record in a few minutes."

"I'm going to the coroner's office at nine, want to come?"

Ian shook his head. He'd never admitted to Rhona that he felt squeamish at autopsies, but Rhona suspected he did. He had opened up enough to admit that he and his mother had identified his brother who'd been killed in a car crash, and ever after Ian had trouble visiting the morgue.

"I'll go. You keep checking. When I come back we'll examine all the security camera records and solicit help to identify as many people as possible."

"Sabrina's journal or notebook. You or me?" Ian asked.

"I'll start it now before I attend the autopsy," Rhona said. "I'll mark any puzzling notations and later we'll interview Ms. Nesrallah and Ms. Wuttenee to see what they can tell us."

Rhona filled her coffee mug at the departmental coffee centre, glad they'd all chipped in and bought a decent machine that dispensed one cup at a time. She didn't approve of the waste using one metal and plastic container for each cup of coffee, but she suppressed her guilt because the coffee was good and she needed those jolts of caffeine to keep her going. Sucking down several mouthfuls, she savoured the flavour and the revitalizing effect before she began Sabrina's diary and made notes for her interview with Ms. Nesrallah.

Here again Sabrina exhibited the level of organization they'd observed in her bedroom. Sabrina had slipped a photo of a quilt, not a traditional quilt but what Rhona had heard described as an art quilt, inside the plastic cover. Having seen Sabrina's detailed plans for her business, Rhona suspected the photo was a constant reminder of the reason for working as an escort and a motivation to do whatever it took to maximize tips.

Rhona began with the most recent entries. On the evening before she was murdered Sabrina had written, *'Dave - opera - Carmen - dinner at Carlu. Pink silk dress and pink coat. Bone up on the opera.'* The security tape would show their return and Dave's departure.

In the afternoon Sabrina had marked *'12 - Brian.'* Nothing else. Rhona flipped through the book. Brian visited every Monday. A regular on his lunch hour.

Three days before the murder she'd noted *'John?'* with a black "x" next to the name. This encounter had not been a success.

Ian, on the phone, covered the mouthpiece and held up two fingers. "Two with records," he said and returned to his conversation.

Rhona continued making notes.

"Guess which two have had brushes with the law," Ian said after he hung up and sauntered over.

"Too early for twenty questions. Tell me."

"Barney Cartwright, the blustery man who huffed and puffed because he had a plane to catch."

"What was the charge?"

"He's in that motorcycle gang, the Black Hawks, and was charged with money laundering. Did two years less a day," Ian said.

"The Black Hawks. They're in a territorial fight to the death battle with the Hell's Angels. The guns and gangs squad have its hands full."

"True. I hate to say this, but if they kill each other that's one thing. But it's the innocent bystanders that pay the price. Remember when a middle-aged woman was killed in the crossfire when the two gangs shot it out on a downtown street at noon. They've kidnapped, tortured — it really does seem to be a fight to the death. "

"High stakes. Big bucks to be made," Rhona said.

"A Black Hawk. Interesting. He said he only recently moved in. I wonder why? Can't see him murdering Ms. Trepanier. Bigger fish to fry but we'll keep him in the picture."

"Who was the other one?" Rhona asked.

"Tim O'Toole."

"The night man. I'd guess he was charged under the voyeurism or trespassing at night provisions."

"Right on. Trespassing at night and photographing through windows. I'd guess he told us he goes out at night because he knew we'd check, and it was better if the information came from him," Ian said.

"Years ago I would have said that wouldn't lead him to worse things, but not any more, not after the murder convictions of that former military commander at Trenton," Rhona said.

Ian tapped his pen on the desk. "That was a case study, wasn't it? Charged with assaults and two murders, and apparently his crime spree began when he stole underwear. Never wise to assume a peeper won't progress to more heinous crimes."

"O'Toole. Ordinary-looking guy but who knows," Rhona said. "For the moment he stays on the list." She glanced at the wall clock. "Time for the autopsy."

No last-minute change of heart for Ian.

The pathology facilities were located in the basement, well away from the daily business of police headquarters. Rhona traipsed from the homicide office to the elevator to the basement and along a lengthy unadorned concrete hall until she reached the unmarked door and entered.

The chill always caught her unawares, and she'd come to associate that particular dank cold with the unpleasantness of the autopsy.

The pathologist, thin, angular Dr. Lee, greeted her and preceded her into the room, where a sheet-shrouded figure awaited them. Dr. Lee had laid out his assortment of scalpels, clamps, and saws. He uncovered the body, turned on his microphone, and began his meticulous inspection of what had been the beautiful Sabrina Trepanier.

"She died instantly. I'd say he clamped a hand on her head to keep her still. That would have woken her, but before she could react he slashed her throat from ear to ear.

"Right- or left-handed?" Rhona asked.

"Definitely right."

"Have you established the time of death?"

"Impossible to be precise, but between one and two in the morning."

Dr. Lee removed and weighed the victim's organs. That done, he examined the stomach contents.

"She ate two or three hours before she died," he said.

For Rhona his information confirmed that Sabrina and her escort had eaten dinner after the opera.

Dr. Lee made more observations on Sabrina's good health and carefully tended body, and Rhona's attention wandered as she considered Sabrina's quilt shop.

"She had a baby several years ago, probably when she was still a teenager. It was a difficult birth."

A baby. Where did that fit into the pattern of Sabrina's life? Was that the reason she was estranged from her family? Did it relate to her murder?

Back in the homicide office Rhona shared the autopsy results with Ian. Knowing that Sabrina Trepanier had died in the early morning helped, as did the information that the killer was strong and right-handed. Whether Sabrina having borne a child was relevant would only become apparent as the investigation continued.

"I heard from the Mounties. Hill has no record with them nor, does Ginny Wuttenee, although the officer I talked to said she could have been picked up many times for being drunk." Ian frowned. "He was really dismissive about Aboriginals. No wonder they have problems out there if there are many officers like him."

"It was early. Maybe he had a bad shift, had a crying baby that kept him up all night. People sometimes say things they don't really mean." Even as she spoke Rhona acknowledged to herself that she knew what he meant. She remembered summers on the reserve. She'd felt embarrassed when the storekeeper or the Indian agent spoke rudely to them. When she'd asked why her grandmother didn't tell them to mind their manners, her grandmother said, "They don't know any better. There's no point trying to change them."

Ian chewed on his lower lip and shook his head. "I don't think there was a reason. He sounded mean. As if he had no use for Aboriginals and hated the policing that he did in Battleford."

"The Sisters in Spirit report claimed that deep-seated prejudice is one reason so many missing women haven't been found and the killers of murdered women haven't been caught."

Ian leaned back, clasped his hands behind his head, and stretched. "Easy enough for them or for us to say, but you've been a beat cop. You know what it's like to pick up drunks who puke all over the car, themselves, and you if they get the chance. It tends to prejudice you against whoever is doing it and in western Canada ..." He shrugged. "Anyway, bottom line, he wasn't any help as far as learning anything about Ginny Wuttenee, but he told me he'd ask around and to phone him again."

"Too bad, but maybe he'll turn up more info. I'm writing up what we've done so far." Rhona was bent over her paperwork — the unavoidable bane of a police officer's life. She pulled the stack of documents requiring her attention out of her in basket and booted up her computer. Thankfully, computers lessened the burden.

"I used Canada 411 to locate Trepaniers in the Oakville area. She may be listed under her husband's name if she has one, but I found two possibilities. Both with the initial M. I've shot off an inquiry to Motor Vehicles, so we'll soon know if a Marie France Trepanier lists either address on her driver's license. The guy I spoke to said he'd get back to me pronto," Ian said as his phone buzzed. "Thanks, got that, very helpful. Thanks again."

He stood up. "Got it. Time to go, although I hate doing this. You ready or do you want to put it off?"

"I'm always ready to postpone paperwork, although I agree with you that informing the next of kin is one of the worst parts of the job." She swivelled to face Ian. "Waiting won't make it any easier. We'll pick up an unmarked from the pool." She opened a file folder on her desk and removed Sabrina's photo.

"I *really* hate this," Ian muttered as they took the elevator downstairs.

"You remember your brother," Rhona said.

"I do. It's a painful experience and everyone's first instinct is to deny, to say that it can't possibly be true, that we've made a mistake."

"If Mrs. Trepanier has been estranged from her daughter for years it will be even more harrowing, because she'll have to face the fact that she'll never have the opportunity to make things right."

As they approached the car Rhona suggested Ian drive out and she drive back. Traffic at nine a.m. would be heavy, not that it ever slacked off much. The Gardiner Expressway and Queen Elizabeth Way, commonly referred to as the QEW, ground to a halt during the morning and evening rush hours but seldom flowed freely. Construction season had begun in May and they could expect delays.

"Maybe on the way home we'll take the Lakeshore. It's stop and go through every little burg, but at least it's close to the lake and it's pretty."

"This isn't bad right here," Ian said, waving an arm at what they could see of Lake Ontario. "The city fathers and mothers sure screwed it up, didn't they? We could have had a lakefront like Chicago instead of railway lines, expressways, and high rises blocking access and the view."

Away from the downtown they made better time, and by ten they'd exited on Ford Drive and headed south toward Lake Ontario and Mrs. Trepanier's home.

When they buzzed the Trepanier condo, Rhona half-hoped no one would be there, although they required information if they were going to solve the case. The chief had emphasized the need for speed.

"Yes?" A woman's voice boomed through the speaker.

"Marie France Trepanier?"

"Yes."

"Toronto Police." Rhona located the security camera and held up their warrant cards, although there would be no way the woman could read them.

"Yes."

"May we come in?"

"What is this about?" the voice asked suspiciously.

To tell or not to tell her over the intercom? "Do you have a daughter, Sabrina?"

"Oh my god," Mrs. Trepanier whispered and buzzed them in.

They walked up the steps to an already open door on the second floor, where a woman and a white-muzzled Golden Retriever awaited them. At one time the woman must have been as beautiful as her daughter. Her hair, shining silver, was twisted into a French knot. Her oval face, remarkably unlined, and her clear dark blue eyes fringed with long black lashes looked very like the photo of Sabrina. Rhona enjoyed magazine articles, usually published to coincide with Mother's Day, of mothers and famous daughters. If Sabrina and Marie France had appeared in such an article, there would have been no doubt about their relationship.

"What has happened to her?" Mrs. Trepanier asked as she continued to block the doorway.

"You are Sabrina's mother?" Rhona said as they clustered around the door.

"I am. We call her Claire." She appeared to realize that they couldn't conduct the conversation where they stood. "Come in."

Followed by the dog, she ushered them through a hall into a bright living room overlooking Lake Ontario. A stiff May wind whipped the water into whitecaps, but, despite this, a few brave and hardy sailors piloted their boats through the waves.

"Please, sit down." She indicated two cream sofas facing one another on either side of a fireplace.

Rhona, conscious as ever about her height, chose a small rose-coloured wing chair while Ian and Mrs. Trepanier sat opposite each other on the sofas. The dog lay at her feet.

"It's bad news, or you wouldn't be here. I haven't heard a word from Claire for almost seven years. Not because I wouldn't have liked to, but when she left here the last time, she said she never wanted to see us again. I tried to trace her but didn't succeed." Her hands gripped her knees as she looked from one to the other. "Tell me," she ordered.

"I'm sorry to bring bad news, but Claire is dead," Rhona said, knowing Ian, despite his years of police work, would have a hard time with the bare, brutal fact.

"How?" Her knuckles white and her fingers indenting her navy trousers below her knees, Mrs. Trepanier gave the impression she was willing herself to hold together.

"She was murdered," Rhona said, hating the words.

"Murdered. Claire was murdered. Who would do such a terrible thing," the woman whispered. Her face had aged since they delivered the news.

"Do you live alone?" Ian asked.

She stared at him as if she'd forgotten he was there. "I do. My husband died not long after Claire left. It sounds melodramatic, but I think his heart was broken. We did the wrong thing but our intentions were good. To lose your only child is a terrible price to pay. He said he couldn't live with himself and I guess, literally, he couldn't."

"Do you have a relative or friend we could call to come and be with you?"

"I have Duchess," she said, bending to stroke the dog's ears. "She was Claire's dog and when Claire left without taking Duchess, I knew how serious the situation was. As you can see, Duchess is old, almost eleven, and for the last seven years I've hoped that if Claire wouldn't come home for us, for me, she'd come back for Duchess." Unshed tears brightened her eyes. "I hope it was quick, that she didn't know. Please don't tell me some sadist tortured her."

Ian leaned toward her. "We can tell you that with absolute confidence. She died almost instantly. Unfortunately, as her next of kin, we have to ask you to come with us to Toronto and identify her."

It was as if Ian hadn't made the request. Certainly Mrs. Trepanier didn't respond. Instead she said, "Where did she live?"

Rhona couldn't imagine the pain this woman had suffered not knowing where her only child lived, let alone how she was or what she was doing.

"In mid-town Toronto, an apartment on Delisle Street."

"So close, it breaks my heart."

Rhona had to ask the questions that would bring back painful memories, but to identify Sabrina's killer, they had to do it.

"What happened that caused your daughter to cut all connections with you?"

Mrs. Trepanier continued to pat Duchess and didn't look at the detectives. "It's a long, sad story."

She'd wear off the dog's fur if she continued. "We have to know because there may be a connection to her murder."

The woman's hand stilled. "He wouldn't have done that."

"Who wouldn't?"

Mrs. Trepanier raised her head and gave a lung-emptying sigh. "Okay. If it will help."

She stared into space as if organizing her words before she spoke. "My daughter was a beautiful child and she matured early into a beautiful young woman. Boys and men found her irresistible and she liked their attention, although she wasn't particularly interested in any one boy. When she was fifteen she told us she was pregnant and asked our permission to have an abortion." She twisted her hands into a knot. "Abortion was a sin for us. We asked who the baby's father was and if there was any possibility they could marry."

She lifted her head and appeared to be looking at a mental image burned into her mind. "I remember her exact words. She said, 'No, and if you won't help I'm going to charge him with rape. I'll stay here, go to school, and have this kid.' Claire's voice when she said it made me shiver. I realized she would do exactly what she said. To her father she was still his little girl and he didn't believe her. He asked why she wouldn't stay with my sister in Calgary and have the baby. I'll never forget it. She stood in the kitchen doorway with her hands on her hips. She said, 'Either you agree that I can have an abortion or you have ten seconds before I call the police.' Her dad tried to placate her but she counted down. When we didn't respond she grabbed the phone book and punched in the number for the police. We were so stunned we just sat there like dummies while she told them she wanted to press charges against a teacher who had raped her." Mrs. Trepanier stopped speaking and peered down at her hands now clenched in her lap.

"What was his name and what happened to him?" Ian asked.

"David Jones. Two other girls supported Claire's charge and he went to jail."

"And your daughter?" Rhona asked?

"She did exactly what she'd promised to do. Stayed and finished her year. Had the baby in July. We asked if we could raise him as our own but she sneered and said no way, that she intended to give him to young parents, not rigid fanatics like us who put God before their own daughter. She gave him, our only grandchild, to the Children's Aid, and left. She said she would never forgive us, would never contact us again, and she never did." Mrs. Trepanier began to cry. "How could we have been so stupid?" she sobbed.

"I'm sure you did what you thought was right," Rhona said. She waited for Mrs. Trepanier to compose herself. "When you're ready, we'll drive you to Toronto and have a car bring you back."

Could the baby's father be Sabrina's killer?

THIRTEEN

THE next morning while the girls hoovered up waffles and blueberries, Hollis thought about the CAS and their reaction if they found out about Crystal. Enough that there'd been a murder in the building. That would be bad, but if they discovered she was harbouring Crystal, all hell might break loose. In her heart she knew it was the right thing to do, but officialdom tended to think rules should not be broken.

"Girls, I think it would be better if you don't say anything about Crystal's aunt going away. But if you do happen to mention it, you may say Mary asked me to have Crystal stay with me."

Crystal put her fork down. "Social Services would take me away, wouldn't they?"

Jay examined Crystal. "Not Social Services — the Children's Aid. That's who's in charge of me. Hollis is my foster mom but the CAS makes the big decisions. I know for sure that if your foster mom complains about you, they move you to another home. Mrs. Cooper always told me if I didn't behave that's what would happen to me. She said some foster homes were awful and if you didn't work out there, they dumped you in a group home where a bunch of bad kids lived. I don't ever want that to happen to me."

Hollis was horrified. Eleven-year-olds shouldn't have a conversation like this. Her respect for Mrs. Cooper dropped like a felled tree. What a terrible threat to hold over a child's head.

She stepped away from the counter, where she'd been feeding waffles into the toaster, and patted Jay's shoulder.

"I solemnly promise I will never ever make a threat like that," she said.

Jay looked up at her. She didn't comment but her raised eyebrows told Hollis she didn't believe her.

"I never tell anyone anything about my life, not that anyone cares," Crystal said flatly.

This statement also shocked Hollis. Her friends' children tended to talk non-stop and to reveal details of their own lives, and even more interesting and often surprising information about their parents' lives. Crystal's assertion revealed how her life differed from other children's.

Barlow gave the short assertive bark that meant he had to go out. Time for all of them to leave.

As they walked toward the school, Hollis said, "I'm visiting the restaurant where your Aunt Mary worked. Did you ever go to work with her?"

Crystal stopped. "No," she said.

"I thought I'd talk to the people there and ask if they have any idea where she might be. It seems like a good place to start."

Barlow spotted another dog, barked, jumped up and down, and yanked on his leash. Conversation stopped as Hollis pulled his collar toward her and administered an open-handed grab on his back, simulating his mother's corrective bite when she taught him manners. Barlow stopped momentarily and Hollis again reined him in.

"Come on girls. I can't let him get away with this behaviour. Keep walking. He has to reach the point where he passes another dog without making any fuss."

"He has a long way to go, doesn't he?" Jay said.

"He does. He's not any easy dog to train. He wants to be the boss, the alpha dog, but he isn't going to be," Hollis said.

When they approached the school, they met other dogs accompanying mothers, fathers, or nannies walking children to school. Busy controlling Barlow, Hollis didn't have another opportunity to question Crystal.

Home again, she let herself into Mary's apartment, opened the refrigerator, and removed the methadone prescribed for Alicia Meness. Why had she been so anxious to learn the name? The pharmacist would know only what she knew — that Alicia lived in this apartment. The information wouldn't help her find Mary.

Back downstairs Hollis booted up her computer and connected to Google. She typed in a number of search terms that she hoped might lead to people who knew Mary but didn't find anything useful. Then she tried Aboriginal Health Toronto and found sites. Several didn't give their location, which seemed odd. If a person desperate for help wanted to see someone face to face, it wasn't possible without making a phone call.

Wild goose chase. Back to plan A: a visit to Mary's workplace.

A quick Mapquest search located the Golden Goose, on Jarvis Street close to Queen. She shouldered her bag, and at the Yonge and St. Clair subway station two blocks east of the apartment building she trotted down the stairs and jumped on the last car as the door closed. She exited on Queen and as she walked, she planned what she'd say.

The restaurant, which advertised all-day breakfast, was a bare bones diner. On one side chrome-and-red-plastic stools ran alongside a scarred Formica counter. A mirror on the wall above the counter gave anyone sitting there a good view of the entire restaurant. Hollis wondered how the restaurant had passed the city health inspection, as cleanliness did not seem to be a priority. Dirty black and white floor tiles, crumb- and food-bedecked tables, and the smeared mirror raised her suspicions about the state of the kitchen, as did the aroma of stale grease and burned toast. A waitress and a waiter, both in black pants and white shirts, scurried from table to table while a man in a black satin windbreaker sitting at the table closest to the kitchen did paperwork and occasionally growled at one of the staff.

At ten thirty the place was hopping. Hollis picked a spot at the counter where she could observe the clientele, slid onto a stool, and ordered coffee and a doughnut. While she sipped she watched the other patrons. At one table, three tired-looking women with long hair, red nails, short, tight skirts, high heels, and leather jackets made desultory conversation as they worked their way through orders of pancakes and bacon or sausages swimming in syrup. The tallest girl had kicked off her red satin stilettos and repeatedly rubbed the arch of each foot with the opposing heel. As Hollis watched her, the woman's cell phone rang. The others fell silent as she spoke briefly, clicked off, hastily stuffed a strip of bacon in her mouth along with a forkful of pancake, and stood up. She collected a gigantic silver handbag ornamented with studs and crystals, fished inside, and passed a bill to the other women before she left.

At an adjacent table, two women, one black and one Aboriginal, similarly dressed, drank coffee, ate greasy fried eggs and toast, and said nothing to one another. None of the women were accompanied by men and no man in the restaurant looked like Hollis's stereotypical conception of a pimp — no bling, no half-unbuttoned shirts or heavy shades. She guessed that most, whether East Indian, black or white, were shift workers, maybe taxi operators or night watchmen.

A heavy-set waitress with deep lines bracketing her mouth, too much blush, and dark blue eye shadow that emphasized the crepey texture of her eyelids, wore a badge identifying her as Bridget.

Hurray. She'd found the woman who'd left the message on Mary's machine. She was one step closer to finding Mary.

When the demands on Bridget lessened somewhat, Hollis crooked a finger.

"What else can I get you?" Bridget asked.

"Nothing in the way of food, but I think you can help me."

"In what way?"

"I'm looking for Mary Montour. I listened to the message you left for her, and I hope you can tell me where to find her. She disappeared before she picked it up."

Bridget assessed her. Hollis recognized an astute women who had dealt with all manner of people and wasn't easily taken in.

Chin jutting forward and eyes narrowed, Bridget said, "Who are you and why are you looking for her?"

Hollis dug into her denim shoulder bag, extracted her driver's license, and offered it.

"Sorry, I should have introduced myself. I'm the super in her apartment building and have a daughter Crystal's age. Mary left a message asking me to take care of Crystal. As you can imagine, Crystal is pretty upset." Hollis took back the license and tucked it in her purse. "I don't know anything about Mary other than she paid her rent on time and kept to herself. Her niece won't tell me anything but thinks something bad happened to her, because when Crystal got home, her aunt was gone and the apartment door was unlocked. Crystal said her aunt would *never* have left the door like that. There was a threatening message on her machine. Mary hasn't come back. That's why I'm here."

Bridget listened but also kept an eye on the other patrons and the man at the back table, who'd raised his head to watch her. "I can't stop to talk right now." She glanced up at the wall clock that hung on the mirror. "I have a break in ten minutes. I'm a smoker, so if you can stand the smell, join me out back and I'll tell you what I know."

Progress. Hollis ordered a second doughnut to celebrate and waited for Bridget to take her break. When her BlackBerry buzzed, she pulled it out and read a text message from Willem.

Would Mary be mixed up in the drug trade? I don't think we should be involved in this but I feel sorry for Crystal. That scream was bloodcurdling. How are you going about your search?

She tapped her answer. *Only beginning. In the restaurant where she worked. Waiting to talk to a co-worker when she takes her break.*

Willem replied immediately. *Be careful. If someone abducted her, she was messing with bad people.*

Touched by his obvious concern, Hollis vowed to be careful, to go to the police if she suspected a crime had been committed.

Bridget waved before she swung through the kitchen door.

Hollis shrugged into her denim jacket and headed outside, down a smelly, garbage-choked alley to the back of the building.

Bridget, who'd wrapped an old stretched Christmas cardigan around herself, perched on a makeshift seat made of plastic cartons, pulled a pack of cigarettes and a lighter from her worn black plastic purse, and lit up.

"I keep trying the patch but I always give up. My kids are at me all the time but quitting is hard."

Hollis nodded. Giving up anything you liked doing was difficult and knowing it was bad for you didn't really help. When she'd decided to deal with being overweight, she'd taken up running and given up many foods she liked. It had been and continued to be a major struggle.

"It's tough and everyone makes you feel guilty if you don't succeed. What can you tell me about Mary?" she said, positioning herself away from the smoke.

"I still don't know if I should. Some things I don't know for sure. I guessed she was doing something that might be dangerous. When I confronted her she didn't deny it, but didn't say she was."

"What kind of thing?"

Hollis felt ambivalent. The more she knew, the more likely it was that she'd have to take action. From past experience she realized this could lead to trouble. With Jay, Willem, Barlow, MacTee, and now Crystal in her life, she mustn't endanger them.

The kitchen door banged open. The man who'd been doing paperwork stepped outside.

"Bridget, your husband is here again. If you don't do something about him, keep him from turning up, I'll fire you."

Bridget jumped to her feet. "Stan, I'm sorry. He has so many problems. Life overwhelms him."

"I run a restaurant. I don't give a fuck about his problems. Get him out of here," he ordered and slammed back inside.

Bridget smiled apologetically at Hollis. "Sorry, my husband has mental health issues. I have to go. Come back again. I'll see what I remember and try to put it together for you."

"Thanks. I will. I hope he's okay."

"He'll never be okay. He's better when he takes his meds, but he says they turn him into a zombie," Bridget said, taking the card Hollis handed her as she disappeared into the kitchen.

Nothing. She was no further ahead. Maybe the Aboriginal prostitute or the waiter could tell her something.

By the time Hollis covered the distance to the front of the building, pulled open the heavy glass door smudged by hundreds of dirty hands, and went inside, Bridget was gone. Again Hollis settled at the counter and surveyed the room. No one seemed upset by whatever had happened, but in this part of Toronto inhabited by prostitutes, drug users, and derelicts, dramatic encounters must happen frequently. The black woman finished eating, rose, tossed a couple of toonies on the bill, and left her friend focused on spreading a thick coat of jam on a second helping of toast. Perfect timing.

Hollis picked up her white china coffee mug and moved to the woman's table.

"Mind if I join you?" Hollis said.

The young woman stopped chewing. She'd added neon red highlights to her long dark hair and wore matching red plastic dangling earrings. Although she'd applied makeup with a heavy hand, she'd failed to disguise her youth or completely cover the triangular scar over her right eye. Hollis guessed she might be in her mid-teens, certainly not yet twenty.

"Why? Who are you?" the girl said, edging farther into the booth away from Hollis.

"Whoa, I'm not here to ask questions about you," Hollis said and realized as the words escaped that she should have phrased the sentence more carefully.

The girl gathered her things.

"No, no. Stop. You don't understand. I'm looking for a waitress who works here, Mary Montour, and I thought maybe you'd talked to her or knew something about her." She held out her hand. "I'm Hollis Grant and I'm anxious to find her, because she's left her little girl behind." She pointed at the nearly empty coffee mug. "Can I buy you another coffee or more toast?"

The girl shrugged into a worn leather jacket that could have come from Goodwill or Value Village. Her dark almond-shaped eyes regarded Hollis suspiciously. "No, I've had enough. Why did you decide to pick on me?"

"No particular reason. I guess because you're here and I had to start somewhere. Do you have a name?"

"Not that I'm going to tell you," the girl said.

Hollis shrugged. "It's easier to talk to someone if they give you a name. May I sit down?"

"Free world. Suit yourself," the girl said. She left her jacket on but seemed loath to leave her unfinished breakfast and returned to piling strawberry jam on her toast.

"Did you ever talk to Mary Montour?" Hollis persisted.

With her mouth full the girl mumbled, "Maybe."

"Is she active in the First Nation community?"

"First Nation. Isn't that fancy? Indian. We're Indians. Wagon burners. Never mind Aboriginal or First Nation. Fucking Indians. That's what we are, and believe me, nobody lets us forget it."

"Must be tough."

The girl raised her gaze. "As if you'd know. Mrs. Rich Bitch. Say all the right things, give to charity, and look down on us like slime."

This girl would tell her even less than Crystal. "Okay, thanks for nothing. I'll leave you alone," Hollis said and slid to the edge of the bench, ready to leave.

"Sorry. Bad night. Yah, I knew her. Since she's a nice lady they'll know her over at the Native Friendship centre too. She treated us good. She worried about us and tried to help."

"In what way?"

"She must have known I was new around here, and one day, when I was by myself, she told me I should never go with a man who made me nervous. She went on about us being animals and knowing more than we thought we did."

Hollis smiled as the girl. "Did you listen?"

"No, not then, but I got beat up by a guy who'd made me feel like that and, after that, I did."

"What did she tell you to do?"

The girl took a gigantic bite of toast. After she'd washed it down with coffee she said, "Say no. Last week I told this guy to get lost, that I didn't want his business." She swallowed more coffee. "He made me feel like that and I knew Mary was right."

"What did he say?"

"That I was a fucking prostitute and I'd be sorry." She finished her toast. "Yah, Mary's an okay lady. I hope she's not in trouble. Hope you find her."

"Where is the Native Friendship Centre?"

"I'm not a fucking phone book. Look it up."

"I can, but since you mentioned it, I thought you might tell me."

The girl stared at Hollis. "It's *not* around here. *Nice* little Indian boys and girls pretend *we* don't exist, and they sure as fuck don't want to see us." She licked strawberry jam off her lip. "You find it. I gotta go." She lifted a shiny purple bag off the floor, dug for a change purse, grabbed five dollars, and headed for the exit.

That hadn't been useful. Probably the boss wouldn't contribute anything either, but she'd try. She slid off the stool and approached his table. He didn't look up.

"Excuse me," Hollis said.

"What is it," he growled, still not raising his eyes.

"I'm looking for Mary Montour. Would you know where she might be?"

The man snorted and stared up at her. "I know where she bloody ought to be." He thumped the table. "Right here doing her job, which, by the way, she doesn't have any more. No phone call. No nothing. She just doesn't show up."

"There could be a reason," Hollis said.

"Reason? The phone lines are down? Her cell phone is broken? Tell me what reason could explain not letting me know. By the time I figured she wasn't coming, it was too late to call in anyone else. Because she wasn't here, did you see how hard my staff worked this morning? Reason? I can't think of one good reason. You tell me." He leaned back, crossed his arms over his chest and lifted his chin. "I'm listening. One good reason."

"She's disappeared. She may have been abducted."

"Lady, you should be making movies — science fiction movies. Abducted. Who by? Aliens from outer space?" He guffawed. "Abducted."

Hollis didn't like being mocked. Her cheeks burned but she persisted. "Did she have any enemies who might have done it?" she asked, knowing that this question would probably unleash more sarcasm.

The man shook his head. "We get more than our share of nutcases in here, people who hear voices, who have radio transmitters in their fillings bringing in signals from outer space. Some are paranoid, think they're being followed. If I was a nice man I'd feel sorry that's the way they think, if you can call it thinking. Someone's after them, out to get them. But I'm not and I don't want them in here. Mary wasn't one of them. I don't know what she did when she wasn't working, but when she was here, she did her job and did it damn well. I'll give her that."

"Anyone who came specially to talk to her? Anyone she was friends with?"

He squared the papers in front of him as he again shook his head. "I can't believe you're serious. I don't monitor my staff and their friends." He bent over the work, clearly finished with the conversation.

No help here. One last try — she'd talk to the waiter. Sandy, according to his name tag.

Hollis left a tip beside her plate and headed for the cash, where Sandy, diamond studs in both ears and in the side of his nose, worked the register and handed change to a young man who pocketed the coins without counting them and headed for the door.

"I might be able to help you if you're looking for Mary," he said in a low voice.

Hollis, discouraged from her run in with the owner, felt a rush of excitement. She handed him a bill.

Sandy murmured, "I finish in twenty minutes. There's a park down the street where I wait until my partner picks me up. I usually zone out for a few minutes before he gets there. Meet me and I'll tell you what I think, although it isn't much."

Late April's unseasonable early warmth had persuaded the trees to send out their leaves. Now, in early May, a broken canopy of green spread over the park. Grass, ragged, untrimmed and dotted with dandelions, invited you to sit, although the ground would not yet be warm. Hollis chose a wooden-backed bench near the entrance, closed her eyes, and relaxed in the warm sun.

"Nice, isn't it?" a voice said and she looked up to see Sandy, wrapped in a too-large man's windbreaker, smiling down at her.

Hollis patted the bench. "Take a load off. You've been on your feet for hours. You must be tired."

Sandy sat down, bent, loosened the Velcro straps on his black shoes, and eased them off his feet. He wriggled his toes and stretched his legs. "I guess sore feet are an occupational hazard in this business."

"I don't think I could do it," Hollis said sympathetically. "I'm happy that you can tell me something about Mary. I was getting desperate."

Sandy swung to face Hollis and leaned toward her. "It isn't much, but it might help. I think she was into religion," he whispered.

Hollis glanced around. No one lingered close by. No need for Sandy to lower his voice.

"Many people are. Do you mean she tried to convert people, to persuade them to go to church, that sort of thing?"

Sandy shook her head. "No. But if we both had a break, if nobody was in she'd ask funny questions and most of them related to the Bible."

"Like what?"

"Last week she asked me if I believed the Bible when it said we should be our brothers' keepers. Then she smiled and said she supposed it applied to sisters as well as brothers."

"What did you say?"

"Well, I was raised a Catholic, although except for weddings and funerals I haven't been in a church for years, and I agreed with her. I said I thought we had a good society because we do take care of one another. Then Mary nodded as if I'd said something really deep and important, laid her hand on my arm, and looked me in the eye. 'We should all take that on as our reason for living,' she said."

"I can see why you'd think she was into religion. Anything else?"

Sandy bent to scratch the sole of his foot and peered up at Hollis. "Nothing specific, but she was always nice and very polite to the drunks and the addicts. Very respectful."

"What about the prostitutes and pimps?" Hollis asked.

"Same for hookers. I seen her give more than one refill and extra jam to women who looked like they'd had a really bad night."

"Pimps?"

"They mostly don't come in. Sit outside revving them muscle cars. They watch their girls but from outside. Them girls knows they're there. Scared shitless most of them are." He pulled his shoes back on and pointed south. "I've been in St. Mike's emerg, and Mary would be right at home there, 'cause they treat street people like they count." He raised his arm and waved.

A red pickup truck idling at the curb blinked its lights.

"Gotta go. I'll think back to things she said and see if anything comes to mind that might explain where she's gone."

Hollis fished in her bag and handed him her card. "Call me if you do."

Sister's keeper. Mary was looking after Crystal. Did that count, or had she meant more than that? Did it have anything to do with her disappearance? The more Hollis learned, the less she knew. Time for the Indian Friendship Centre. She needed a phone book, and they were hard to find.

Hollis had forgotten that she could find addresses using her BlackBerry. Standing on Jarvis Street she glanced above the restaurant's door and typed in the address as her starting point and the Indian Friendship Centre as her destination and waited. A late model Ford station wagon pulled up to the curb. The driver rolled down the window and leaned toward her.

No doubt some tourist looking for help. Hollis walked over.

"How much," the man said.

My God, he thinks I'm a hooker. Hollis didn't know whether to be flattered or insulted. She stared into the car, noting two car seats in the back.

"I'm not a hooker. I was waiting for my BlackBerry to load an address," she said.

"Sorry," he said as the window rolled up and the car began to move.

A tall woman dressed entirely in magenta from the spikes that made her seem even taller to a tiny satin mini-skirt, a low-cut silk top, and a leather jacket, nudged Hollis none too gently.

"Get your own patch," she said.

Hollis was astounded. In her worn running shoes, blue jeans, black T-shirt, and jean jacket, she asked herself how anyone could mistake her for a prostitute. She waved the BlackBerry. "I was waiting for an address to download. I'm out of here," she said, already moving away.

Spadina Road. The number was low, so it must be just north of Bloor Street, close to the University of Toronto.

She looked at her watch. Because of Calum Brownelly's insistence that she deliver and pick up Jay, time mattered. That morning Crystal had resisted going to school and finally admitted to Hollis she was terrified that if someone had grabbed her aunt, he might come back for her. Hollis reassured her that she and the dogs would be waiting and would protect her. Both girls wanted to come home for lunch because they knew that if they remained at school, the kids in the lunch room would question them about the murder.

Hollis sympathized and planned to offer macaroni, everyone's comfort food, and time for the girls to zone out and forget the chaos in their lives. While she was happy to do it, she had an ulterior motive. If she was lucky and probed carefully, she might discover more about Crystal's background.

The need to reach the school in time spurred her to rush to the subway, take the Yonge line to St. Clair, and half run to collect the girls. Seemingly they'd dismissed their early morning fears and chattered about an upcoming school visit to the Ontario Science Centre. Hollis had volunteered to be one of the adults accompanying the class and didn't know whether to look forward to or to dread the assignment. At home she heated the macaroni and cheese. Standing at the stove she talked to them as they waited at the kitchen table.

"Crystal, I visited the restaurant this morning."

With her back to the room, she couldn't judge how her Crystal had reacted, except to note that she hadn't responded. Hollis turned the heat down and swung around.

"I talked to Bridget, Sandy, and the boss. You ever meet any of them?"

"No. I already told you. Mary never took me there."

"She ever talk about work, about people she knew, people she might have been helping?"

"Nope."

Hollis dished up the pasta, retrieved ketchup and salsa, from the refrigerator, and piled mandarin oranges in a blue bowl.

Crystal hunched her shoulders and stared at her plate when Hollis lobbed questions at her. Hollis couldn't believe that an eleven-year-old didn't know or suspect what was going on in her own house.

If she couldn't get any information, perhaps if she had a quiet word with Jay, she might persuade her charge to investigate. She'd need to word the request carefully. Most children resisted spying or being tattle tales.

"Before you came to live with your aunt, did you live on a reserve?"

Crystal spooned salsa on her macaroni. She muttered an almost inaudible, "Yes."

Hollis hated badgering the child, but she needed answers. "Which one?"

This time Hollis could not hear Crystal's reply, which she whispered.

"Would your repeat that?" Hollis asked.

"Hollis, you must have wax in your ears. I heard her. Crystal said Oneida. I'd like more macaroni," Jay said.

Enough questions. At least she had one answer. From long-ago history courses she dredged up what she knew about Ontario's Aboriginals. Surprisingly, she remembered that the Oneidas belonged to the Iroquois Confederacy, Indians granted land along the Grand River after they supported the British during the American Revolutionary War. She thought back to university, when she'd learned some of this. There had been six. What were they? Oneida, Mohawk, Cayuga, Seneca, Onondaga, and Tuscarora. She smiled. Sometimes factoids stuck in your brain. Only the Mohawk and Oneida came north after the war. She'd google the Oneida and find out more than she wanted to know from Wikipedia.

"Girls, finish your lunch while I check something on my computer."

A quick flip and she learned that the Oneida reserve was located close to London, a southern Ontario town known for its university and cultural life. That wasn't much help but it was a starting point. After she walked the girls back to school, she'd head down to the Friendship Centre.

The apartment building's glass door swung shut behind them and they walked down the circular driveway toward the street. A black town car with tinted windows crept up the curve behind them. Hollis whirled around, grabbed the girls' hands, and sped back into the apartment lobby and away from the doors. She might be paranoid, but that driver had intended to cut them off before they reached the sidewalk.

Hollis shooed the girls into the garage, where she loaded them into her Mazda van and locked the doors.

"What was that about?" Jay said. "That car spooked you. How come?"

"I know *how come*," Crystal said. Without waiting for either of the other two to comment, she continued. "You really *do* believe something bad happened to my aunt and you believe whoever did it is coming after me."

Hollis hadn't thought about Crystal when she'd reacted to the black car. Feeling a little silly, she turned to the two in the back seat. "It *did* spook me. I have no idea why, but it's always better to listen to your instincts. I didn't connect the car to Mary. The truth is I just didn't think. I'm sorry if I scared you."

She swivelled back and started the car. "I'll drive you to school, double park, and walk you to the door. After school don't leave until I arrive."

"It's all my fault," Crystal said in a flat voice.

"No, it isn't. Why would you think it was your fault? Children aren't responsible for the things that happen to adults," Hollis said firmly.

"If you weren't looking for Aunt Mary I bet that car wouldn't have been there. It had something to do with her. If I wasn't with you, nothing would have happened."

Hollis slowed for a jaywalking pedestrian and didn't respond to Crystal until she'd navigated a tricky left turn and cruised toward the school.

"Crystal, that's guesswork. Stop doing that or you'll make yourself sick. I repeat, children are *not* responsible for things that happen to adults."

Nevertheless, in spite of her reassuring words, she checked for the black car before they left the van. When she had determined everything was okay, she flicked on the car's flashers and shepherded the children into the school. Once they were safely inside, she parked the car and returned to the school intent on speaking to the principal. The woman in the outer office raised her eyes from her computer and asked what she could do for Hollis.

"I need to speak to the principal on a matter of some urgency," Hollis said.

The woman raised an eyebrow as if to indicate she'd heard overwrought parents say exactly the same thing many times before.

"He has someone with him." She looked up at the wall clock. "Probably be about ten minutes if you want to wait."

Hollis regretted her impulsive dash into the school. What was she going to say? On one hand she didn't want to spill the beans about Crystal being in her care, about her concern about Jay's father, or about the suspicious black vehicle. On the other hand she didn't want the girls to ever leave the grounds or be released to anyone else. She'd stay and try to get the point across without alerting the principal to the actual situation.

She settled on a hard wooden chair. There were no magazines, old or new, so she pulled out her BlackBerry and tidied her mail.

The door to the inner office opened and a large, visibly upset woman exited, nodded to the receptionist, and slammed out of the office. Seconds later the principal, a beanpole-thin worried-looking man in his thirties followed her. He looked surprised to see Hollis, who stood up when he appeared. She stuck out her hand.

"Hollis Grant, I'm Jay Brownelly's foster parent."

After he shook her hand, he said, "What can I do for you."

"There already have been many disruptions in Jay's life. Now there's been a murder in our apartment building. I've assured the Children's Aid Society that I will always pick her up from school, and I wanted to make sure that you knew that and that I can count on you not to allow anyone but me to collect her."

The principal nodded to his assistant. "Ms. Broadbent will do that. Jay isn't the only child in this school whom we guard. We'll make sure all our teachers know that Jay is only to be picked up by you."

As she thanked him Hollis backed toward the door before he asked questions. Outside she discovered a yellow parking ticket tucked under her windshield wiper, stuffed it into her purse, and headed home. No point driving to Bloor and Spadina. Any lot in the area would be hideously expensive and probably full. She'd take the subway, but first she'd make sure no black cars lurked in the driveway.

Emerging from the subway at Yonge and Bloor she walked along Bloor Street, one of Toronto's major east–west arteries, to Spadina Road. The Indian Friendship Centre, located steps from Bloor, must have once been a lovely private home. The front entrance and foyer panelled in heavy dark wood seemed a tad gloomy, but in contrast the young man staffing the reception desk at the entrance smiled warmly when she approached.

"How can I help?" he asked.

"I'm inquiring about a friend from the Oneida of the Thames reserve. I know she's in Toronto but I lost her address."

A frown creased the young man's broad face. "To tell you anything about anyone who uses our centre would violate her privacy. If it's any help, there's a new Internet service for Aboriginals. Often when young people come to the city, they want to connect with other Aboriginals." He waved his arm toward the south. "Although specific institutions like the University of Toronto have clubs, young men and women who arrive for nursing or for work find this new service helps them." He pulled a pad of paper toward him and wrote on it before handing it to Hollis. "This might help. If she attends U of T you could check out their group or the ones at Ryerson or York." He gestured toward an adjacent room with dark wood wainscotting and a plate rail. Probably a dining room at one time. Now bulletin boards covered two walls.

"Check the boards. Often individuals post messages and leave contact information. There are notices of meetings and other events."

Hollis did as she was told but knew Mary's name would not be there. When she glanced quickly at the board, a poster caught her attention. In June, Norman Thompson would be exhibiting at the Zanandu gallery.

Norman Thompson was a Mohawk from Brantford. She knew that because she'd studied with him at the Ontario College of Art and Design. Over the years since their graduation she'd attended each of his shows and maintained a desultory email relationship. She hadn't contacted him for several years but should have thought of him. This had not been a wasted trip — she had a new lead, a possible new source of information.

At home she emailed Norman, hoping he hadn't changed his address. She'd never known where he lived, since their contacts had been in cyberspace. *It's a voice from the past. I need information about an Iroquois woman who is missing. She's an Oneida. Do you know anything about Mary Montour?*

FOURTEEN

NORMAN must have been sitting at his computer for he replied within minutes.

On the Oneida reserve, Montour is a very common name, as are Doxtator, Antone, and Cornelius. On the Six Nations at Oshwegan, it is also common as is Johnson, Jamieson, and Maracle. Mary is the Christian world's most popular name. Tell me something about her?

That wasn't too helpful. First she'd share her reaction to his last show. She'd meant to email him at the time but something had distracted her.

Before I do I wanted to say that your series "Residential Schools" made me weep. Technically it's glorious but the emotional impact really affected me. How come you didn't come to the vernissage? I've attended your last three shows and you're never there. Have you become a recluse?

Waiting for his reply, she wondered why she hadn't asked before, why she'd allowed their friendship to falter. She plugged in the kettle.

You might describe me that way. I have my reasons. What about Mary Montour?

Back to business. She lives in the apartment building I live in and manage on Delisle Street. She works as a waitress at a diner on Jarvis Street. Her sister's daughter, Crystal, lives with her. Crystal's mother is dead. Mary has other women stay in her apartment for various periods of time. That's what I know.

Norman did not reply immediately. Hollis took time to make tea and was drinking her second cup when the red light on her BlackBerry flashed.

I know who you mean. We should talk. Do you want to come to my studio? If so, then you have to promise you will tell no one, and I do mean NO ONE, where I live.

Not another person with a secret. This was too much. But it was a chance to find out more about Mary. Anyway, other than Willem, who would she tell?

Sure, I agree to that. Mary left Crystal with me, so I am very anxious to know if she's okay and where she is.

I live in an apartment at Harbourfront. The doorman will expect you. He'll request photo identification. Bring your driver's license or passport.

Decidedly weird. Something strange was happening to Norman. The Norman she'd known would never have been so jumpy or careful. He must be in trouble, serious trouble.

I have a foster daughter and Crystal, so I'll come during school hours. Too late today. Do you prefer a morning or afternoon visit tomorrow?

Morning. Be sure no one knows you're coming or follows you.

Following this bizarre email exchange, Hollis rushed to fetch the girls. Dogs and kids in tow, she walked toward home knowing decision time approached. Wednesday and time to deal with Jay and the Eaton Centre? Given everything happening at the moment, this was the last thing she wanted to cope with. But for Jay the decision loomed large. Having so recently lost her foster mother, she intended to maintain contact with and hang on to her father, the elusive man who drifted in and out of her life.

The witching hour was seven o'clock tomorrow.

In the apartment she ignored the blinking message light until she'd provided the girls with string cheese and apples.

She left them at the kitchen table with the dogs drooling beside them and went into her bedroom to play the messages.

When she pressed play, a gruff voice growled, "What the hell is happening there? I don't want my daughter in danger. Phone me immediately."

Hollis didn't like being told what to do. The second message was a hang-up.

What to say to Brownelly? She'd think about it. She entered the kitchen to see Jay breaking off bits of cheese and giving them alternately to MacTee and Barlow. So much for her rule that under no circumstances were the dogs to be fed at the table. Jay quickly closed her hand as Hollis stared at her.

"Where do the dogs get their treats?" she asked Jay.

Jay shrugged. "What does it matter?"

"It matters a lot. If you feed them at the table, they hang around waiting for you to give them something, and they drool. It's revolting how much they drool. Don't do it again." Even as she said this she knew her smart dogs had pegged Jay as a soft touch and would never forget what the child had done.

Crystal, always hungry, ignored both of them and peeled back the plastic on another cheese strip.

"Well, I don't think it matters and it's time," Jay said, pushing back her chair and standing up. Hands on hips, her entire body challenged Hollis.

"Time for what?" Hollis said.

"You know what. Tomorrow I'm supposed to go to the Eaton Centre. I *have* to let my dad know whether you'll let me go."

Hollis absentmindedly stroked Barlow's bony back and wondered if she was feeding him enough. "Your father left a message on the machine. I haven't phoned him back yet. We could meet at the Children's Aid Office. That's the way visits are supposed to work."

"That's stupid."

"Why? It's perfectly reasonable for him to visit you there. Why the Eaton Centre?"

Jay frowned. "I don't know. That's what he said when he phoned. When I lived with Mrs. Cooper we met there, and I guess he thought we'd always meet there." She focused a level stare at Hollis. "He can only come now and then. Dad says he'd like to see me more often, even have me live with him, but because of what he does it just isn't possible."

"The social worker told me that but didn't say what he did. Do you know?"

Jay shook her head. "Dad says it's better if I don't know."

"You may go if Crystal and I come along."

"No."

"That's my offer. I'm not allowing you alone on the subway and in the shopping mall at night without me. And we certainly aren't going to leave Crystal at home."

Jay crossed her arms over her chest and hugged herself. "It won't work," she said in a flat voice.

"We don't need to be right by your side," Hollis said. "If you meet your father in the food court you can find a spot at the back and Crystal and I will have milk shakes or fries or something sinful and sit at the front near the escalator. That way, if something goes wrong you know where to find us."

"If something goes wrong?" Jay's voice rose. "What can go wrong?"

Hollis shrugged. "Probably nothing, but we'll be there. When you're finished you and your father can join us."

Jay picked at a scab on her wrist and said nothing.

"Your father's number is on the phone list. I'll call and tell him what we've arranged." Hollis went to the kitchen phone.

"Hollis Grant here," she said and listened.

"With the police presence in the building I'm sure Jay is fine. She tells me you want me to allow her to go alone to the Eaton Centre to meet you, but I'm uncomfortable doing that. In fact, the CAS told me they only allowed you to see her at their offices. I realize that if the meetings have to be in the evenings, this doesn't work and I'm willing to be flexible. We'll meet you in the food court. You can have a private conversation but I want to be able to see her."

She listened to Brownelly for a moment or two before she said, "Mrs. Cooper may have agreed but I'm amazed that you would risk what could happen to her travelling alone on the subway and meeting you downtown. I'll pass the phone to Jay."

Crystal, who'd been following the conversation said, "I like the Eaton Centre. So many different people. Everyone always seems to have a good time. I'm glad I'm going with you." Her lips turned down. "It will keep me from thinking about Aunt Mary and what's happened to her."

Hollis passed Crystal another cheese string and watched while the child carefully prepared to eat it. "Have you been there often?"

"No, Aunt Mary said it was a bad place, not somewhere young girls should go. When I needed clothes we went to the Bay at Bloor and Yonge."

"She was partly right. Young girls from the suburbs cruise the mall looking for excitement. Sometimes they find more than they can handle. We'll be fine. I want a chocolate milkshake. You may have anything you like."

Crystal's eyes sparkled like her name. "Thank you, that will be great."

Jay's lower lip stuck out and she glowered at Hollis with narrowed eyes. "I still don't see why you have to come, but I guess it's better than nothing."

Hollis felt uneasy. Was it just that talking to Jay's father had that effect, or were her instincts telling her to be careful? Why was Calum Brownelly so obsessed with Jay's safety?

After her confrontation with Jay, Hollis poured herself half a glass of wine and added soda, left the girls to do their homework, and took herself across the hall to her office. She fielded calls from nervous residents anxious to hear if the crime had been solved, and arranged for a plumber to attend to a problem in 307. Phone calls over, she leaned back, turned to watch the security cameras and sipped the spritzer, her favourite drink.

"Drinking on the job. Does your employer know?" a woman's voice asked.

Hollis swung around to see the two detectives. Rhona grinned at her.

"What can I do for you?" Hollis said.

"We're seeing Ms. Nesrallah in five minutes, but we need more tenant information," Rhona said.

"What I can do?"

"There are two apartments where we haven't been able to contact the tenants."

Hollis's heart flipped.

"On the third floor, we didn't get a response from Martin Palliser in 318."

"He's in the hospital. He had a heart attack but plans to return," Hollis said.

"And apartment 202, Mary Montour."

Hollis didn't look at the detectives but picked up a pen on her desk. "She called to say she'd be away for a while but didn't say where she was or when she'd be back." She held her breath, waiting to see if they'd ask if Mary lived alone. She'd be forced to tell them about Crystal if they did."

"Interesting that she'd tell you. I thought tenants only did that if they might miss a rent cheque, but I suppose she wanted you to put her mail aside if it piles up," Rhona said. "We also thought we'd check and see if you have any insights about your tenants that might help us."

"Not so far. Every person in the building is looking suspiciously at every other resident, but as far as I know there haven't been any revelations."

Ian straightened. "Please inform us immediately if you do hear rumours or accusations."

Hollis didn't know whether she should have said anything else. She had told the truth — she didn't know where Mary was, but her disappearance had been abrupt and unexplained.

She gave herself a time limit. One more day and she'd tell the detectives everything she knew about Mary.

If she only had twenty-four hours, she didn't want to wait until the next day to see Norman. She couldn't leave the girls alone if she was out of the building, but Agnes Johnson, the feisty octogenarian on the fourth floor, was always willing to keep an eye on Jay and surely wouldn't mind if Crystal was there too. She punched in Agnes's number.

After the preliminaries were taken care of she said, "My apologies for calling you on such short notice, but would you join us in a few minutes for an early supper of lasagna and then keep an eye on the gang for a couple of hours?"

"I'd never turn down an invitation like that," Agnes said.

Hollis emailed Norman. *Okay if I come down tonight? I have time and I really want to talk to you.*

Minutes later, Agnes, pushing her walker, appeared in the doorway. Hollis closed the office and led the way across the hall, where the girls sat at the kitchen table talking. Both looked up.

"Hi, Mrs. Johnson," Jay said and introduced Crystal.

"Glad to meet you, Crystal. I hope you like to play Monopoly, because I'm dying for a game." She waggled a finger at them. "It's only fair to warn you that I fight to the finish and am partial to railroads."

The girls giggled.

"Homework finished?"

"Yes," the girls said in unison.

The aroma from the lasagna Hollis had tucked in the oven earlier filled the apartment, and the dinging timer told her to take it out and let it rest for a few minutes. While it did, she gathered lettuce, peppers, and avocado from the fridge.

"Take Mrs. Johnson into the living room and set up the board. I'm making a salad before I put supper on the table. After that I have to go out for an hour or so."

She checked her BlackBerry. Norman's reply. *Sure. Make sure no one follows you.*

She couldn't imagine why anyone would.

After walking the dogs she left the apartment shortly after five, squeezed on the subway jammed body-to-body with rush hour travellers, rolled out with the crowd into Union Station, left most of the mob heading for the commuter trains, and broke away to wait in the underground terminal for the streetcar that would deliver her to the buildings along Queen's Quay. When she arrived on the platform three people waited. Clearly none of them had followed her as she'd just arrived. The streetcar swung into the underground station and they climbed on. Just as it was about to leave, two men to whom middle age had not been kind dashed into the station and flung themselves aboard.

Hollis, who'd chosen a seat at the back, examined them. Both wore black jackets, black jeans, and black boots. Too old to be Goths, they certainly weren't businessmen, but with the Boomers' attraction to motorcycles, they probably worked as accountants or stockbrokers and lived on the wild side evenings and weekends. Neither looked particularly dangerous, nor did they exhibit any interest in the other passengers.

When they got off when she did, she paid more attention.

Given Norman's paranoia, she decided it was unwise to proceed directly to the apartment and turned east walking toward the ferry docks. She passed the two apartment buildings, Harbour Square and Harbourside, without a sidelong glance. A Golden Retriever on a leash sideswiped her, and she bent to pat the dog while checking behind her. The two men, deep in conversation, sauntered slowly along. She strolled to the cement walkway leading down to the Island ferry dock.

There she lined up behind three women with bicycles, their panniers filled with groceries, an elderly man puffing on a pipe, a rare sight in today's smokeless world, and a mass of high school students going home to the Island. At the wicket she dug into her purse and bought a ticket which included a return. A trip to bucolic Centre Island had definitely not been on her agenda, but she wasn't about to lead anyone to Norman.

When the gate creaked open and the crowd poured onto the ferry, she made for the back of the upper deck and perched on a slatted wooden bench where she could watch the other travellers. And there they were, Tweedles Dee and Dum.

The ferry hooted and set out for island. Normally she loved this trip, but not today. Should she disembark and see where they went? Not a chance, she'd ride back, go to the Eaton Centre and lose them. She yanked out her BlackBerry and phoned Norman.

"I'm on the ferry. I may be weird but I think two middle-aged guys are following me. I don't know how they knew where I was going, but I'm not coming to see you. I'm going home and I'll shake them on the way."

"It must be the computer — they've hacked into it or my cell phone. I'll call you later. Don't email me, but I hardly ever go out, so come when you can. Thanks for leading them away. You may have saved my life."

My god, he can't be serious. Saved his life. What was he hiding from?

The ferry slowed and the deckhands grabbed the thick hausers and made ready to tie up the boat. The disembarking passengers bunched and crowded in the lower gangway. Hollis didn't move.

She remained anchored to her seat and wasn't surprised to see that her two thugs didn't get off either. A crowd of returning passengers flooded on as soon as the gangway emptied. Hollis sat where she was on the return trip and watched the men, who ignored her.

Once ashore she decided to give them some exercise, so instead of taking the streetcar she walked briskly past the hotel adjacent to the docks, under the train underpass, and back to the cavernous vastness of Union Station. Time for some fun.

She headed down to the bowels of the building and over to the subway entrance, where she dropped in her token and made for the north platform. A glance behind told her they were still with her. She pivoted on her heel and marched up to them.

"Why have you been following me?" she demanded.

The taller man, who had a silly-looking Fu Manchu moustache, shrugged. "We weren't following you."

"No. You took the streetcar, went to the island, and didn't get off. We were the only people who didn't get off. Well, let me tell you I'm going to Sears to buy a new pair of sandals, a bra, and maybe a dress. Now you know and you can follow me there too."

The short one, who needed to lose twenty pounds and do something about his very yellow teeth, bared them. "Don't threaten us, sister. We can go wherever we fucking want to go."

"Fine," Hollis said and jumped onto the subway car that had screeched into the station.

When she got off at Dundas, the two men did not come after her. But she had no doubt that they had followed her. Given Norman's reaction, she worried about what kind of trouble he might be in. If he was in a mess, did the fact that she'd contacted him place her in danger? If they'd hacked into his computer, they knew she was searching for Mary. Was that significant?

She worried that the thugs might know where she lived. Could they have been in the black car that had spooked her? Had that happened before or after she emailed Norman? She hadn't given that information in the email, or had she? Had she said she lived on Delisle? Was it possible to use sophisticated techniques to ferret out locations? She didn't know but didn't think so. Facebook was a different thing. Often individuals who carelessly or inadvertently gave away names and addresses placed themselves in danger.

In case the men still lurked about, she rode up the escalator to the lingerie section. Then she found the elevator and zipped to the basement, where she scurried to the food court, back up the escalator, out the doors to the church yard and over to Bay Street, where she popped through one entrance to the bus depot, out another and caught a cab to the apartment.

Six thirty and she hadn't been missed. Agnes and the girls, hunkered down in front of the Monopoly board, looked up when she said hello. She left them to continue the game and went to the office. One message on her machine. Her breath quickened. Maybe Mary had called, maybe she was returning and all would be well.

"It's Miss Tilly Green in 401. You're supposed to be there when things break. My toilet is plugged," a voice snapped.

Hollis pulled out her list of service providers, contacted the plumber, and insisted that since they advertised twenty-four hour service, they come immediately. Then she called Miss

Green, a retired teacher who must have run a no-nonsense classroom if her current insistence that everything be exactly right in her apartment was any indication. After her initial huffiness, Miss Green thanked Hollis for acting quickly and persuading the plumber to make the call a priority.

Too bad, Hollis really had hoped it would be Mary or even Rachel, her fellow waitress, who called. She hadn't exactly lied to the detectives, but she hadn't exactly told the truth. If only Mary would contact her.

FIFTEEN

MRS. Trepanier didn't speak on the ride into Toronto. Rhona, intent on the detours and the heavy traffic, didn't say anything, nor did Ian. Chit-chat or small talk had no place in the car. Rhona took Mrs. Trepanier's arm as they emerged from the underground garage. She did it not only with the intention of leading her through the maze of corridors to the morgue, but also to provide physical and emotional support. She felt tiny tremors pass through Mrs. Trepanier's body. Rhona couldn't imagine what it would be like to be in Mrs. Trepanier's situation, to take a journey knowing that at the end you would face the worst nightmare a parent could imagine.

They entered the identification area. Mrs. Trepanier breathed quickly and almost imperceptibly held back as if her body was resisting, putting off the terrible finality of death.

Rhona still held her arm, and she gave a tiny squeeze before the moment arrived when Mrs. Trepanier would have to face the reality that the body could be her daughter's.

One quick look sufficed. Mrs. Trepanier lurched back and swung away.

Her head dropped and she took deep, steadying breaths. For some moments she said nothing. Finally she raised her head and turned to Rhona. "It's Claire," she said.

Rhona never got used to the moment when hope was extinguished. No matter the circumstances, family always hung onto the flimsiest of reasons to explain a loved one's disappearance. Even when travelling to view a body, they persuaded themselves it wouldn't be the person.

Mrs. Trepanier stood, dry-eyed, and stared into space. The desolation in her eyes was painful to see.

Was there anything they could do to help?

"Would you like to come with us and sit quietly while we make you a cup of tea?" Rhona offered.

Mrs. Trepanier flinched as if she'd forgotten they were there. She focused on them and considered Rhona's words. "No. Take me home. Duchess's bladder isn't as reliable as it used to be and it will be an hour before I get there."

Once they'd seen her into a car and on her way, they returned to the homicide office.

"David Jones, the teacher she testified against, the man who spent time in jail because of her, would have reason to kill her if he was set on revenge. Let's find out if he's done his time, and if he's out on parole, what address he left with the Parole Board," Ian said. He tapped a few words into his computer, waited for the information to download, and reported, "Out for three months and living in Oshawa."

"It might have taken him that long to find her, although she didn't change her surname. Time for another trip. Does he live in a halfway house?"

Ian tapped again. "Yes, and there's a phone number." He picked up the phone, asked for David Jones, and arranged to meet him at the house in an hour and a half.

"Too easy," Rhona said.

"Perps aren't brilliant, or they wouldn't spend so much time in jail," Ian replied.

"What would he gain by killing her?" Rhona asked.

"Revenge."

"Not enough. He'd know we'd learn about his rape conviction."

"He had good reason to hate her."

Rhona offered to drive the sixty kilometres to Oshawa, a small city close to Toronto noted for its car plant — a working class community. On Highway 401 out of Toronto, Rhona kept her attention fixed on the road. With a multitude of lanes and an overload of tractor trailers, the traffic challenged even the best of drivers. There wasn't a GPS in the car, but before they left, Ian had downloaded a map from the Internet and directed Rhona through a maze of downtown streets to a roomy, turn-of-the-century brick house.

Five men occupied the shaded front porch. Bundled in jackets despite the May weather, two sat on wooden kitchen chairs tipped back against the wall, and two slouched on an old bench car seat. A third man lounged on the concrete steps.

All conversation stopped and five pairs of eyes checked out the two detectives as they made their way up the cracked cement walk.

Rhona greeted them pleasantly and said, "Where can we find David Jones?"

The man sprawled on the steps muttered, "Living room, inside the front door."

They skirted him and entered the living room, where a slim, athletic-looking man sitting on one of three overstuffed dark blue faux leather sofas was reading the paper. He stood when they entered and proffered his hand.

"David Jones. What's this about?"

Ian launched the conversation. "We're here to talk to you about Claire Trepanier."

"God, not again. I've done my time, at least I've done two-thirds of it. I want to get on with what's left of my life," Jones said and exhaled a huge sigh. "She ruined me. No one wants to believe me, but although she may have been fifteen, it wasn't rape. I didn't even know she was pregnant until she charged me."

Ian waited to see if Jones had anything more to say. When it appeared that he didn't, Ian said, "She wasn't the only one."

Jones sighed again. "I know, I know, I abused a position of trust. I deserved to lose my job. God knows I'll never get another one unless it's teaching adult males. It was wrong, but I didn't figure I was doing anyone any harm. The girls led me on, let me know they wanted sex."

Rhona took her turn. For a long moment she simply stared at him. "Of course you realize that all rapists use that line. There is no justification for forcing yourself on a fifteen-year-old girl."

"You won't believe me, no one does, but I didn't force myself on her," Jones said, his voice reflecting his resignation. He stood up. "I don't know why you're here other than wanting to know about Claire, but I've put the whole sorry mess behind me. I don't know where she is or what she does and don't intend to find out. I've lost years of my life, as well as my vocation, my wife, and my self-respect. I applied for parole because I needed time in a halfway house to get help putting my life back together."

"Very commendable." Rhona, who had been standing throughout the interview, leaned toward him. "But hard to believe. Difficult to think you wouldn't want to punish the person who caused this," she waved at the room, "to happen to you."

Jones considered the two detectives. "I may have been a fool, but I'm not an idiot. Why this sudden interest?"

"First, tell us what you did Monday night?"

"Monday night? You know all about parole. We have a curfew. Early Monday evening I went to the library, borrowed two books and a DVD, came back, signed in, went to my room, and watched the DVD on my computer."

Ian's eyebrows must have expressed his disbelief.

"My brother gave me his old one and bought me a new printer. He said I couldn't job hunt without them. He doesn't love the idea that he has a jailbird for a brother, but he hasn't deserted me, nor has my mother."

"Do they do a bed check here?" Rhona asked.

"They do and there's no way to leave without setting off an alarm. Now will you tell me what this is about?"

"Claire Trepanier was murdered Monday night," Rhona said.

Jones looked from one to the other. "Poor Claire. Such a pretty, bright girl with so much promise. She wrecked my life, but I'm sorry she's dead."

Rhona recognized the sincerity in his voice, but the best liars could be very convincing. She didn't intend to drop him off the suspect list.

In the early afternoon Rhona and Ian arrived back from Oshawa. The boss, Frank Braithwaite, wanted to see them.

He sat behind his gleaming desk admiring a new GPS. "In case we get lost. Have to check that it works in remote locations, but since it bounces off a satellite I assume it does," he said.

Rhona had forgotten about the adventure camping trip Frank planned to take with his dog. Time to make an intelligent remark. "Won't your human guide know where you are?"

"Of course, but you always have to be prepared for the worst, for something to happen to the guide or for him to lose his equipment. In the wilderness there are no second chances." His eyes sparkled as he spoke, and Rhona felt he hoped something dramatic would challenge him.

He pushed the GPS to one side and tapped it lightly. "Never mind this. We're here to discuss the case. You know that this afternoon the paper will have the victim's name. Are we closing in on anyone?"

"We interviewed several possible suspects. One, a man she accused of rape, has just come out of jail, a second has a peeping tom conviction and lives in the building. A profiler would say he's operating in the neighbourhood where he's comfortable, but we think his own building is probably a little too close. A third man interests us because he too lives in the building, used the services of the fifth-floor women, and frightened them. We're also considering the idea that Sabrina Trepanier wasn't the intended victim, and we're doing a background work-up on the apartment's tenant, Ginny Wuttenee."

"Any johns who might have done it?" Frank asked, his hand reaching again for the GPS.

"We have a list of Sabrina's clients and we're talking to Ms. Nesrallah, who owns all the apartments and sometimes screens possible clients for the women. That's what we have so far," Rhona said, resisting the urge to tell him to stop fiddling with his newest toy.

"Okay. I'll give a noncommittal press release. Working through a number of possibilities, etc. etc. By the way, there's no chance that this is a serial crime, is there?"

"I checked unsolved crimes looking for similarities, and it doesn't look like it," Ian said.

"Good. I don't want any surprises," Frank said.

Back in the homicide office, Ian shook his head. "He should retire and concentrate on his trips. Except for the necessity of avoiding unfavourable publicity, he really doesn't seem to care."

"Never mind, as long as the press doesn't make it a major issue, it keeps him off our back. Time to go and talk to Ms. Nesrallah."

Rhona loved the variety in her job. It had its bad moments, but she enjoyed never knowing what was coming next, getting out and interviewing, investigating odd possibilities.

"We'll stop and talk to Hollis Grant on our way to the interview. She may be a wingnut, but in the past she's given us useful leads."

"I've made Turkish coffee," Ms. Nesrallah said as she let the detectives into her apartment, her multi-coloured silk caftan swirling about her legs. Dangling silver earrings composed of discs that gently tinkled as she moved added to her exotic appeal.

Rhona and Ian seated themselves in the living room. Again Rhona felt she'd been transported to North Africa. She'd never travelled there but knew she'd find it intriguing. She already loved the food — humus, tabouli, black olives, falafel — all delicious. Maybe on her next holiday she'd join a tour and see Marrakesh, Casablanca. The names conjured up mystery and intrigue.

Fatima returned and lowered a brass tray with a tall, ornate china coffee pot, small cups, and a plate of pastry to the table.

When they each had coffee and a sinfully rich pine nut baklava, Fatima led off. "You asked me to think about Sabrina, about her clients and about her murder." She sipped her coffee. "First, can you tell me if she was raped?"

"Why?"

"There are clients who come here to visit us and, despite Viagra and the skillful ministrations of our women, they can't perform. I suspect these men are very angry and might direct their fury at the woman who was supposed to help and only made them feel more inadequate."

"Interesting. You think like a psychologist," Ian said.

Fatima smiled. "You'd be surprised, or maybe you wouldn't, to know how much psychology we employ. The women on the street don't have to do that, but we accompany our clients to social functions, we provide the comfort and support they often don't receive at home. We need skill." She leaned forward and refilled their cups.

"If she wasn't raped, can you think of a client who might have hated her enough to kill her?" Rhona asked.

"I'll think about it and consult the other women. I do know both she and Ginny saw a man who called himself John. He frightened them and they refused to entertain him again. Unfortunately, he contacted them directly and they didn't check him out as well as I would have."

"How do you do that?"

"There are websites that rate escorts and others that rate johns. I go online frequently and keep up to date with what's happening out there. Word gets around about undesirables. In our business there is an underground network where those who've had bad experiences share names. If his had turned up, I would have warned the women here not to deal with him."

Interesting. Like a better business bureau. It was a business, and like any business it was wise to know your customers, to know who had liens against them and complaints about their work. "How did he get their names and contact information?" Rhona asked.

"We never did figure that out. I'm thinking about it because it doesn't happen often."

"If you think he was a possible killer, can you describe him?"

Fatima shook her head. "You'd have to talk to Ginny."

"She's not here, is she?" Ian asked.

"No, she has a toothache and I sent her to my dentist. She left more than an hour ago and should be back in the next few minutes."

"Any other thoughts you'd like to share before we show you the information we found in Sabrina's diary?" Ian asked.

"I'm sure you've already figured out that if he was a client who used the door, there will be a photo of him on the security camera." She smiled. "Most clients never mention the cameras but others, mostly prominent men, fear that having their photos on record could be compromising. We assure them the photos are used to keep the building safe and to record any problems that occur, but I don't think we make them feel better." She licked the crumbs of her baklava from her fingers.

Rhona saw Fatima's action as unconsciously lascivious. Had she intended to titillate, she could have made it even more provocative. Rhona wondered if the woman's blatant sex appeal had any effect on Rhona's metrosexual partner. She sneaked a peak but he was making a note in his book and seemed unaffected.

"Yes, we have a complete set of tapes. Fortunately, when this building was updated they installed the best of security systems and all cameras were working, so we have a good record," Ian said, looking up from his note-making.

Fatima hadn't finished. "If the attacker came in through the window, he had to be relatively young and agile as well as very determined. Those characteristics would rule out ninety percent of the clientele. Many of our customers are regulars, businessmen in mid-life and often from out of town. They want the sex and the company without any attachments. Not many could or would scale four floors of scaffolding to climb through a window and slash a woman's throat. I'm happy to help you with Sabrina's book, but I don't think it will tell you anything useful."

Ginny entered the room and said hello.

"Get yourself a cup from the kitchen and have some coffee," Fatima instructed.

"No thanks, my mouth is frozen," Ginny said and produced a lopsided grin. "The coffee would dribble out and make a mess."

Fatima nodded. "Quite right. I told them I knew nothing about the john, that only you could describe him as I never saw or spoke to him."

"Scary. Big man but in good shape, lots of body hair, really, really ugly and not clean. Bad breath. I was stupid and let him use handcuffs, even though Fatima and Sabrina warned me not to do that. He punched me in the stomach. He hit me so hard I doubled up and collapsed on the floor. But I screamed really loud and I think that scared him off. He called me a fucking bitch and left. He had a look in his eye that frightened me." Ginny shivered. "I think he would have killed me right then if he thought he'd get away with it."

"Thanks," Rhona said, thinking that the man sounded as if he could navigate the scaffolding. If they saw him on the security tapes they'd see if they could find out more about him. Wouldn't he be pleased if they ran his picture on TV as a "person of interest" in the case? He might have a wife who would punch *him* in the stomach. She wondered how Ginny would react if she shared her idea? Instead she returned to more mundane matters. "Fatima's about to tell us the meaning of the notations in Sabrina's book."

"I need Tylenol," Ginny said and excused herself.

Rhona handed Fatima the list of clients' initials and the notations after them. Just as she'd thought they related to individual's sexual preferences or in the case of "t" and "0" meant talk and no sex. Fatima explained the initials and gave thumbnail sketches of Sabrina's regular clients. She expressed no suspicion of any except for the man who'd called himself John.

"Did she ever talk about men she refused to have as clients?" Rhona asked.

"Everyone has those. Residents approach you in the lobby. Somehow they believe that living here makes them eligible." Fatima smiled. "I've had a few too."

"Anyone in particular?"

"I refused Barney Cartwright after the others didn't and regretted it. He's a mean man. Threatened to sic the Black Hawks on me, but that isn't the way motorcycle gangs operate, so he didn't scare me. Sabrina said some creep approached her and she told him she'd have to be starving to death before she'd consider him. She laughed and said he was really pissed off. That he'd taken for granted that he could use her services. She said that after what she said to him, she didn't think anyone else would have to worry about him."

"You don't know who it was?"

"I don't. I'm sorry. For the sake of the others I should have asked, but Sabrina convinced me he wouldn't go near any of us."

"Later today we'll ask you and the other women on this floor to come downstairs to the party room. We're running the security tapes and want you to identify as many men and women as you can." Rhona checked her watch. "Please have everyone there at eight."

"I'll arrange it."

Step by slow step, the elimination process ground on. Rhona only hoped the killer wouldn't strike again and send the city into a frenzy.

Eight o'clock — time for the detectives to meet the fifth-floor residents in the party room. With a screen set up, the techies prepared to show the security video, hoping those present would identify everyone they knew, particularly their clients.

Ian and Rhona arrived a few minutes late. When they entered the room the buzz of conversation stopped. Women perched like birds waiting to fly. Fatima, leader of her flock, stood up and stepped forward. "We don't need to introduce ourselves, since you've spoken to each of us. We're to identify people, particularly men, but how should we let you know when we recognize someone?"

Ian flashed the boyish, off-kilter smile that melted Rhona's heart and brought answering smiles to the women's faces.

"Shout 'bingo' when you recognize a face. The technician will freeze frame the person and I'll record the name. If you'd like to say something else about the person, we'll note that and Rhona will talk to you after we've seen the tapes. How does that sound?"

Rhona watched the group. Their appearances varied but not one resembled the women who stood waiting for pickup on Jarvis, Church, or Sherbourne Streets. Even dressed casually, they would fit in almost anywhere in the city.

Fatima, in flowing black silk pants and a long-sleeved leopard-print top, scored top marks for the most exotic. Glancing at the woman's feet, Rhona wondered how she managed to walk in the platform-soled shoes. She'd wondered where to find shoes like these until she'd walked downtown from Bloor Street to Dundas and seen two shoe stores that specialized in what had to be called "hooker" shoes. Always keen to increase her height, she'd considered trying on three pairs that appealed to her. She would not have worn them in the office. She imagined the reaction of her fellow officers if she'd teetered in on red leather faux jewel-encrusted platform shoes. Even in her off hours she suspected she'd be unable to walk well, and explaining a sprained or broken ankle resulting from falling off her shoes forced her to give up the idea. Despite her decision, she still coveted the dark green crocodile sandals with cork platforms.

Ginny, with her inky hair, olive skin, and enormous brown eyes, would win runner-up in the ethnic category. Dressed in blue jeans and a sweat shirt, she wore little or no makeup.

A third exotic-looking woman stood no more than five feet and had long, dark hair, fair skin and a childlike body guaranteed to appeal to men who travelled in Asia looking for lithe young Asian women. She too wore blue jeans, probably bought in the children's department, and a white T-shirt that revealed minuscule breasts.

Unlike this androgynous woman, two others epitomized the football cheerleader with their long blonde hair, blue eyes, large breasts, and long legs. They sat together and appeared to have consulted on wardrobes, since they both wore navy miniskirts, clinging red jersey tops, and armloads of silver cuffs. As Rhona surveyed the group, one of the cheerleaders, like a schoolgirl, raised her hand.

Ian gave her the nod.

"What will you do if we tell you someone's name?" she asked in a breathy, little girl voice.

Given their business, this was a legitimate question. Nothing would scare their clients faster than knowing that the police knew who they were. Rhona suspected that many men, reading their morning papers and noting the murder location, would thank the powers they believed in that they hadn't been caught in any traps and would vow not to visit their favourite women until the police solved the murder and the building returned to normal.

"We want to find the killer quickly. We will investigate, but if a man or men had nothing to do with the killing, they will be eliminated from our list."

The young woman cocked her head to one side. "So they will know that we named them?" she said in her whispery voice.

"They will," Ian acknowledged.

Rhona sensed one or two women might at that instant think of their incomes and resolve not to identify clients. Time to step in and speak to them, woman to woman, to persuade them to be honest.

"You may be tempted to hide a client's identity, but we must eliminate all possibilities in our search. We also need each of you to provide the names of clients who made you uneasy. We value your frank opinions." She gave them her "girl talking to girl" smile and lowered her voice. "We all remember the times someone or something made us uneasy and we crossed the street or didn't enter the elevator or took some other evasive action. It sometimes makes you feel you're overreacting, but we need to listen to the warnings our bodies give us when they read almost invisible signals given by men intending to harm us." She saw small nods as they recognized the truth of her remarks. "We don't want to interfere with your lives but we need your help."

A tall brunette in form-fitting black slacks and an expensive black silk cowl-necked sweater rose, turned to face the others, pulled the sleeve of her sweater up and revealed a jagged scar running from her shoulder to her elbow. "This is what happens when you don't listen," she said in a deep voice.

She swung around to face Rhona and Ian. Her green eyes bright and her gaze intent, she said, "I nearly died because I failed to pay attention." She again addressed her peers. "For all we know, one client has decided to pick us off one by one. I for one intend to name every man or woman I recognize." She leaned forward. "We never," she paused, "let me repeat, never, lack clients. If we lose a few because of this, there will always be others. Don't pretend not to know someone when you do, because that someone may come back and kill you or me or …" Here she lifted a long, elegant hand and pointed at various women, "… or you, or you or you. I'm not a big fan of the police, but I sure want Sabrina's killer caught and every one of you must help."

Sometimes people surprised you. Rhona hadn't been expecting a real cheerleader in the crowd.

"Thank you. You put the case very well," Rhona said.

The technician, who'd watched with admiration and lust written on his face, turned to the task at hand.

"We're starting the tape from last Saturday and running it through Tuesday. We've patched tapes together and eliminated repetition and moments when they photographed no one," Rhona explained. "We've tried for a good face shot of everyone, but sometimes we only got the back view. In that case, we included a stretch of the person moving, because people have distinctive gaits and mannerisms." She waved to the back of the room where she'd arranged with Hollis to have the party room's coffee urn bubbling and bottles of water set out, along with a box of Tim Hortons doughnuts. She didn't expect these slim beings, whose bodies represented their capital, to pig out on sweet stuff, but coffee or a cold drink never went amiss.

After they collected what they wanted, the women settled back to watch. Five seconds later someone shouted "Bingo."

"That's me," one of the cheerleaders said.

The group laughed, as did Rhona. "No need to identify yourselves," she said and decided that either this woman wasn't one of the brighter lights in the room or had taken on the tension reliever role.

As the tapes rolled the detectives garnered a list of names for Saturday and Sunday. Sunday night the numbers dwindled. At ten on Monday morning, a tall man and a short woman entered the elevator. Dark wraparound glasses covered the man's eyes and a baseball cap jammed on his head obscured his hair, and the stand-up collar of his jacket masked his face. He had his right arm wrapped around his companion's shoulder and his gloved left hand held a bag close to her body.

No one shouted "bingo."

As the pair left the elevator the woman looked directly at the camera.

"Bingo," Ginny said. "Did you see that? I think she was saying, 'help.' I don't know her."

Ian directed the technician to rerun the sequence. The women in the room verbalized the silent "help" as the woman said it.

"Are you sure you don't recognize either of them?" Rhona asked.

No one did.

"With that baseball cap, dark glasses, and the collar of his jacket turned up, he could be anyone," Ginny said. "I bet he knew about the cameras and didn't want anyone to see his face."

"He can't hide his height," Fatima remarked. "Easy to figure out how tall he is if you project his image against the elevator wall and measure it. Either he's exceptionally tall or the women is as short as I am." She looked directly at Rhona. "Or the good detective."

Rhona ignored the remark but it registered that Fatima had read her body language and sensed her sensitivity about her height. No doubt figuring out people was a finely honed skill that she used every day.

"I wish we'd invited Hollis to sit in on this," Rhona said quietly to Ian.

"I'll go and get her," Ian volunteered.

The technician held the tape while Ian left the room. When he returned, Ian said, "She's gone out. Her boyfriend's watching the kids and said she'd be back very soon. I asked him to send her in when she returns."

Why was the unknown woman begging for help? Did the man's tight grip indicate love or hate?

SIXTEEN

BACK in the apartment Hollis again thanked Agnes for taking care of the girls. Willem was due in half an hour. She just had time to change into grey cargo pants and a grey-striped fisherman's shirt and refresh her makeup.

She'd given herself twenty-four hours to find Mary, and her mission to see Norman had failed. Should she ask Willem to babysit and make another attempt to visit Norman, who not only could answer her questions but also might make an informed guess about Mary's disappearance? Much though she would have preferred to spend the entire evening with Willem, this was not the time to choose romance. She would ask him to do it. When she returned she'd try to make it up to him.

Willem arrived and enveloped her in what he called his "famous bear hug." "You look great," he said.

When they heard his voice, both girls emerged from Jay's bedroom. Willem produced two more gigantic hugs accompanied by a bear imitation, complete with growling and gnashing teeth, that sent the girls into fits of giggles.

"I have a favour to ask," Hollis said after he'd disengaged himself. "I have to leave for an hour or so and hoped you'd keep the girls company."

Willem stopped horsing around, walked over to her, cupped his large hand under her chin, and lifted it. He stared unblinkingly into her eyes. "You're involved. You're going to do something dangerous." It wasn't a question, it was a statement.

"No, I'm not. I'm meeting with a long-time Aboriginal friend of mine from the Brantford Six Nations Reserve who keeps up with what's going on there and on other southern Ontario reserves."

"Does he know Aunt Mary?" Crystal asked.

"He does, but he didn't want to talk on the phone, so I'm going to see him," Hollis said.

She removed Willem's hand from her chin but held it tight as she gazed into his eyes. "Willem, I *must* know where Mary is and when she plans to come back, or I can't keep Crystal. I don't want Crystal to suffer through a bureaucratic nightmare, but she can't stay with me unless I know *exactly* what's happening."

Willem tightened his grip on her hand. "I understand and," he looked at Crystal, "I'm sure Crystal appreciates what you're doing. But I've seen you involved before, and somehow bad things happen to you." He drew her into his arms. "I won't ask you where you're going, but stay safe," he said and kissed her.

"Yucky," Jay said.

Hollis gathered her denim bag and headed for the door.

"You driving or taking the subway?"

"Subway, and I've got my BlackBerry," Hollis reassured him. She'd wondered if it would be safer to drive, but she didn't know where to park.

The walk along Delisle and down Yonge Street to the subway was uneventful. She got off at Dundas with the crowd heading into the Eaton Centre, lollygagged through Sears, detoured into the food court, slid out of the building, and back into the subway, where she leaped on a southbound train. Again she pushed through Union Station and took the light rail to Queen's Quay. Most of those who entered the waiting space after she did appeared to be legitimate businessmen and women returning home, but she wasn't taking chances. Instead of making her way directly to Harbour Square, she strolled to the main shopping concourse, drifted through it, and then sauntered to the apartment building.

"I'm here to see Norman Smith," she said, offering her driver's license. The security man on the desk took a careful look at her and the document before he buzzed Norman and allowed her through the doors to the elevators.

Norman stood in the hall waiting for her. They hugged and said all the usual things about it being too long and how good it was to see each other before he drew her into his apartment.

He lived on the north side of the building, which faced the city skyline and didn't have the endless views of Lake Ontario that filled the south-facing windows. He'd converted what must have been the living room/dining room into a large studio. Three easels with paintings in various stages, along with two long tables loaded with paints and other supplies, filled the space. He'd removed the wall between the kitchen and the living room and installed a large industrial sink. Hollis took all this in.

"Norman, why didn't you buy a loft? You'd have higher ceilings."

Norman, who watched her survey the room, nodded. "True, but lofts don't usually have good security, and their fire escapes can make them too accessible."

"What are you hiding from?" Hollis said. They still stood in the middle of the studio.

"You don't waste any time, do you?" He ignored her question and continued. "I live in what was the master bedroom. I'll pour you a glass of wine and we'll sit down before we get into the serious stuff. Red or white?"

"White. Sorry, it's none of my business and I was too abrupt, but I'm under the gun as far as time goes. I have to learn everything I can about Mary Montour and where she is."

As Norman moved to the kitchen, Hollis noticed that his gait was uneven, as if he wasn't sure of his footing. When he turned from the fridge carrying a bottle, she observed his grey hair and stooped shoulders. Norman seemed like an old man, but she knew he was forty, far too young to look like that. Was he ill? Had he suffered a serious accident? What had done this to him?

"If you're hungry, I can dig out crackers and humus to go with the wine," Norman said.

"I've eaten dinner, but if you're hungry go ahead,"

"I'm never hungry," Norman said, leading the way to the bedless master bedroom where a slip-covered sofa, book-laden coffee table, wall-mounted TV, and a small pine table with two chairs worked with a wall of bookcases, a brilliant Oriental rug, pillows, and throws to create a cocooning nest.

Probably a mixed metaphor, as cocoons didn't have nests, but the lovely warm room enveloped her and made her feel cozy.

Hollis sank into the sofa and Norman chose an ottoman.

After she sipped Hollis, swallowed and said, "Lovely wine. Now tell me why you're hiding and who you're hiding from."

"You don't want to know," Norman said. "It sounds melodramatic, but it's true that keeping myself hidden is a matter of life and death, so I don't mess around. If I wasn't an artist with a reputation, I would have changed my name, but I couldn't do that. Instead, I'm a prisoner in my own home." He picked at a spot of yellow paint on his fingernail. "Bet that wasn't what you were expecting."

"No, but I knew when those men followed me that it must be serious." She put down the wine glass and reached across the table to clasp his hands. "Keep safe. If you want company

I'll opt for the most circuitous route, maybe drive to Buffalo and back, to make sure I don't lead anyone to you."

Norman squeezed her hands. "Thanks. I may take you up on that. Back to the reason for your visit. You want to know about Mary, don't you?"

"I do. She lives in my building, and yesterday she disappeared, leaving behind her eleven-year-old niece, Crystal, who is my foster daughter's friend. I've taken Crystal in because Mary left a cryptic message asking me to care for her until she returned."

Norman nodded. "That sounds straightforward."

"It isn't. There also has been a murder in our building. I'm harbouring a child whose aunt disappeared and for all I know may be involved. If I keep her without telling the authorities, I risk losing Jay Brownelly, my eleven-year-old foster daughter, and that's not an option. Now you know why I have to find Mary or know what she's up to."

"Did you say Jay Brownelly?" Norman asked. His brows drew together and he narrowed his eyes.

"Yes, do you know her?"

"I'm not sure. What's her father's name?"

Not her parents' or her mother's but her father's. What did he know?

"Calum Brownelly."

"Describe him." Norman's frown had deepened.

"I can't imagine why you want to know, but medium height, thick-set, big hands, very curly hair."

"Raspy voice?"

"Yes. Why."

"Unbelievable, absolutely unbelievable." Norman shook his head. "He doesn't know you know me, does he?"

Hollis felt uncomfortable. This wasn't the way the conversation was supposed to go. "No. I met him and we talked about Jay and my fitness to foster her. I can't understand why he isn't looking after her himself, although his work takes him away for long periods. It's not as if she's a baby. He could find after school programs, sitters, a housekeeper."

Norman continued to frown.

"Actually, he asked to meet Jay tomorrow evening in the food court of the Eaton Centre. I've insisted that Crystal and I be there too. By the terms of the CAS agreement, he's supposed to see her at their offices."

"Did the men who followed you discover where you lived?" Norman said, leaning forward with wide eyes.

The urgency in his voice alarmed Hollis. "No. I lost them in Sears. I confronted them and said I was buying a bra and asked if they wanted to come."

A grin spread across Norman's face. For a moment his youthful exuberance peeked out from behind the grey facade he now presented to the world. "Very funny. But this is serious." He thought for a moment. "You sent me an email. They have hacked into my computer. Do you have a webpage, a Facebook profile?"

Hollis nodded. "Both, and I sometimes tweet."

"They can find you. Even if they knew you were coming to see me, I didn't think you were in danger, but fostering Calum Brownelly's daughter is something else again. Do not take her to the Eaton Centre. Phone Brownelly and give him any excuse, but do not go."

A wave of panic swept through Hollis. What had she done? Too late to undo her past actions. Time to figure out a new course.

"I hear your warning but not the reason behind it. I promised him and I promised Jay. Her heart will break if we don't go."

Norman lurched to his feet, bent over Hollis, and grabbed her shoulders. "She could be dead if you do go. And you may also be a target. Don't do it. Look at me."

Hollis pushed his hands away but met his gaze. "This sounds like a police matter."

"It isn't, at least I don't think so. It's more like going into the woods in hunting season. You take the chance of being mistaken for a deer." He frowned. "Yes, it's more like that. Nothing much the police can do except warn you to be careful. Don't go out alone if you can help it. Do the girls walk to school by themselves?

"No. The dogs and I accompany them, and then I take the dogs to the reservoir to run."

Norman appeared to visualize the site. "Big dogs?"

"Retrievers."

"Too bad. Anybody who knows anything about dogs knows retrievers of all varieties never cut it as watch-dogs. Luckily the world's villains don't know much about dogs. They usually only take an interest in large, aggressive ones like pit bulls, Rottweilers, Dobermans, or some other breed that complements a thug's image. Do you park in a secure garage?"

My god, what was this all about? "Yes, monitored by state-of-the-art video cameras."

Norman nodded. "Drive the girls to school and drive to the reservoir. Drive wherever you go. Zoom into a parking garage, get a ticket, and drive out again if you think someone is following you." He stopped. "What else? Make vigilance your watchword."

He scared Hollis. "Tell me what this is about. I came here to talk to you about Mary, not about Jay or her father."

"I know how to contact Mary, and I'll do it. Sometimes she involves herself in dangerous stuff. I'll find out exactly what's happening and get back to you. I'll send you text messages, They're harder to intercept than emails. BlackBerry security beats all the competition." He collapsed on the sofa beside Hollis and covered his face with his hands, mumbling. "Never, it's never going to end."

"What, *what* are you mixed up in?" Hollis almost screamed.

Norman shook his head. "Go home. Don't go to the Eaton Centre," he whispered.

His agitation and insistence that Hollis take great care frightened her more than she cared to admit, as did his comments that her safety was up to her, that there was nothing the police could do. Creeping out of Norman's building, she scanned the driveway and the nearby promenade along Lake Ontario. No one struck her as suspicious. She'd forgotten to ask Norman if the men to fear all looked like Tweedles Dee and Dum. Unlikely, but she should have pinned him down to describe the kind of men to watch out for. Although she'd not done that, she remained hyper-aware of her surroundings. She'd always thought tailing a victim into the subway during rush hour and giving the person a good push as the train roared into the station would be the best way to kill someone. In the confusion and horror, the killer could fade away or brazen it out and claim not to have done it. She thought of this scenario each time she stood on the platform and imagined others considered it too. From now on she planned to glue herself to the wall or maybe, given Norman's advice, avoid the subway altogether.

She shook her head as if listening to an internal conversation. Sometime in the next twenty-four hours, Norman's text about Mary would arrive and, depending on what he told her, she might be able to turn the whole puzzling problem over to the police.

Meanwhile she loitered outside the entrance to the underground streetcar until a group of chattering teenagers flooded down the steps. Sticking close to them, she descended and hopped on the train. In Union Station, she shot to the platform that served north and south lines and pressed herself against a pillar as far from the tracks as possible. Again, she surveyed the crowd but no one appeared either threatening or interested in her. When she disembarked at St. Clair Avenue, she emerged on Yonge Street and walked north with a stop to look in the Roots window, then another to read the menu outside the Thai restaurant, before she crossed at the light and made her way south. She wished Gowans, the high-end home products store on the corner, was open because she loved walking through it and it would provide one more chance to assure herself no one was interested in her. Since it was closed, she employed no more diversionary tactics and trotted up Delisle. All this subterfuge had taken time, but it reassured her knowing she wasn't leading home the men Norman feared, men connected to Brownelly.

Brownelly. From the start he'd made her uneasy. For the CAS to remove Jay from his care meant something had been very wrong. What reason had he given Jay? Probably the "I did it for your own good" line. Given Norman's fear, Brownelly had told the truth. But what was he doing now that made it impossible to reclaim his daughter?

She ran through various possibilities but none convinced her.

At home she let herself in, shouted hello, and endured Barlow and MacTee's enthusiastic welcome before she entered the living room where Willem, Crystal, and Jay played Uno.

The three card players raised their heads and smiled.

"How'd it go? The detectives want you to check in with them right away," Willem said.

Oh, no. Had they found out about Mary and Crystal? Hollis remembered Rhona's past anger when she withheld information, innocuous or not.

"They're waiting in the party room," Willem added.

No time to tell Willem about Norman. She turned and reluctantly walked to the party room, wondering if prisoners marching to an interrogation felt like this.

"There you are," Rhona said.

Hollis resisted the urge to say that they were mistaken. This was no time to be a smartass.

"The women from the fifth floor viewed images on the security cameras, and we want you to do the same and identify everyone you recognize."

Not Mary and Crystal. Hollis breathed again.

She grabbed a bottle of water and, amazed that the women hadn't gobbled up every doughnut, gave in to her passion for the coconut-covered chocolate ones.

"The women said 'bingo' to stop us when they recognized someone. Please do that," Ian said.

Bingo? You'd think it was a game.

She identified those she knew. In one sequence she watched a man in a baseball cap and oversized dark glasses and a woman he was holding close move into the elevator.

"Hold it," Ian said to the technician. "What about this man and woman? Do you recognize either one of them?"

"Run it by again," Hollis said.

The technician froze the frame in which the woman looked at the camera and appeared to mouth a word.

"Hard to know if I've ever seen the man, but the woman looks familiar. Not a renter but she may be a visitor I've seen. Is she shouting something?"

"When we watched earlier, Ginny Wuttenee decided the word was 'help,' and we agree. That's one reason we wanted you here, to see if you knew her."

They played the remainder of the tapes as Hollis continued to name renters and any visitors she knew.

"As I said, I've been on the job three months and I don't collect the rent cheques — they go to the company that owns the building. If friendly tenants stop to talk, I meet them as well as those who've had problems with something going wrong in their apartments. I'm sorry I can't be more useful."

When she returned to her apartment, the Uno game was over and the girls were watching TV.

"So, how'd it go?" Willem said.

"What?"

"Whatever you had to do when you went out and whatever the detectives wanted to see you about?"

"I looked at security camera videos and identified those I knew. How about a beer?"

"I have to go but you're very jittery. What's bothering you?"

Initially, after she'd seen Norman, she had planned to talk to Willem, but what would that achieve? He was already worried about her. Once the twenty-four hours passed she'd tell him. "Nothing much. A murder in the apartment building you run is enough to make anyone a little jittery." She threw her arms around his comforting body. "Thank you for looking after the girls. When will I see you again?"

Willem pulled her tight and kissed her. "I'd like to stay but I can't. Please take care of yourself. I'm worried about you. Tomorrow I'll be here as soon as I can get away."

SEVENTEEN

"THAT woman is hiding something," Rhona said to Ian as the door closed behind Hollis.

"I agree."

"Having dealt with her on three previous cases, I know she makes assumptions about what is and isn't important. And she goes off on her own investigating and interfering." She shook her head. "Most annoying, but we can't beat information out of her."

"It could have nothing to do with this case. Maybe she's broken a law or taken an action she believes is illegal. It's not an uncommon reaction. Remember that before they co-operated we had to reassure the women on the fifth floor that we only wanted information, not to bring them in or to charge them with a crime."

Rhona gave the technician the high sign to pack up and go.

"Clearly, some didn't want to deal with us. But that speech made them realize that whoever killed Sabrina could have marked one of them as the next victim," Ian said as he collected his gear.

"What now?" Rhona asked.

"I'm heading back. The RCMP officer responsible for Red Pheasant reserve promised to call me before he left work. Seven-thirty here is five-thirty there, so I'd better step on it. He said if he didn't have any information, he'd pass me on to a band member who might."

Rhona swung her bag over her shoulder and joined him at the door. "I'll see if the fingerprints in the room where Sabrina slept matched any perps on the register. Because he didn't rape her or touch anything except for the weapon, we don't have any DNA, but they may have found fibre fragments on the bedding, if he leaned over and braced himself to slash her throat with such force. So far nothing, but I'll keep checking."

They parked the unmarked in the vehicle pool and took the elevator upstairs. The homicide office never closed down completely, but tonight no other detectives were working at their desks.

Ian put through his call to Red Pheasant reserve. A man answered.

"I'm using a speakerphone so my colleague, Detective Rhona Simpson, can listen and add anything she thinks is relevant. As you know, we're looking for background information about Ginny Wuttenee. She told us she completed high school in North Battleford, but that's all we know about her.

"Her mother, grandmother, and sister live on the reserve. I'll tell you what I have and give you their numbers. You can talk to them yourself, although you won't be able to talk to her grandmother."

"Why is that?" Ian said.

"Her grandmother ..." The man paused.

Rhona suspected he'd been about to make a politically incorrect remark and had thought better of it.

"Her grandmother is mentally incapacitated, but even before she took sick, she refused to talk to white men and particularly hated ministers."

"Because of residential school," Rhona said.

"Everything goes back to the residential schools. They blame *everything, everything* on that."

Rhona felt her Cree grandmother urging her to intervene. "It's Rhona Simpson here. Everything *does* hinge on those schools. They poisoned generations." She wanted to bang her fist on her desk and shout at the officer, one of thousands over the years who had refused to see.

"Look, I don't want to argue with you, but kids from all over the British Empire got sent home to boarding school in England, and you don't hear them demanding an apology, demanding a royal commission." He spoke as if this was the definitive answer.

"Are you crazy?" Rhona demanded.

Ian's face registered surprise and shock.

"I beg your pardon," the man said huffily.

"Let me spell it out. Those children from the Empire came to England to be educated in *their* culture. To have the values of *their* culture inculcated in them. Some of them suffered severe physical punishments, some were sexually assaulted, but the difference was that they were not having *their* culture, the very essence of their beings, attacked, were not being told that they were worthless Indians, were not forbidden to speak their native languages, did not have their personal possessions ripped from their hands. I am appalled that a person like you, a person who deals with the Cree every day, would say something so asinine, so stupid."

Ian intervened. "My colleague feels very strongly about this subject."

"No kidding."

"We do want to know more about Ginny Wuttenee," Ian said.

Rhona put her head in her hands. Good thing she hadn't faced this racist officer. She would have liked to kick him in the groin, or worse. Pretty bad attitude toward a fellow cop.

"Like I said, her grandmother did and does not like white men. Her mother, who works as a Cree teacher in the community centre, isn't much better. But it was her grandmother who insisted the girls, Ginny and her sister, finish high school. She believed Indian kids needed a really good education to succeed competing with white men and women."

"When Ms. Wuttenee finished high school, what happened to her?" Ian said.

"She got into trouble, but what can you expect from women like her?"

Rhona raised her head and said quietly. "Please tell us what happened. Don't editorialize, just tell us." She expected a story of an early unplanned pregnancy or a descent into alcoholism or drug dependency.

"She stole her boyfriend's truck and money he'd saved and disappeared."

"Did anyone in her family or anyone on the reserve know why she did this? Do they know where she is? Has she contacted her family?" Ian asked.

"She'd committed a crime and it was our business to track her down. When I asked her mother and her brother why she'd done it and where she might be, they shrugged and said she must have had her reasons. They wouldn't give me a 'yes' or a 'no' to any other questions."

"Did you follow up? What about the boyfriend?"

"His family swore they'd teach the girl a lesson, but when they say things like that, it's usually all talk. I reminded them that this was a police matter, but I wasn't too worried about them *actually* doing anything. Often they get upset and then throw a party or drink themselves into oblivion and forget about it. Like last year. Remember those two babies who froze to death. Alcohol does it every time."

"How long have you been in Saskatchewan?" Rhona asked.

"Seven years."

"Isn't that a long time for a posting? I thought it was usually three?"

Ian stared at her.

Rhona knew she appeared tense, appeared to have activated every muscle, to be poised to spring.

"That really isn't our business," Ian intervened.

Oh, yes it is, Rhona wanted to scream but kept her voice level. "It's time we made it our business to expose men like this as the Indian haters they are and demand that they be moved somewhere else."

"I don't have to listen to this. I've told you what I know," the officer said and hung up.

"My God, Rhona have you lost it or what?" Ian said. "Good thing Frank didn't hear you or you'd be in deep trouble. We're supposed to maintain civil relations with other police forces, not attack their officers."

"I heard every word." Frank Braithwaite, who'd been standing behind them in the doorway to his office, beckoned to Rhona. "Come into my office."

Rhona, still rigid and gripping her hands together as if to stop herself from doing something she'd regret, stood and followed Frank into his office.

"How do you explain that unwarranted attack?" he demanded.

Rhona interlocked her hands behind her back. "I'm sorry. I got carried away."

"To put it mildly. Whatever possessed you? I thought you prided yourself on your professionalism, your calmness under fire."

"I do."

"I'd like an explanation," Frank said.

Rhona heard curiosity rather than anger in his voice. Should she explain? Would he understand her conflicted emotions? She had hardly sorted them out herself. Was it worth it to try to make him see how someone with Aboriginal ancestors felt? It was. Where to begin?

"Remember the report on missing and murdered Aboriginal women written by the Sisters in Spirit? The one you asked me to read because I'm part Cree. Then you sent us off to check to see if there were Toronto cases that had fallen through the cracks?"

"Of course. What does that have to do with what you just did?"

Rhona took a deep breath. "That report affected me in ways I hadn't anticipated."

"How so?"

"Although it probably wasn't impartial, the women who drafted it felt strongly and their emotions came through. They reported on the hundreds of Aboriginal women, lost souls, individuals society didn't care about, didn't search for when they went missing, and didn't insist that the police find the killers when the women were murdered. I don't need to tell you about Robert Pickton, the highway of tears, the missing women in Edmonton. The effects are ongoing and widespread. Those women had families, and even more important, they often had children."

Elbows on his desk, Frank tapped his fingertips together and listened.

"You're probably thinking that this isn't news, and it isn't. Nor is the poverty and degradation on some reserves. What is news is the long-term impact of the residential schools. We have the reconciliation commission, the government, and church apologies. That's all very well, but I don't think we can imagine what it must have been like for those children. If the adults running your life treat you as a worthless piece of shit and tell you that everything distinctive about your family and their life is bad, you'll have no self-esteem. You'll live your adult life feeling like that, looking for escape from the pain, the sense of worthlessness. Your children will inherit these feelings. It goes on and on and on. *That's* the problem."

"I understand all that, but why are *you* so upset? Why did *you* launch into the officer like you did?"

"Why? The western Indians signed treaties in the 1870s because the buffalo had disappeared and they were starving. The government undertook to change them from hunters and gatherers to farmers, to make them into mock whites. It didn't work then and it's not working now, and no one is willing to say that we took the wrong course. No government proposes the kind of changes that will make a difference."

Frank sighed and leaned back in his chair. "Strong generalizations. Maybe true, maybe not, but I don't see why *you're* so worked up."

"Because those *were*, those *are* my people, and *I* feel guilty as hell. I've never volunteered in the community, never offered to help, never acknowledged that as an educated, privileged woman I should act, should speak out, shouldn't allow others to make racial slurs in my presence. I haven't done it, haven't wanted to draw attention to my Native heritage."

Frank stared at her.

"I know. Because I'm a police officer I shouldn't be emotional, and usually I'm not, but he really set me off with his remarks. He was *so* smug, *such* a know-it-all, that I lost it. I'm sorry and it won't happen again, but that's why I went off the deep end. It was guilt, my guilt.'

"Okay. I admire the fact that you've owned up to the reason you reacted like you did. It wasn't acceptable, but I understand. I could initiate disciplinary action but I won't. We'll forget about it. No report. It's a good thing that only your partner heard that exchange, or I would have had to do something."

Even if he didn't plan to take action, Rhona had blotted her copy book, but she couldn't feel bad, because she'd finally articulated the feelings that had swirled around in her head for months. When she emerged from Frank's office, Ian raised his eyebrows. She considered giving a thumbs-up but thought better of it.

"Sorry he hung up because of my rant. We still need to know the boyfriend's name, and if he lives on the Red Pheasant reserve. I could phone ...." she paused.

"Of course you can't. I'll do it and apologize for you."

"Just don't say it was a female thing," Rhona said.

"Why? That would get you off the hook. Hormones can be blamed for many things."

"You know how often misogynists use hormones to justify not having women in the police force. Don't you use that. Say something innocuous like 'she was up all night on a case.' Or, better still, don't offer an explanation."

"Do you want me to use the speakerphone?"

"No. he'll only enrage me again. Let's find out who the boyfriend is and where to find him."

After Ian finished the brief conversation, he said, "The boyfriend's name is Larry Baptiste. He left the reserve after Ginny stole his worldly goods. The family told the police they don't know where he went. Maybe you'll have better luck talking to them. I'll give you his father's phone number if you want to call."

Rhona recognized a peace offering, an acknowledgment that her outburst, while unprofessional, had not offended her partner. She reached for the paper on which Ian had scribbled the name and number. "Speakerphone?" she said.

"Why not."

Should she introduce herself as a detective? She could expect one of two reactions if she did. Whoever took the call would fear that either a terrible accident had befallen a family member or that the person had committed a crime. Rarely did the police phone anyone, Aboriginal or otherwise, with good news. She remembered reading that during the Second World

War, bad news came in yellow telegrams hand-delivered by the telegraph company. To open the door and see a man standing on the doorstep holding the yellow telegram almost always meant bad news. Today, when a member of the Aboriginal community received a call from the police, they must feel much the same way. She'd introduce herself without any rank and ask to speak to the son, which would tell whoever replied that she wasn't calling to say he was dead.

"This is Rhona Simpson. May I speak to Larry Baptiste?"

"He doesn't live here," a gruff voice responded. "What's this about?"

"Who am I speaking to?"

"John Baptiste. Larry's father."

"Officer Rhona Simpson, Toronto Police. Do you know where we can find your son?"

"What is this about?"

No point in dragging Ginny Wuttenee into the picture. Any reference to her would likely anger Larry's father. "My business is with your son, who's not in trouble. I want to ask him some questions."

"It's about that bloody woman, isn't it? That bitch was the worst thing that ever happened to him."

Rhona neither confirmed nor denied, she just repeated her request.

"Right after she hightailed it out of here with his stuff, he up and left his job in North Battleford. Didn't give notice or anything, just left. That sure does a lot for our reputation for reliability. Didn't tell us, not even his mother, that he was going. Broke her heart. He was her hope for the future."

"What kind of work does he do?"

"He's a mechanic, a damn good one too."

"Wherever he's gone, that's what he's likely to be doing?"

"Who knows?"

"If you hear from him, will you call me?"

"You still haven't told me why. I can't see turning him over to you without knowing what you want," the man said in a voice dripping with suspicion.

Time to admit the real reason they wanted to talk to Larry Baptiste. "You were right. It's about Ginny Wuttenee," Rhona said.

"That bitch can only bring him bad luck. If I hear from him, I won't call you. Find him yourself," the man said and hung up.

Rhona looked at Ian. "Is this going to be a needle in a haystack situation?"

Ian raised an eyebrow and pushed the lock of unruly black hair out of his eyes. "Assuming he figured out she'd gone to Toronto, followed her, used his own name, and signed up for a landline tapping into Canada 411, we'd locate him. Lot of ifs, but if he's here we can find him. However, I'm wondering if we should bother, since no one has attacked Ginny. Shouldn't we focus on Sabrina's contacts?"

Rhona leaned back in her chair and clasped her hands behind her head. "I still suspect the perp killed the wrong girl. If he intended to murder Ginny, a client could have a motive, but a man she 'wronged' is more likely."

"We won't find him tonight. Time to pack it in. You want to get some food?"

Rhona didn't allow her hopes to rise. Not exactly an overture for a heavy date with flowers and soft music. "Sure, gotta eat."

"Let's go to Spring Garden for Thai food. Bit of a hike but a walk will do us good."

Rhona shrugged on her black trench coat and joined Ian. Outside a fine drizzle and a lowered temperature compelled them to turn their collars up and trot briskly along College Street before turning onto Dundas Street and entering a restaurant that hummed with the buzz of a hundred conversations.

Usually a line-up snaked away from the entrance, but not at this late hour. The hostess led them to a table and their server appeared almost immediately. Rhona decided against a drink. She'd wait until she got home for her vodka martini.

After they ordered soup, hot and sour for Ian, coconut chicken with lemon grass for Rhona, they chose three mains — one with shrimp, one with chicken, and one vegetarian, along with two helpings of rice.

Rhona wanted to talk. Always curious about Ian and his life, she longed to lob questions at him. He didn't open the conversation. Instead he sagged back on his chair and stared off into space. She followed his lead, settled back, and didn't speak while they waited for the food to arrive.

Rhona adored Thai soups. When she chose to cook, her repertoire included them. At the same time she usually whipped up bannock, Scottish oatcakes, or cornbread to accompany the soup. She called it her international cuisine.

They spooned up the fragrant broth.

"Where did you first have Thai food?" Rhona asked.

"In Thailand," Ian said without elaborating.

"Me too. Did you love Thailand?"

Ian looked at her. "I hope this isn't going to be another one of your inquisitions."

"My god, it's small talk. Do you want us to sit here and say nothing?"

Ian put his spoon down and blotted his lips with the paper napkin. "That would be okay."

"Well, it wouldn't be okay with me. Conversation is part of civilized eating. Not bolting and running. If you don't like my topic, you introduce one."

"You seem pretty touchy today. I guess I'd better not ask about ..." He raised an eyebrow.

"No. You better not," Rhona muttered.

EIGHTEEN

WHEN Hollis took the dogs outside on the lawn, she increased her vigilance while waiting for the dogs to do what they had to. She felt like the Secret Service men around the U.S. president. Their eyes darted everywhere and they focused on everything going on around them. She did the same but also took time to ask herself questions.

What had the Children's Aid hidden from her? What did they know about Calum Brownelly that they hadn't told her? If danger threatened Jay, the CAS should have forbidden her father's visits. But maybe they didn't know. They'd told Hollis that they'd taken Jay into care as a toddler without explaining the background. Why hadn't Hollis asked? Perhaps the fault was hers?

Why did they take children? What had she read? That the law charged parents or guardians with not providing the necessities of life, of endangering a child's welfare. The cases mostly related to neglect, to drug-addicted parents who didn't look after their children. Time to go online and see what other causes she could find. Tomorrow morning she'd phone the case worker and persuade her to reveal why they'd removed Jay from her father's care. She'd assumed Jay's mother had died, but assumptions could be wrong. Time to inquire. She couldn't believe the CAS had lied, but omission could be as big a sin as commission.

First, she'd phone Brownelly and tell him they weren't coming to the Eaton Centre. That done, she'd inform Jay that the Eaton Centre meeting was cancelled. Whatever course she chose she could only claim that a friend had warned her they might be in danger. When her mother had used the line, "just because I said so," Hollis hated it, but it might be her only option.

Back in her apartment she found the girls getting ready for bed.

"I have to make a phone call. I'll join you in a minute," she said.

In her bedroom with the door shut, she pulled her BlackBerry out of her handbag, and tapped in Brownelly's number. She'd couldn't bring Norman into the equation, so she'd cite Rhona.

"A police officer I know told me that Jay and I will be in danger if I take her to meet you at the Eaton Centre," she said.

"A police officer? You have to be kidding." Brownelly's voice registered his amazement.

"Yes. She didn't spell out the reason. She's worried about my connection to you. When she said you were in danger and not to take Jay to meet you, I believed her. What I want to know is why the CAS allows Jay to see you."

"Because she's my daughter."

"Is the officer right? Are you in danger?"

"Listen, smartass, I wouldn't risk my daughter's safety, but she's been meeting me for years and nothing's happened."

"Maybe, but my friend says that the situation has changed. From now on, if you want to see her it has to be at the CAS offices."

"Jesus, she's my daughter. I could take her with me any time I wanted."

"I don't think so. If you plan to do that, deal with the CAS," Hollis said, hoping forcing this confrontation had been the right thing to do.

"You'll hear from me," Brownelly growled.

Hollis took a moment to collect herself before she went to see the girls.

"Jay, come into my bedroom. We have to talk."

The child looked from Hollis to Crystal and back. "Talk away. Crystal knows all about our life." Her hands on her hips, her head back, her eyes said *I dare you.*

A challenge.

Jay's sensitivity to Hollis's moods initially had unnerved her, but now she believed that a child desperate to continue to live with a foster parent developed an accurate barometer for reading moods. In this instance Jay sensed Hollis's reluctance to deal with an issue. Crystal's presence would provide moral support and might prevent Hollis from taking a hard line. Smart child.

"No. I want to talk to you, not to you and Crystal."

Hollis smiled at Crystal, who had troubles enough of her own without finding herself in the middle of a squabble between Jay and Hollis. "Crystal, finish up in the bathroom. We'll be back in a few minutes."

Crystal didn't wait for a second invitation. She bolted from the room, leaving Hollis and Jay face to face.

Hollis pivoted, headed down the hall to her bedroom, and held the door ajar to allow Jay to follow before she shut it.

"You aren't going to like what I have to say."

Jay flopped on the bed. "So. Say it."

"We are not meeting your father at the Eaton Centre tomorrow."

"What?" Jay bounced off the bed and grabbed Hollis's arms. "What do you mean? You promised. My dad will be waiting for us."

"I called your dad and told him."

"What did he say? He wanted to see me. I bet he was really, really mad." She released Hollis's arms, straightened with her arms at her sides, and her mouth set in a straight line. "My dad will make you *really, really* sorry you did this."

"What do you mean?"

Jay maintained her stance. "He can be *really* scary. I've seen him when he's like that and you better watch out." She crossed her arms over her chest, lowered her chin, and dropped her voice. "Mrs. Cooper tried that once, and my dad made sure she never did it again."

My god, what was she dealing with? Who was Brownelly that even his daughter knew he could intimidate and enforce?

The set-to with Jay upset Hollis. She felt it might indicate that she was failing to give Jay the security she needed. She wanted to be sympathetic, to recognize the effect that losing Mrs. Cooper must have had on the child. Most of all she wanted Jay to be happy about coming to live with her. Reneging on the agreement to go to the Eaton Centre certainly hadn't helped establish a rapport between them.

What had Brownelly done to Mrs. Cooper when she crossed him? Why hadn't she reported him to the CAS? But maybe he hadn't done anything. Who knew if Jay's angry threats were true? Children frequently accepted their parents' omnipotence. Hollis guessed that it was vital for Jay to believe that whatever her father did was so important that he'd had no choice but to leave her in foster care.

Meditation usually calmed Hollis down and helped put her life in perspective. In her bedroom, crowded though it was, she'd designated one corner for the purpose. Here, a floor cushion and small statue of Buddha provided the framework for meditation. She sank to the floor, thinking that crossing her legs in the lotus position might soon be impossible if she didn't get back to Pilates and running. Because of her busy life she'd neglected both. She centred herself, focused on the air coming in and out of her lungs, and worked to clear her mind.

Twenty minutes later she rose and acknowledged that it had worked once again.

Breaking Mary's black book code seemed a manageable task. She checked on the girls, who lay in bed talking in low voices. Jay refused to look at her.

"Girls, I'm working in the office. The monitor is on and I'll leave the office and apartment door open and the dogs on guard. If you need me give a shout."

She bent across Jay, who slept in the first bed, and kissed Crystal. She then brushed her lips against Jay's cheek, ignoring the fact that Jay did not reach up for a hug or return the kiss.

"Turn out the light in ten minutes and sleep well," she instructed, walking to the door.

Fastening the gate in the apartment's doorway, she crossed to her office, pulled a pad of paper from her desk drawer, and opened the diary. She paused for a moment to watch the security monitors as tenants and visitors came and went.

Facing away from the distraction of the cameras, she unfolded the downloads she'd printed from Google and tucked into the diary. Taking a copy of the alphabet and moving a second copy any number of letters to the right so that "a" became "c" or another letter for purposes of the code was one way to do it. Another was to reverse the alphabet's order and make "z" correspond to "a." Before she tried any options, she examined the entries looking for vowels, the letters that occurred most frequently.

The first entry began, zdurolkhjdfglxjdoomxov09qhuhhq.

A month might precede 09, but which one? She tried various combinations before she reached July. If m was j, x was u, o was l, and v was y, would it work? She printed the alphabet and then overlaid those letters above their regular counterparts.

Eureka. Mary started with x, y, and z then moved all the letters three steps to the right. Hollis printed a copy of the first page. Then she used the guide to decipher the notations.

Caroline MacDougall July 09 three weeks could not kick the habit pimp intervened Caroline back to the street. Pimp intervened. Innocuous words that spelled trouble. A good reason to keep her activities secret, to protect Crystal from knowing what she did or the identity of the women.

Sheanna Robinson August 09 started methadone on for one month back to North Bay registered in the preparatory studies program to upgrade, connected with their aboriginal learning program

Page after page of women's names and details of their attempts to leave the street and the life of drugs. Not a high success rate. One or two woman at a time, year after year.

Why had she fled? Had the caller Bridget mentioned been an angry pimp looking to drag Alicia or Veronica back to the street?

Hollis moved to the last entry looking for the reason, but found no mention of either Alicia or Veronica. Of course. Mary only made her comments *after* her clients finished.

When she left, had she taken Veronica, with her hooker's clothes, and Alicia Meness, the woman well on her way to methadone salvation, with her? After she heard from Norman she'd turn this information over to Rhona.

"Working late?"

Hollis looked up to see Barney Cartwright, the man from the sixth floor whose cold gaze made her feel as if she was an insect to be crushed if she interfered in any way with his life. He had never threatened, but nevertheless he frightened her and to have him blocking the doorway scared her. Where were her dogs when she needed them?

Unless well-trained as watch dogs, most canines retire for their beauty rest at nine, and her dogs, both retrievers, a breed noted for its laissez-faire approach to life, did exactly that. She glanced at the gated doorway to her apartment, but they hadn't chosen to nap there. Instead she knew they'd both be curled up on their beds, legs twitching as they dreamed of exciting chases through the woods.

"What can I do for you?" Hollis said, working to keep her voice level and businesslike.

He stepped into the room "That looks like code. Now why would a woman like you be doing something like that?" he said.

Hollis flipped the sheet over. "Nothing to do with you," she said.

"You might be surprised. I have many interests, some of which may relate to you," he said, shutting the door behind him.

Hollis looked around for a weapon, but only a heavy three-hole punch tucked away in her desk drawer filled the bill. She couldn't imagine he'd give her time to open the drawer, grab it, and whack him.

"What interests? Is there something in your apartment that needs attention?"

"I'm not talking about the apartment," he said, narrowing his eyes and looming over her.

Hollis ran through other possibilities: Sabrina? Calum Brownelly? Norman? Events in her past life? "I have no clue what you mean," she said and looked at her watch. "It's late. Could we postpone this conversation until the morning?"

He moved directly in front of her desk.

She removed her hands from the top lest he notice the tremors.

The man bent forward, leaning his elbows on the desk with his face close enough for her to count the acne scars that pocked his face. His stained teeth resembled fangs and his yellow eyes indicated his liver's unhappiness with the life he led. When he spoke, his foul breath made her gulp.

"You have no clue what I mean," he said, repeating her words and spacing them out.

"No. I have no idea and I don't like your attitude."

He cracked his knuckles. "No idea. My, my, aren't you the little innocent?"

Hollis lied badly and celebrated that on this occasion she truly had no idea what he meant and didn't need to lie. "Act like a threatening bully all you like, but I don't know what you're talking about, and I wish you'd get out of my office," she said, crossing her arms over her chest and using her firmest voice.

Cartwright removed his elbows, straightened up, and reared back. "I don't believe you."

"I don't lie well. I'm telling you the truth."

He mimicked her action, crossed his meaty arms over his chest, and rocked back on his heels. "If I say *motorcycles*, will that jog your failing memory?"

Motorcycles. Where had they come from?

"I know nothing about motorcycles. I've never ridden one, never had the urge to own one, never known anyone who had one. Motorcycles mean nothing, nada, zero to me."

He stared at her. "Nothing."

"No. When I was a kid my mother took me to Bermuda where we rented a scooter. She drove badly, and right after we rented it and they showed her how to operate it, she loaded me on board and drove straight from their lot and over an embankment. We landed upside down with everyone nearby screaming and running to rescue us. Now you know my one and only experience."

Cartwright's eyes reflected his confusion.

Time to press her advantage. "Now what's this all about? Why are you threatening me?" She pulled the phone toward her. "Maybe I should phone my friend, Detective Rhona Simpson. She's interested in anything odd going on in the building that might relate to Sabrina's murder."

"Sabrina's murder. What the fuck does that have to do with anything?"

"Isn't that why you're here?" Hollis said.

"I know and care fuck-all about the bitch's murder." He considered her with icy reptilian eyes.

Hollis shivered.

"Okay, okay, maybe I was wrong. But if you're lying to me and I find out," he smashed one fist into the open palm of the other, "you'll be one sorry lady."

After he was gone Hollis waited until she stopped shaking. She called Rhona's cell and left a message.

"Barney Cartwright threatened me tonight and I thought you should know."

NINETEEN

IN the morning, Rhona's fitful sleep, probably attributable to one too many vodka martinis, left her exhausted. The temptation to push the snooze button for another ten minutes was high, but she resisted, staggered out of bed, and yawned her way from task to task until she stood staring at the coffee machine, waiting for it to finish its work and provide her with a hit that would get her going.

Fortified with a dark blend made at maximum strength, she surveyed herself in the mirror beside the balcony door, where natural light revealed her true appearance. Her black pantsuit matched with red cowboy boots and a white shirt looked professional and bore no stains of culinary lapses. She taken care with her makeup and managed to direct the eyeliner to the edge of her lashes, not riding high on the lid as if trying to escape, and the carefully applied concealer hid the circles under her eyes. She'd tamed her unruly curly hair and forced it into a chignon pinned relentlessly in place. She'd do.

Opie swirled around her legs, agitating for a tasty breakfast, and guilt-ridden about her long absences, she gave in and shovelled an overly generous portion of his favourite food into his dish.

Seven o'clock and time to head for the shop, where she never managed to beat Ian to work. They needed a break in the case. A mounting fund of information and nothing to tie it to anyone. Maybe they'd locate Ginny's ex-boyfriend, who had cause to seek revenge.

She loaded her travel mug with the strong brew. As usual she saw Ian working away when she walked into homicide. Before she could greet him or even park her bag in her desk drawer, Frank burst from his office. What had brought him in at this hour? He spoke directly to her.

"We have another one. It could relate to your case if your killer intended to murder the Aboriginal woman. Come into my office," he said.

Rhona's breath caught in her throat. Not Ginny. They should have done more than warn her, should have put a guard on her apartment or sent her somewhere safe.

"Ginny Wuttenee?" she said, hoping for a negative answer.

"Who?" Frank stood in front of his window.

"The woman we thought might have been the intended victim," Ian said.

"Could be. This woman — we haven't found any ID — received multiple stab wounds. The perp threw her in the water at the far end of the dogs off-leash section of Cherry Beach. It rained last night, so we have tire track prints going through the park. A cement block tied around her waist should have taken her to the bottom, but the body was wedged under an old half-submerged picnic table. Although they say she's tiny, it must have been a job to dump her into the water."

"Aboriginal woman?" Rhona asked.

"Looks like it, although we won't know for sure until we get an ID. The marine unit divers secured and removed the body and conveyed her to the marine station on Queen's Quay. Go there first before you go to Cherry Beach, where I have officers conducting a ground search looking for evidence and taking casts of the tire treads. The coroner is on his way to Queen's Quay."

No guarantee that it wasn't Ginny. Rhona felt like crossing her fingers or touching wood, a very unprofessional way to think.

"You take the case until I determine that it isn't related to the apartment murder." As he spoke, Frank performed an annoying exercise Rhona believed he was unaware of. First he balanced on one foot and then on the other. Rhona noted that he had more difficulty on his right than his left. He stopped alternating feet, rose on his toes, and rocked back on his heels.

"Who found her?" Ian asked.

"A dog, which isn't surprising in an off-leash dog park. I think it was a retriever. Of course they breed them to find things in the water. At any beach they race into the lake no matter how cold it is. It's only May and Lake Ontario must be freezing, but that dog jumped in, and I know that mine would do the same thing."

Frank loved to talk about dogs. With no encouragement, he would launch into lengthy and excruciatingly boring stories about the brilliant or amusing antics of his dog. Rhona held her breath. At this early hour she didn't want to hear a dog story, particularly as Frank forgot who he told his stories to and tended to repeat them.

"I remember once …"

Oh no, not again.

He stopped and stared at Rhona. "After yesterday's outburst I need to know you can deal with an Aboriginal woman's murder."

"One reason I lost it yesterday was because I hate it when cops or anyone else speaks disparagingly about Aboriginals. I always feel that they are including me in their generalizations, which is stupid because most people in multicultural Toronto have no idea what ethnic mix I represent. To answer your question, I want to get the perp. I only hope the victim isn't Ginny Wuttenee."

Frank nodded. "I thought you'd say that. You're on both cases as long as we think there's a connection."

Ian and Rhona collected what they needed. Rhona refilled her travel mug. The department's weaker coffee didn't recharge her like the high test she made at home, but she needed more java to keep her going.

"Although the weatherman called for a nice day today, it'll be cold down by the lake. I need a jacket from my locker," she said.

Ian also collected a jacket and they headed from College Street to University Avenue, where they drove south to Lake Ontario.

A brisk wind blowing from the water chilled them as they moved from the parking lot to the station.

Inside, the clerk at the desk directed them through the building to a room at the rear. They found the medical examiner suited up and ready to go. He blocked their view of the woman on the gurney. Rhona held her breath as he turned to speak to them and they saw the body.

It wasn't Ginny. Rhona breathed a silent thank-you.

Ian stepped closer. Long, wet black hair spread around an unmarked face. Only multiple gashes in her acidic yellow shirt told the tale.

Rhona joined Ian.

"She look familiar to you?" Ian asked.

They both stared down.

"The security camera. The woman marched out of the building. The one who mouthed *help*," Rhona said.

"Was Frank prescient or what?"

The medical examiner, studying the woman's feet, looked up. "You can identify her?"

"No, but we have a record of her whereabouts on Tuesday," Rhona said. "Did the stab wounds kill her?" she asked, sure they had, but sometimes the coroner surprised them.

"I'd say so but we won't know for sure until we have her on the table." He pointed at the slashes. "Any one of those could have hit her heart, aorta, lungs, or an artery."

"We'll check back after we visit the crime scene," Rhona said and put her hand on Ian's arm. "Time to head over and see what the divers found in the water and the officers on land. With luck they may find her handbag."

Ian scrunched his face. "If I rerun the video in my mind, I see something glittery tucked under her arm. Let's hope it turns up or someone hands it in. If they don't and we have a clear image, we can appeal to the public to bring it in."

In the car they headed along the Lakeshore and turned south on Cherry Street.

"Ever go in there?" Rhona said to Ian as they passed T&T Chinese supermarket.

"Never," Ian said without adding that he might find it interesting or hate it.

"They sell the greatest Chinese prepared foods. On the weekends women heat and offer samples. I love it."

"Something to add to my list." Ian said. His voice conveyed that if he did, it would take last place on a long list.

They turned into the pot-holed lot crowded with police cars and emergency vehicles. A few early morning dog walkers clustered at the far end near the sandy beach. Officers must have told them to leash their animals, for no dogs roamed the area. A young officer, not recognizing the unmarked car, leaned in the window Ian opened.

"Crime scene, sir, sorry, but you can't park here."

"Homicide," Ian said and the young man waved them in without requesting a badge.

After the night's rain, low spots remained muddy. Although Rhona had sprayed two cans of leather preservative on her red cowboy boots, she didn't have total faith in the product.

She hated getting the boots dirty, and picked her way around the puddles and the worst muddy patches. Ian, wearing heavy black brogues, clomped along seemingly unaware of his feet. Rhona knew plastic booties awaited them at the actual scene and regretted that when they left the car, she hadn't slipped on the ones she carried with her.

A bright day, but the wind blew steadily, carrying the chill of recently melted ice. The divers' boat rocked, pitched, and rolled as the crew waited for the divers to return. Several officers in booties and coveralls, heads down and eyes fixed on the ground, scoured the shore as they searched for evidence.

Rhona, after she donned protective footwear, gingerly picked her way down the bank, where huge slabs of concrete lay randomly deposited as if a giant had flung them from above. Rebar and lengths of rusted cable protruded from most of them. These leftover remnants indicated that at one time they had formed part of a substantial dock or building.

"Have the divers found anything?" she asked the officer in charge.

"Her handbag and a bunch of stuff from it. No wallet. No I.D. They retrieved a cell phone, not that it'll be any good."

"Along the bank?"

"We made casts of the treads and a couple of shoeprints that could be connected. The man who found the body told us he climbed down to see if she was alive. When he verified that she was dead he moved off. He showed us his footprints."

"Where is he?" Ian asked.

The detective pointed up to the right, where a man was hunkered down on a bench watching the police and absent-mindedly patting a dog.

Rhona and Ian walked over. "We'd like to speak to you," Rhona said.

The man nodded and stood up.

"Let's get out of this wind." Rhona led Ian and the man back to the parking lot, where they huddled in the lee of a beach building boarded up for the winter.

"I'm sure the officers got your name and particulars," Ian said. "But would you tell us?"

"Certainly. Denton Dennison, and this," he patted the dog's head, "is Denby. I've always liked alliteration."

Ian bent and patted the dog, who swiped his hand with a slobber-laden tongue. Rhona decided to forego the pleasure.

"Tell us what happened."

"Well, as soon as I let Denby off his leash, he headed for the beach." Denton pointed to a broad swath of sand that ended in leafless bushes rimming a narrow stretch of shoreline that curved out to a point. "We walked." He grinned. "I'll amend that. I walked and Derby retrieved balls." He flourished a long blue plastic stick with a ball holder at the end. "I carry this, a chuck-it, and use it not only to throw the ball a long way but also to keep from getting my hands covered in saliva. In May the water's cold and your hands freeze quickly if you don't use one. Anyway you don't want to know about that. I walked and threw and he swam and retrieved."

He waved at the point. "We usually walk around there, come up on the gravel, and then continue to the back where that high fence topped with barbed wire separates us from an industrial site. I like going around there because Denby gets to do some serious swimming. On this side the water is too shallow for that." He bent to pat the dog again. "Denby ran ahead of me. Not many people here at five thirty, it's barely light. I heard Denby barking frantically and hurried to see what was wrong, and that's when I saw her in the water." He shook his head. "I briefly debated whether to go down the bank, but I worried that she might still be alive, so I did." He smiled. "You can't watch crime shows without realizing you shouldn't muck up the scene, but I did show the officers where I stepped, and I got Denby out and leashed him as soon as I realized what he'd found."

"Did you recognize the woman?" Rhona asked.

An expression of horror crossed the man's face. "You don't think that I knew her? Of course not. Never seen her before."

"Did you notice anyone leaving as you arrived?"

Denton frowned and cocked his head to one side as if the action might jog a memory. "Let me see. There were two cars in the lot when I arrived." He moved to one side and glanced behind them before he pointed. "That black Ford Explorer and the silver Toyota van. I didn't see anyone when Denby and I walked along the shore. No. Nobody left as I came in."

"The officers took all your particulars?" Ian asked.

"They did and I'll do like they say on TV. I'll call you if I think of anything else."

After Denton left, Rhona told the officer manning the parking lot to run the two vehicles' plate numbers and interview the owners if they returned.

"We could get lucky but probably these two vehicles have nothing to do with the crime. I suspect the killer dumped the woman in the middle of the night and took off. Whoever did it either didn't see the table or figured that with the weight tied to her body she wouldn't drift that way."

"Someone in that apartment building must know her identity. Get the techies to photograph her and doctor it up so she looks less dead and have an officer take it door to door in the building. You and I will talk to Hollis Grant. We'll also post the photo in the mail room." Rhona liked to have a plan. "Let's go. Get an officer to deliver the photo to 68 Delisle when it's done."

TWENTY

HOLLIS, who seldom used an alarm clock, realized she should have set hers when she opened her eyes and saw the time. Coping with an excess of adrenalin released by Cartwright's threatening visit along with the time spent deciphering the entries in Mary's diary had kept her sleepless until the early hours. She rushed to get the girls up and fed, the dogs out, and the whole tribe off to school on time.

Crystal smiled when she came into the kitchen, but not Jay, who stomped into the room, glared at Hollis, and clomped to the table.

"Sorry to rush you but I slept in," Hollis said as she provided cereal, milk, blueberries, and juice. That done, she foamed milk and poured herself a cup of coffee. Everything always looked brighter after that first rejuvenating cup.

"You'll both eat lunch at school today," she said, whipping together tuna sandwiches and tucking them, along with an apple and a granola bar, into their backpacks. I'll pick you up after school."

"You told us we'd come home for lunch until the police solved the murder," Jay said in an accusing voice. "You never do what you say you're going to do," she added.

"I did say that, but I have to go out this morning and I'm nervous that I won't be back in time to collect you." She wanted to defend herself against Jay's accusation, but trying to change minds already made up was pointless. Putting herself in Jay's place, she knew how disappointed she would have been about the cancellation of a visit with her father.

With the dogs walked and the girls safely at school, Hollis went first to the office to deal with any issues that had arisen overnight. To her relief no one hovered at the entrance and no demanding messages waited on the machine. She swung away from the door and watched the screens from the security cameras as she punched in the number for Ms. Young, her contact at the CAS.

Pleasantries dealt with, she said, "I've received information that Jay's father's background may make him and her and possibly me a target for violence. If this is true I should have been told."

"We didn't believe it was true," Ms. Young said.

"*Didn't believe?* You *knew* there was a possibility?" Hollis heard the outrage in her own voice.

"A remote one, and had we learned that anything had changed we would have told you," the woman said huffily. "We do not put our wards at risk, but we also don't want their foster parents to worry unnecessarily or to refuse to take them because of perceived risks."

"What was it that Brownelly did or does that makes him a risk? Furthermore, why didn't you tell me that you removed Jay from his home?"

"I'm sorry, but that confidential information could endanger him if we told you and you happened to tell someone else. As for Jay's removal, it was not his bad parenting but because we felt the circumstances were not conducive to bringing up a child in a healthy way."

Hollis clenched her teeth. Bureaucratic gobbledegook. How she hated a runaround. "Not good enough. I have to know what we need to fear, what I'm protecting Jay from, where the threat comes from. It appalls me that you would allow me to walk blindly into a situation endangering Jay and me."

A pause at the other end. "I'll speak to my supervisor and get back to you."

Always *the supervisor*. Like buying a car and the salesperson's charade that he could make no decisions about giving you a deal without consulting the manager. Not that they ever gave you one, but they liked to make you feel you might get one.

"I guess that will have to do. I'll be here." Hollis slammed the phone down.

"Problems?" Fatima said. Wearing black tights and a loose, patterned silk top with metallic dangling earrings, she balanced on high-heeled sandals in the doorway.

Hollis wondered how much of the conversation she'd heard. "Fostering children is challenging. Always something to worry about," she said. "What can I do for you?"

"But lucky for them there are women who will care for them," Fatima said. "Have the police finished with Ginny's apartment?"

Hollis shrugged. "I don't know."

"Too bad about the other murdered woman," Fatima said.

A rush of adrenalin placed Hollis's body on high alert. "What woman?"

Fatima took a step back. "Sorry. Didn't mean to shock you. As a news junkie, I always think other people share my passion. I heard on 680 News radio that the police fished a woman's body from the water at Cherry Beach and suspect foul play." She pivoted into Cartwright, who'd come up behind her as she spoke.

Hollis did not want to deal with him again this morning. "Fatima, come in and sit down, don't rush away."

One of Fatima's eyebrows rose quizzically and a small smile curved her lips. A quick study, she recognized a cry for help when she heard one. In one fluid motion she entered the office and perched on a chair. "Our talk is long overdue," she said and turned to gaze meaningfully at Cartwright.

His head swung from side to side as he looked from one woman to the other. His thick black eyebrows lowered and his eyes narrowed. "I came to talk to *you*," he said to Hollis.

"Come in this afternoon," Hollis replied, hoping he'd choose the time she collected the girls. "I have several appointments between now and then."

"Goddamn it, why the fuck should I have to make an appointment to talk to the fucking building super," he said.

"Because other people also need to talk to me," Hollis said, meeting his angry gaze.

"Don't screw around with me," he threatened and lumbered out of sight. Hollis watched him reappear in the camera monitor focused on the elevator.

"Mr. Charm," Fatima muttered.

"One of your clients?" Hollis asked.

Fatima nodded. "Twice. Blacklisted now. A bad client, and we don't do business with men we dislike," she said.

"Thanks for staying. He scares me."

"I'm here to tell you Ginny moves today."

What if Ginny had been the real target? Would the killer strike again?

Hollis wished Ginny would postpone her move back into her own apartment until the police nabbed Sabrina's murderer. However, she could do nothing to stop her, and it was none of her business. Indeed, as the saying went, she had other fish to fry. Time to text Norman and find Mary.

"I know Mary tries to rescue Aboriginal women from drugs and the street. I'm guessing she ran afoul of someone who did not want this to happen to one particular girl. Have you contacted her and do you know when she plans to return?"

Hollis laid her BlackBerry on her desk, where she'd see the light flashing to indicate the arrival of a message. While she waited, she caught up on office filing. Minutes later the light alerted her.

You've got it right. I talked to Mary, who contacted one of her boarders, Alice Meness, who was visiting family in Golden Lake. Mary told her not to return to the apartment. The threat still exists, so Mary will stay on the reserve. She asked me to thank you for looking after Crystal.

Two women lived with Mary.

What happened to the other woman? she typed.

Hollis filed more papers while keeping an eye on her phone.

Mary repeatedly called her cell phone and left messages. The last time she called she didn't even get the answering machine.

Hollis made the connection. This must be the woman the police had asked her about. The one on the security camera who seemed to be shouting for help.

Tell me her name?

Mary didn't say. She told me nothing else. Are you watching your back, not taking risks?

I am.

Time to call Rhona Simpson.

First she needed the number. She fumbled through a raft of business cards she kept in the top drawer of her office desk. As she thumbed through them, she wondered why she'd saved some of them. Why had she thought a company that sold restaurant equipment specifically geared to vegetarian restaurants would interest her? Or the card for skydiving. What had she been thinking?

She located Rhona Simpson's card near the bottom. Once she placed it on the desk in front of her, she had second thoughts. How would she phrase her call?

First, she'd tell Rhona that Mary Montour in apartment 202 tried to rescue Aboriginal women from the streets and had two tenants and her eleven-year-old niece, Crystal, living in the apartment. Hollis could almost hear Rhona sizzle and demand to know why Hollis hadn't given her this information earlier. Hollis would say Rhona should wait until she finished, and then she'd know. That would be part one.

In part two she'd say that Mary and the two tenants had disappeared, left Crystal behind, and later Mary phoned, leaving a message asking Hollis to care for Crystal. Apparently, Alicia Meness and Mary were okay. Alicia had left to visit her family but someone had threatened Mary, who'd run away without the other tenant, who remained unaccounted for.

"May I speak to Detective Rhona Simpson?"

Voicemail, bloody voicemail. She couldn't recite the story on voicemail.

"It's Hollis Grant. I have information that I believe might help you with your investigation."

That should do it. Now all she had to do was keep the girls and herself safe until Rhona and her sidekick arrived.

TWENTY-ONE

THE two detectives headed back up Cherry Street, along the lakeshore, up University Avenue and Avenue Road, turning off into the maze of streets north of St. Clair. Inside 68 Delisle, they buzzed Hollis.

"You got my message?" she said.

"What message?" Rhona said.

"I have information that might help you. I don't think it's related, but I'll leave it to you to decide."

They collected in Hollis's office. She waved them to the visitors' chairs and plunked down behind the desk.

"Information for us. How long have you been keeping it?" Rhona grumbled. "Tell us."

Hollis related the story of Mary Montour and her one-person campaign to save Aboriginal women addicted to drugs, and told Rhona about her disappearance.

Rhona didn't comment immediately. Instead she glowered at Hollis and pursed her lips. Finally she spoke. "Where *is* Mary Montour?"

"She's gone to ground but she's okay," Hollis said, and from the look in Rhona's eyes, she wished she hadn't decided to tell them.

"How do you know she's okay?"

"As I said, she phoned and asked me to take care of Crystal until she returned."

"That was a couple of days ago. How do you know she's okay now?"

Hollis knew she mustn't blow Norman's cover. In his situation he didn't need the police swooping down on his apartment, drawing attention to him. She shrugged. "A friend told me."

Rhona steepled her fingers and contemplated Hollis. "A *friend*. That's the kind of information we like to get. A *friend*. Could you be a little more specific?"

Crunch time. "No. I can't reveal his name. He lives a very private life and found this information for me as a great favour. I'm sorry, but I can't."

Rhona and Hollis glared at one other.

"What about the unknown woman in the apartment?" Ian intervened.

"I don't know about the other woman. As far as I know, I never saw either one of them."

Ian's phone rang. He listened. "I'll come to the front door." He stood up. "The photo's here. I'll collect it."

After he left, Rhona considered Hollis. "Why did you wait so long to share this information?"

"As I said, I was afraid if I told you, you'd feel compelled to have Crystal taken into care, and I didn't want that to happen. She's had an unsettled life and Mary bolting upset her terribly. My foster daughter lost the foster mother she'd lived with for years, and since she's only recently moved in with me, I wanted to give both girls stability and continuity."

Rhona's expression softened. "I understand that, but you've got to stop making decisions that aren't yours to make."

Hollis said nothing.

Ian appeared and handed Rhona an envelope. She opened it and removed several photos.

"Not a brilliant job. A half-blind person could tell that this woman is dead," she said.

"Very dead. Do you really think we should post it in the elevators?"

"Here? In the elevators here?" Hollis said.

Rhona nodded. "And go door to door."

Hollis reached for a copy. "My God, she looks awful. Why are you putting up her picture here?"

"We saw her on the security tapes we ran yesterday. You saw them."

"I didn't recognize her. Why don't you freeze the frame from the tapes and make a photo from that? It would look like her and not like this gruesome thing," Hollis said, waving the photo.

Ian nodded. "Good suggestion. This photo," he flipped it over, "belongs in the morgue."

"Don't know why we didn't think of that," Rhona admitted. "Okay Ian, over to you, get it done as fast as you can."

"Many of the people who live here are out during the day. You'll have better luck getting an ID when they arrive home from work or college," Hollis said. She stared at the photo. "Do you know her name?" she asked.

"Not yet."

"It could be Veronica," Hollis said.

"Veronica? Where did that name come from?" Rhona asked.

"The other woman living with Mary left a necklace on her dresser with the name Veronica on it, and Mary hasn't been able to reach her."

Rhona rose. "Let's see that apartment."

Hollis grabbed her master keys. In the elevator she said, "I checked it and it looked okay."

"Did you change anything?"

Hollis sniffed. "I'm not stupid. Of course not. The apartment remains exactly the way I found it."

"You didn't *think* to report this to the police?" Rhona said.

Hollis heard the accusation in Rhona's voice. Since she had considered it but had refrained because of Crystal, she understood the detective's exasperation.

"I didn't have enough information to report anything. If I had I would have done it." Hollis thought about her search through the apartment without wearing gloves and concluded she'd made a mistake.

After Hollis let them into the Montour apartment, she stood back as the two detectives slipped on gloves and booties. Rhona waved her dismissal. "We'll deal with this," she said.

Hollis turned but didn't leave. Instead she drifted along behind them. Going through the apartment, she watched them discover the same things that she had, particularly the difference between Mary's two boarders.

"This one, Alicia Meness," Ian indicated the tidy side of the bedroom, "seems to have been on the road to a normal life." He flicked through the methadone pamphlet as he spoke. They'd already spotted the drug in the refrigerator. "Anyone allowed a week's supply is well on the way to conquering her addiction."

Rhona patted the top of the bureau. "Alicia Meness. Her clothes, her tidiness, and the methadone indicate recovery. The other bureau tells a different story."

Ian pointed to the necklace spelling "Veronica" that lay on the bureau.

"If that belongs to her, we've moved a step closer to identification," Rhona said as she went systematically through the contents of the half-open bureau drawers. She found many credit card receipts but no documents, nothing personal.

"We can find out who she is using these," Rhona said, holding up the slips of paper.

Ian examined the cupboard contents. A pile of dirty or discarded clothes lay on the floor. He picked through them. "She was one messy lady," he said.

From his use of the past tense, Hollis realized he'd decided the police had found Veronica, the missing woman, in the harbour that morning. He reached up and checked each hanger's clothes. He stopped at a black leather jacket, removed it from the hanger, and laid it on the bed to examine it more closely.

"Look at this," he said.

Rhona noticed Hollis hovering in the hall. "Police business. This is a crime scene," she said, waving a hand dismissively and shutting the door.

Ian pointed to patches sewn on the jacket. "These indicate she was the girlfriend of someone in the Black Hawks," Hollis heard him say as she left.

"Living with Ms. Montour, she was trying to escape from him or from drug addiction or from both," Rhona said.

"This could be the reason for her murder, but it's hard to believe. These men don't like women leaving them, but I don't think I've ever known a biker to kill an ex-girlfriend for that reason."

"Maybe he intended to rough her up and ended up killing her," Rhona said.

"There had to be more to it than that." Ian picked up the jacket. "Do we have infiltrators in the gang who could tell us anything about the girlfriends? Usually they aren't important."

"The force protects the identity of the undercover guys, but Frank could channel our questions."

"We have the security video. How did he get in? Hell of a lot of chutzpah to walk in, nab her, and walk out knowing the security tapes would record it."

Rhona nodded. "We need to take another look at the garage tapes and see if we see them leaving. If we don't that means he walked her out the front door without anyone being any the wiser and without her screaming for help."

"A gun in your side gives you a big disincentive to yell," Ian said.

"Time to go downtown and check out the tapes, but first we'll ask Hollis a few questions."

TWENTY-TWO

DISMISSED by the detectives, Hollis returned to her office. She left both the office door and the door to her apartment open. The dogs settled on the other side of the baby gate. When she stood up to retrieve a document from the files, they also rose, and only when she returned to her chair did they sink back to the floor. Administrative work awaited her, but tenants appeared in the doorway one after the other, and she spent endless minutes reassuring them.

Another confrontation with Cartwright rated last on the list of things she wanted. After an hour, she relaxed but she should have known better. Cartwright loomed in the doorway. No Fatima to run interference for her this time. Now, when she wanted visitors, none appeared.

Cartwright, in his leather jacket and dark glasses, slid into the room and close to her desk. He leaned forward.

Hollis smelled sweat and garlic overlaid with heavy expensive cologne. She leaned back in her chair, poked her hands under the desk and regarded him with a steady gaze.

"What can I do for you?" she said.

He tapped lightly on the desk with a manicured finger that looked strange on his heavy, meaty hand. The black hair made her think of gorillas, or maybe of the mythical mountain yeti, infrequently sighted beings reportedly covered in hair.

He regarded her unblinkingly. The malevolence in his gaze unsettled her. "You know more than you're telling me, don't you," he said.

It was a statement, not a question.

"I didn't know what you were talking about last night, and I still don't. Nothing has changed overnight," she said.

He leaned his full weight on the desk, bringing his face close to hers. "Women who lie to me regret it," he said in a low, ominous voice.

Hollis wanted to push her chair back, leap out, race into her own apartment, and slam the door. What use were dogs if they didn't sense trouble and make a racket?

As if she'd sent them a message, both dogs began to bark. Cartwright swivelled to face her apartment door. His body language told Hollis dogs frightened him, but this would do her little good unless she owned a dog trained to lunge, grab a man, and hang on — a pit bull, German Shepherd, or Doberman Pinscher.

Rhona appeared in the doorway, trailed by Ian. "What's up with the dogs?" she said.

"You must have surprised them," Hollis answered. She asked herself if Cartwright's remarks could be taken as a threat and should be repeated, but decided that Rhona already knew Cartwright had threatened her and decided not to intervene.

Cartwright, his face expressionless, regarded the two detectives.

"We spoke yesterday," Ian said.

The man nodded.

"We have more questions," Rhona added.

Cartwright didn't twitch or frown or give any indication of nervousness. "Ask them," he said.

Hollis jumped to her feet, nearly upending her chair. "Feel free to use the office," she said. Her wide eyes and quick reaction reflected her fear.

Rhona remembered Hollis's call reporting that Cartwright had threatened her. In the past little had frightened Hollis.

In fact, she'd ended up in dangerous situations because of her lack of fear. Yet Cartwright, sitting in Hollis's own office, clearly terrified her. She'd deal with this later.

Hollis probably had work to do, and there were other empty rooms.

"Thanks, but I think we'll use the party room," Rhona said.

She and Ian accompanied Cartwright out of the office and down the hall.

In the party room Ian placed three folding chairs in a triangle and told Cartwright to sit facing them.

"You said business took you out of town," Rhona said. "What is your business and where were you?"

"Investments," he said.

"The name of the firm?"

"I invest for various people."

"Do you have a record of your transactions?" Ian asked.

"My accountant does."

"We'll accompany you to your apartment and wait while you get a copy of your most recent transactions and the details of your Monday night business trip. Credit card slips, your boarding pass, anything to prove where you were."

Barney regarded them unblinkingly with eyes that reminded Rhona of alligators she'd seen in the zoo — cold eyes that focused on prey and judged to a millimetre the amount of speed and energy needed to kill. Presuming his business was Black Hawk business, she didn't think he'd like revealing any details.

"Don't you need a search warrant?" he said, his tone mild but his eyes revealing his rage.

Only a man with something to hide and a wish to delay an investigation required a search warrant.

"We thought we might need one and prepared accordingly. Coming right up," Rhona said cheerily. Ian stood up and

left the room. Cartwright waited in silence until he returned.
"It's in the works. Should be here soon," Ian said.

"Now we'll see what you have to hide," Rhona said and watched Cartwright suppress the rage her remark engendered.

Cartwright and Rhona waited while Ian went to meet the courier bearing the search warrant. Rhona had spoken to Frank before they left and told him they would need one, so they didn't have long to sit in silence before Ian returned waving the piece of paper.

Cartwright said nothing. He lumbered to his feet and preceded them into the hall and to the elevator.

"Strong, silent type," Rhona murmured to Ian.

Cartwright lifted his head and regarded her with a cold-blooded stare. Rhona knew he would have no qualms about taking her out if he thought he could get away with it.

"You live alone," Ian said as they followed him into his apartment.

"I do. I rent it furnished. Moved in a couple of weeks ago."

Rhona looked around.

The apartment, a combination of inoffensive neutral colours and textures designed to soothe, please, and offend no one, must normally rival a high-end boutique hotel in attractiveness. However, in a week or two Cartwright had turned it into a sewer. He'd strewn dirty and discarded clothes everywhere. Empty beer bottles and the remains of take-out meals and overflowing ashtrays covered all flat surfaces, including the floor. The apartment smelled of stale food and beer but most of all of an unwashed man who hadn't changed his socks for too long.

Rhona wrinkled her nose and breathed shallowly. They'd entered a predator's lair and the stink revolted her.

"We want to see a boarding pass or a hotel receipt for Monday night and what financial information you have," Rhona said.

"We have the authority to search everywhere," Ian said.

Cartwright didn't move.

"Well," Ian said.

Rhona suspected Ian loathed the prospect of burrowing through this man's belongings as much as she did.

Cartwright frowned, and his black furry eyebrows edged toward each other like caterpillars in a mating dance. He moved across the room in exaggerated slow motion and plucked a navy blue sports bag from the desk chair.

"I must have chucked the receipts in the garbage. I don't have them," he said.

"Chucked them in the garbage," Rhona repeated. "How convenient. Where were you? The airline will have a record."

Cartwright frowned. "Maybe it was the week before," he said. "Nothing much here," he muttered, swinging the bag.

"So you were here on Monday night," Rhona said.

"Guess so," he said and thrust the bag at her.

Rhona took it, walked to the dining room table, then pushed aside and stacked empty pizza boxes to make a space. She took a notebook and pen from her bag before removing a sheaf of papers from the briefcase.

"I'll go through these. See if you can find other papers or anything else of interest," she said to Ian.

Ian looked unhappy, but he pulled on gloves and headed for the apartment's depths.

Rhona cleared a chair of debris, sat down, and began her inspection.

Cartwright walked to the kitchen, opened the refrigerator, and grabbed a beer. He didn't offer any refreshments to the detectives, which did not surprise Rhona. She would not have wanted to eat or drink anything in this apartment.

She read documents but made few notes. Cartwright had told the truth when he claimed to have nothing incriminating. She learned that he dealt with the bank of Nova Scotia, where he had three accounts. Although they'd search these, she suspected they would find no evidence of money laundering. Time in prison would have honed his concealment skills.

Ian walked out of the bedroom. "You belong to the Black Hawks," he said to Cartwright.

"What about it?"

"A senior member. I know from the patches."

"So. Not a crime, is it?" Cartwright said as he grabbed another beer from the fridge.

"Depends what you do with them."

"Ride around. Meet at the clubhouse. Nothing much."

Did he classify the murders, gun battles, kidnappings, and the heightened violence resulting from the two rival gangs' war to control the drug trade, prostitution, human trafficking, as *nothing much*? They'd freeze his bank accounts and analyze the transactions. Rhona hoped they'd collect enough evidence to put him away again.

"We'll be back. Don't leave town," Rhona cautioned as they left. Outside the apartment building she took a deep breath. "That man thinks personal hygiene doesn't apply to him," she said.

She stopped walking and clapped a hand to the side of her head. "We've taken the wrong track. He may launder money but I think we just interviewed Veronica's murderer. We should have caught on when you talked about the Black Hawks. Her killer lived in the building, that's why he didn't have a problem getting in. I could be wrong but I don't think so." She pulled out her cell phone but before she put in her call she said to Ian, "We need the team here to check his vehicle inside and out. We need him down at the shop to measure him and see if his height matches the man in the elevator."

"He won't wait around for us to make the connection," Ian said and sprinted back into the building. "I'll head him off in the garage," he shouted over his shoulder.

Rhona, assured that backup was on the way, shot into the elevator. At Cartwright's door she pressed the buzzer.

"Police. Open the door," she said.

Nothing. She called Hollis.

"Bring up the master keys. I have a warrant to enter Mr. Cartwright's apartment."

Had Ian stopped him?

TWENTY-THREE

AFTER Cartwright and the detectives left, Hollis composed herself. Time to text Norman.

If I'm in danger tell me about your connection to motorcycle gangs.

She knew Norman never left the building and expected an immediate reply.

Nothing came.

Should she worry? Despite her care, had she led someone to him? She hoped he wasn't responding because he was working.

If he was like her and most artists she knew, his work came first. Involved in a painting going well, she turned off her cell phone and allowed the answering machine to record calls on the land line. Could Norman have taken this approach? She sighed as she realized that she couldn't hide away anymore, in case the school or the CAS phoned about Jay. Perhaps her recent inability to shut herself off from the world had diminished her creativity.

A change in media provided another technique to surmount a creative roadblock. Fibre artwork, along with her money-making creation of papier-mâché animals, kept her working and allowed her subconscious to deal with a painting problem. Right now she'd assume Norman's creative process had taken over and led him to ignore his cell phone and computer.

With only an hour until she locked the door and collected the girls, she needed to be there not only to work but also to reassure worried tenants. An unsolved murder created anxiety. Again she left her apartment door open so the dogs could see her and the office door ajar to indicate her readiness to talk to tenants.

Fatima showed up first. Hollis heard her before she saw her, since the woman's pointed slippers sported bells on the toes.

"Good thing you don't want to sneak up on anyone," Hollis said as Fatima wafted into the room on a cloud of spicy perfume reminiscent of Biblical frankincense and myrrh.

"Ginny moved to Sabrina's apartment. The police allowed her to collect her clothes, toiletries, and anything else she thought she needed. She's happy she's moved but ..." She settled herself on the visitor's chair. "I think she wants to go home, to leave Toronto."

"She suffered a terrible shock. Maybe it convinced her that she should reconsider her life."

Fatima nodded. "Not everyone is cut out for this business. You have to consider it just that, a business. If you can't think of it that way, and many can't, you turn to drugs or drinking to make yourself feel better, less guilty." She smiled. "On the other hand, many are already on drugs and need money to pay for the habit."

Hollis had always wanted to know how call girls felt about what they did. "How did you come to think of it as a business?" she asked.

Fatima spent ten minutes revealing part of her history. Hollis held her BlackBerry while Fatima talked. She willed the red light to flash but nothing happened. After Fatima left Hollis fiddled with files and absentmindedly watched the security cameras.

Finally, when the phone rang she grabbed it. Maybe Norman had found a safe phone or Brownelly had decided to return her call.

"This is Ms. Young. I spoke to my supervisor."

Hollis perked up. Would she discover Brownelly's secret?

"She asked me to inform you that the information remains confidential. Only Mr. Brownelly can provide the information you want."

Prissy bitch. "I have a good mind to talk to one of the investigative reporters I know. I can't believe that you would knowingly withhold information that might endanger a child's life, let alone mine," Hollis said.

"There's no need to be huffy. I certainly don't think you should go to the press. Speak to Mr. Brownelly. Share your concerns. As a good father he wants his daughter safe and would not take any action that might hurt her."

No point continuing this conversation. Bound by bureaucratic rules, this woman would drive Hollis crazy if she continued to hammer away. She hung up and immediately felt ashamed of unleashing her anger against a woman who only acted as the messenger.

Okay. She'd do it. She punched Brownelly's number into the phone and listened to him tell her to leave a message. "Please call me" was the only message she felt comfortable leaving.

Hollis found it hard to concentrate and ended up tidying her desk drawers and half watching the security cameras.

A figure running in the garage drew her attention. She peered at the screen. It looked like Cartwright. She verified this when the camera caught his face as he leaped into his car, backed, turned, and sped away. At that moment Detective Gilchrist burst into the garage, stared after the vehicle disappearing through the door, pulled out his cell phone and spoke rapidly.

This action movie mesmerized Hollis. In the next shot the detective raced from the garage and another camera picked him up as he emerged from the elevator on the ground floor. At that moment a flying wedge of police entered the lobby.

Before she took it all in, her cell phone rang. She jumped, hoping again to hear from Norman or Brownelly. Instead Rhona instructed her to bring the master keys upstairs to Cartwright's apartment. Following instructions, she locked the office and zipped to the elevator, where she joined several police officers.

At the apartment she stood back while Rhona, now backed by other officers, demanded entry and then, gun drawn, proceeded cautiously into the apartment. Her actions surprised Hollis but she guessed the police didn't want to find someone else there.

Rhona emerged and holstered her gun. "Treat the apartment as a crime scene. Look for anything to link the resident to the murder victim in the harbour or to money laundering," she said to the officers. Her phone buzzed. She raised her hand to detain the group while she listened. "Detective Gilchrist got his license number. We have an all points bulletin out for the car. I have business at the shop. Let me know if you find anything."

Hollis returned to the office and kept an eye on the cameras, half-expecting more dramatic activity. Creak, bang, creak, bang. Hollis recognized the sounds made by one of several possible tenants navigating a walker down the hall.

Agnes Johnson, her accommodating child minder, thumped into view.

"I saw the police arriving. Do they know who killed Ms. Trepanier?" she asked.

Hollis shook her head. "Not yet."

"Why are they here? Has something else happened?" Agnes leaned on her walker. "Certainly keeps us on our toes, doesn't it?"

Hollis recognized the glint of excitement in the woman's eyes. No doubt the need for vicarious experience along with insomnia motivated her to keep tabs on the building's late night comings and goings.

"It does, but I'd much prefer a quiet life."

Ms. Johnson's eyes sparkled. "Time enough for a quiet life when they put you in a box. Myself, I like activity."

Agnes edged into the room and settled on the seat of her walker. She leaned toward Hollis as if she intended to stay and talk.

"Have you remembered anything else that you saw when you looked out the window on Monday?" Hollis asked.

Agnes flipped her purse into the basket, straightened her wire-rimmed glasses, and repositioned herself

"I thought I told the police everything, but I forgot that I went to bed about two and woke up at four with a migraine. I took a pill, made myself a cup of hot milk, and parked at the window while I waited for the medicine to work. No one was about at first, but then I noticed a man in the shadows to the right of the portico. He simply stood there. I thought he might have a dog that had needed to go out, because I saw something beside him on the ground." She checked to see that Hollis was listening. "Then the little Asian man who delivers the *Globe and Mail* arrived. The man I was watching stepped back and, if I hadn't noticed him before, I wouldn't have known he was there." She paused and Hollis waited rather than interrupting the flow. The woman didn't look at Hollis. Rather she seemed to be focusing on an invisible screen.

"I waited. The paper man takes a while because, as you know, he delivers the paper at each subscriber's door. Finally, he emerged and left. The man bent down and grabbed what I had initially thought was a dog but seemed to be a bundle. He rearranged it, hunched over and hid whatever it was with his body before he rushed inside. Of course I didn't see where he went, but he must live here. It struck me as odd."

A shiver of excitement ran through Hollis. "Did you recognize him?"

Agnes frowned. "Not right then. Being up high distorts my view. I saw the top of his head covered by a dark flat hat."

Hollis's initial excitement disappeared.

"An hour ago I came down on the elevator with a man wearing a black cap. I felt sure it was the same man. I told him that if he was the man I'd seen, I didn't think much of people sneaking around at night."

"His name?"

"That's the trouble. I don't know. I decided to talk to you and see if you thought it important enough to tell the police."

"It is. I'll contact Detective Simpson. If that man had anything to do with the murder, you must be careful. He knows that you saw him outside."

Agnes's lips twitched into a smile. "I will, but it's exciting, isn't it?"

Hollis shook her head. "No. This isn't a TV show. It's serious. Promise me that you'll be careful."

"I will," Agnes said dutifully, but from the look in her eye Hollis knew she was relishing the moment. She called Rhona and once again got her voicemail. Bloody voicemail. If the detective carried her cell phone, why didn't she answer?

"I have new important info for you. Call me."

Later that evening Willem returned. After the girls went to sleep, Hollis and Willem snuggled in bed, Hollis traced the outline of his face with her finger. Willem turned his head, kissed the finger, and reached to pull her close again. His arms tightened around her.

"Why don't we move in together?" he murmured.

Had he really suggested that they live together? Could it work? Would it be like her marriage? Exciting at first and then a disaster.

"You're not throwing your arms around me and shouting, yes, yes, yes," Willem said.

"I'm in shock," Hollis said before she kissed him. For some time the question remained unanswered.

Relaxed and happy, she sighed, "It would be wonderful," she breathed.

"I hear a *but*," Willem said.

"I have so many questions I have to answer first."

"Such as?"

"What about Jay? Would the CAS allow her to stay if you moved in? I'm committed to her and can't and don't want to chuck her out. She needs the stability, needs to know that no matter what she does or says, she's here for the long run."

"Could you ask about their policy? I can't believe that a good number of their foster parents don't live together in common law relationships."

Hollis had hoped he'd respond with a proposal. She'd always believed that the man got all the perks in a common law relationship.

"You're going to study law. Why don't you find out?"

Willem leaned over and kissed her. "I sense a decided lack of enthusiasm. Forget I ever mentioned it."

Now he was put out, the last thing she wanted. She loved him, loved everything about him. The thought of lazy Sunday mornings, of long walks or runs with the dogs, filled her with joy. But what would Jay do when they did couple things? How would the child feel about sharing her home with Willem?

Hollis returned the kiss and then pulled away. "I love the idea, but you surprised me. I worry because in the past I've rushed into situations and later regretted my impetuousness. You mean the world to me and I don't want to blow this." Should she admit how much she loved him? What the heck. "More than the world. I love you and can't bear to think of life without you."

Willem rolled over and sat up. "That's what I wanted to hear. I love you too. We can make this work." He bounded out of bed. "My God, it's two a.m. I have to go."

Hollis slid out of bed and pulled on her terrycloth robe. "Do you want anything to eat?"

A scream ripped through the air followed by a metallic crash and a second scream. Not Crystal — the noise had been outside.

Hollis grabbed the flashlight she kept in the bedside table, ran to the window, and threw it open. She stuck her head out. The flashlight's weak beam flickered over the scaffolding but showed nothing amiss.

"Shout and see if anyone answers you," Willem suggested, already pulling on his shirt.

"I hope that whoever yelled can answer." Hollis hallooed out the window. "Who screamed? Where are you?"

At that moment Hollis's cell phone rang and she grabbed for it.

"Ginny. Did you scream?" Hollis listened. "That's terrible. I'll call the police and then come up."

"What did she say? What happened?" Willem said, sitting on the chair to pull on his socks.

"She woke up and saw someone's hand pushing her window up. She slammed the window on the fingers."

"Whoever it was fell and then gave the second scream," Willem said.

Hollis tapped in 911 and delivered the information. "I can't stay on the line. It isn't happening in my apartment. I'll unlock the downstairs doors for the police." She hung up. Her shoulders slumped.

They heard a second metallic crash.

"What the hell is happening out there?" Willem said.

"Whoever planned to attack Ginny must have dropped something. He's still out there."

"If Ginny smashed the window on his fingers, she likely broke them. Whoever it is has one or maybe two hands severely damaged. It's unlikely he can climb down or back up with mangled fingers. The police will get him." Willem thrust his feet into his loafers.

Hollis grabbed jeans and a sweatshirt and stepped into her slippers. She headed for the door but before she reached it Jay appeared.

"What are you doing? Who screamed? What happened?"

Crystal stood behind her saying nothing, but shivering.

Hollis saw the panic in the girls' eyes. She couldn't leave them and couldn't bring them in case Sabrina's murderer had returned. What to do?

"Ginny phoned. She screamed because something scared her. She asked me to come up. I phoned the police. I have to open the door for them and then go upstairs," Hollis said.

"We can't stay here. We'll come with you," Jay volunteered.

Willem recognized her dilemma. "Probably better for you girls to stick with me when I unlock the front door for the police. I'll keep you company back here until Hollis returns and we find out what frightened Ginny."

Hollis hugged him and the girls before she headed out the door, dreading what she might find on the fifth floor.

TWENTY-FOUR

THE search for Cartwright had been fruitless. Rhona and Ian had both called it quits and gone home. A vodka martini and a snuggle with Obie helped Rhona relax, as did a warm bath. She lay in the water and reviewed what they now knew. They had used credit card slips to identify the murder victim as Veronica Horn. She appeared to have been the women they'd seen being hustled out of the building, and Barney Cartwright appeared to have been the man with her. His car could provide forensic evidence to link him to Veronica.

As for Sabrina's murder, they were no closer to a solution, unless they could connect Cartwright to that murder. David Jones, the newly released con who'd spent years in jail for raping Sabrina, remained on their radar. His alibi had checked out, but possibly he'd managed to slip out of the halfway house and travel to Toronto. A video of him walking might correspond to that of one of the many men who had taken care not to expose their faces to the security cameras. On the other hand, if Ginny, not Sabrina, had been the intended victim, a former wronged boyfriend stood first in the line of suspects. Not much to go on, but all they had for now.

Rhona climbed out of the tub. Just before she went to bed, she'd discovered that her cell phone had run out of juice. It had done this several times lately. It was time for a new one and she would put in a requisition in the morning. No way to know what she'd missed.

Before she bedded down, she left it recharging on the bedside table beside her land line. She stretched, relaxed into the soft bamboo-fabric sheets, and wondered whether to watch TV or read. She fell asleep before making a decision.

The clamorous "William Tell Overture" brought her from a deep sleep, fumbling for the phone.

"Simpson here," she muttered in a sleep-choked voice.

"Another event at 68 Delisle," the dispatcher said. "Thought you'd want to know. We've responded to a 911."

All vestiges of sleep disappeared.

"What happened?"

"Report of an attempted break-in through a window on the fifth floor."

"I'm on my way. Have you called my partner?" Rhona asked. Assured that they would, she snapped the phone off and struggled out of bed. Grabbing the outfit she'd worn the day before, she dashed into the bathroom, cleaned her teeth, washed her face, slashed on lipstick, and headed for the door.

Unless they had a copycat killer, Ginny had been the original target. Two suspects in the frame. Her boyfriend and the john who had punched and frightened her.

At the apartment building, emergency vehicles littered the street. Rhona couldn't abandon her car, so she backed up until she reached the driveway of the next apartment building and snaked into their visitors' lot, where she double parked. She trotted along the sidewalk, identified herself, and marched into the building.

The officer standing at the door motioned to her.

"The action's out back. Somebody's hung up on the scaffolding."

Rhona didn't wait to learn whether the body was young or old, male or female, dead or alive. She raced for the back of the building.

TWENTY-FIVE

WHEN Hollis emerged from the elevator, Ginny rushed forward and threw her arms around her. "He must have come back to kill me," she sobbed.

It seemed likely but not the time to say so. Patting Ginny on the back, Hollis made reassuring noises before disentangling herself.

"Do you want to come down to my apartment, or do you want me to go and have a look in your apartment?"

Ginny stared as if Hollis had suddenly morphed into a madwoman. "Are you crazy? Of course I don't want you in there. He probably climbed back up and he'll kill you." She pushed the elevator button. "Downstairs. Not in your apartment. In the lobby, where I can give my key to the police." When the elevator door opened, the wail of approaching sirens heralded help's arrival.

They emerged in the lobby as emergency workers poured through the door. Hollis watched Willem, who'd been waiting, step forward and hand over the key. Jay and Crystal clung to his arms.

"I wanted to do that," Ginny said, fingering her key.

"One key is as good as another. Ginny, come into my apartment. You'll only be in the way here."

Ginny, her white terrycloth robe pulled tight around her, shook her head. "I want to be here when they bring him down, want to see the man who wants me dead."

Hollis understood how Ginny felt. She should stay with her, but she wanted to make sure all was well in her own apartment.

"I agree, but come with me while I check that the girls aren't too shook up."

Ginny looked across the lobby. "They look fine. Who's with them? Is that your boyfriend? "

Hollis patted Ginny's shoulder. "It is. Come and meet him."

Reluctantly, Ginny agreed.

When they reached the apartment, Hollis introduced Ginny. When Hollis opened the door, Barlow, seeing the crowd in the lobby, streaked between Willem's legs, and before anyone could stop him rushed up the emergency crew, tail wagging, tongue lolling, hoping someone would play with him.

"Get that dog out of here," a firefighter shouted.

Hollis ran, grabbed the dog, collared him, and looked up to see Rhona striding into the lobby.

"Out back, the dispatcher said out back," a man shouted and the group circled as one and headed for the door, Rhona in the lead.

Out back. What did that mean? The three adults stared at one another. "We're all awake. We might as well follow the crowd, but we need jackets," Willem said. He turned to the girls standing behind him. "Kids, grab something warm for yourselves and for Ginny, it'll be chilly outside."

With coats and jackets over their pyjamas, they trooped out into the hall. Hollis pocketed her keys before joining the others.

They rounded the building and found organized mayhem. The firefighters had trained powerful lights on the side of the building.

A thin man dressed in dark clothes held onto a horizontal steel bar and rested the toe of one shoe on a lower horizontal bar as he dangled from the fourth-floor scaffolding, alive but in grave danger of plunging to the ground.

"We think it's the killer, that he came back," someone whispered.

"Did he get another one?" a voice responded.

As they murmured to each other, the rumoured identity of the hanging man circulated through the crowd. It amazed Hollis that at this hour of the morning so many people had found their way to the scene.

Firefighters charged past carrying long extension ladders.

"Careful, careful. Don't jar the scaffolding or he'll lose his grip," the leader shouted as the crew jockeyed the ladder into position.

Other firefighters positioned themselves to hold a net to catch the man if he did release his hold on the bar.

Hollis glanced around. At least forty people crammed the edges of the scene. After the whispered identification had circulated, an eerie quiet, broken by the wind sighing through the nearby evergreens, settled over the scene. Only the firefighters' grunts as they manoeuvred their equipment sounded in the silence.

"Hang on, buddy, we're just about there," one said as the men mounted the ladders.

"I can't hold on any longer," the man yelled and let go.

The crowd gasped.

He flipped downward and his head smacked against the board platform on the third floor. It sounded like a watermelon being dropped on concrete. The impact flipped him further away from the scaffolding. The men holding the rescue net moved back quickly and braced themselves. The man landed on his arms and somersaulted over onto his back with an audible slap. He lay still. The crowd sidled forward to watch the next act of the drama.

After they carefully lowered the net, a paramedic jumped forward and bent over the inert form. Hollis couldn't see what he did and neither could the onlookers who moved forward again.

"He's unconscious, weak vital signs," the woman reported as she motioned for a stretcher.

Rhona Simpson spoke to the detective beside her, who waved two police officers over. "Go with him and make sure he's secure. My partner will go too in case he regains consciousness," Rhona ordered.

They loaded him on the stretcher and wheeled him away, but not before Hollis and her pack saw his still-white face.

"Oh my God," Ginny breathed.

At that moment the young man opened his eyes. "Ginny," he sighed as he was moved toward the waiting ambulance.

Rhona, standing close to the stretcher, stepped over to them. "You know him," she said to Ginny.

Ginny buried her face in her hands and sobbed.

When the excitement ended, the crowd recovered its voice and noisily swarmed toward the street. Rhona grasped Ginny's elbow.

"Come with me to the office," she ordered, ignoring Hollis, Willem, and the girls.

Hollis hated to relinquish Ginny. Whatever his identity, seeing the man on the stretcher had deeply affected but not terrified the young woman. Not the reaction Ginny would have had if she thought she'd seen a killer. Odd. Who was he?

Hollis shrugged and was heading back into the building when she remembered Agnes Johnson and their conversation. She surveyed the rapidly departing throng knowing that if Agnes had come outside, she would be moving slowly on her walker. She didn't see the woman. That too was odd. She couldn't imagine the curious woman sleeping through the sirens and noise. Maybe she should check on Agnes. But first she needed to catch up with Ginny and the detective.

"Ms. Simpson," she said, touching Rhona's shoulder.

"What is it?" Rhona said, half turning and not stopping.

"Did you get the message I left on your voicemail?"

Rhona thought about the hours that her cell phone had not been receiving messages. "No. What was it?"

"I have more information that might help identify Sabrina's killer."

Rhona stopped. She kept her hand on Ginny's elbow and pivoted to face Hollis. "I expect you're too late. The probable killer is in the ambulance."

"Maybe not. I think you should hear what Agnes Johnson has to say," Hollis insisted.

Rhona's eyebrow rose. "Agnes Johnson, the woman on the walker, the insomniac who sat looking out the window half the night."

"Right."

Rhona surveyed the dispersing mob. "Surprising not to see her here. What did she remember?"

"I really think she should tell you herself," Hollis said

"If you think I should, then I will, but first Ginny and I need to chat," Rhona said and hurried the girl toward the door.

Willem stepped forward. "Let's get these kids back to bed," he said.

Inside the girls wanted to talk.

"Why was the man on the scaffolding?" Jay asked, hugging MacTee, who leaned against her.

"If Ginny knew him, why did he try to get in her window?" Crystal said, flopping on the sofa. "She screamed. Do you think she saw who it was that scared her?" She fiddled with the piping on the sofa. "I don't think so. I saw her face when she looked at him and she wasn't scared."

"Out of the mouths of babes," Willem said, settling on another chair.

Hollis checked her watch. "It's the middle of the night. Maybe we should forget about sleeping and cook up a big breakfast." She thought the girls would leap at the chance to do something different, something they could tell their friends about when they went to school later in the morning. "Well? Want to do that?"

Jay sat on the floor with MacTee collapsed next to her. "Crystal can but not me. I'm tired. Hollis, why don't you wait for Ginny and tell us what she says when we get up in the morning."

"Good suggestion," Willem said. He looked at Hollis. "You want to see to Ginny when Rhona is finished. Why don't I bed down here so the girls won't be alone."

"Great idea. I want to check on Agnes as well," Hollis said, grateful that Willem had anticipated her needs.

Willem yawned. "You kids head for bed so I can go too."

Surprisingly, the girls did as he asked. Hollis hugged Willem. "Maybe the CAS will be glad you're here. Nothing like a strong man in a young girl's life."

When Hollis found the door to the office closed, she settled down to wait. By the time the door opened, she'd slid to the floor and leaned against the door frame, nodding and wishing she could go to bed.

"Ginny, would you like to sleep on my couch?" she offered.

Rhona stared at her. "Have you been waiting all this time?"

"I didn't want Ginny to have to go back to her apartment alone."

"Ms. Wuttenee is suffering from shock," Rhona said. "Make her a cup of tea with lots of sugar. I have to get downtown and see what's happening at the hospital."

Ginny roused herself. "I hate tea. I want to come with you." She clutched her hands together so tightly the knuckles shone white. "I need to be there when he wakes up, need to apologize, need to tell him how sorry I am," she said.

Sorry! What was going on?

Rhona assessed the woman. "It's against my better judgment, but you may come. Maybe if he regains consciousness he'll tell you why he climbed the scaffolding in the middle of the night."

Hollis had her hand on the doorknob when she remembered she'd received a message from Norman.

"I have something else to tell you," she said to Rhona.

"True confession time. Shoot," Rhona said.

"You may already know this, but my friend says Mary told him Veronica's last name is Horn and she's a Mohawk."

"Thanks. We do have that information. I'll talk to you in the morning."

Trailed by Ginny, Rhona walked down the street feeling as if a weight tied to each foot was slowing her steps.

As always, in a scene of organized chaos, Emerg operated in high gear in the middle of the night. Ambulances stood under the archway and response workers waited with the stretcher cases they'd rushed to the hospital. She'd read somewhere that whoever took charge of emergency response services planned to change the procedure so the responders would not have wait until hospital medical personnel saw the patients but would transfer them to hospital stretchers and get back on the road. She couldn't remember if legislation had passed, but since the attendants waited patiently, she assumed it hadn't.

"Detective Gilchrist?" she asked the harried triage nurse sitting in the glass-enclosed booth at the entrance to Emerg.

"Inside in the hall," the woman said.

Rhona pushed through the swinging door and walked past a string of gurneys lining the hall until she found Ian, who'd commandeered a chair he'd placed beside the intruder's stretcher. The other officer leaned against the wall.

"He came around once, but only for a second," Ian reported. "They took him to X-ray. He has a severe concussion, three broken fingers, and a broken right arm." As if answering Rhona's unspoken question, he said, "No guesses about when he'll regain consciousness. No ID either." He looked at Ginny, who stood behind Rhona with her eyes fixed on the young man.

Rhona put a hand on Ginny's arm. "He's Larry Baptiste, Ginny Wuttenee's ex-boyfriend."

Ian glanced from one to the other. "Are we charging him with Ms. Trepanier's murder?"

"Not yet. He remains a person of interest. Ms. Wuttenee has permission to sit with him." She turned to the police officer. "Call us if Baptiste regains consciousness."

Ian rose and Ginny took his place. She stared at Larry's face as if she intended to memorize it.

"Ms. Wuttennee," Rhona said.

Ginny raised her gaze to meet Rhona's. "Thank you for letting me do this," she whispered.

Rhona produced a facsimile smile. "We'll talk to you later," she said.

Wending their way back through the noisy hospital corridor, Rhona felt the depth of her fatigue. Ian's drawn grey countenance revealed his exhaustion.

"We'll call it a night," Rhona said. "Hollis Grant told me Agnes Johnson, the woman on the walker, has information for us, but it's too late to talk to her tonight. We'll speak to her in the morning." She glanced at the wall clock. "It's three. Time for a few hours' sleep. When Baptiste regains consciousness, we'll interview him, but I don't think he killed Sabrina. By morning I hope Cartwright is in custody. We're a long way from being finished but we have made progress."

"Anything on Veronica Horn?" Ian asked.

"Nothing else."

"More to work on tomorrow," Ian said, yawned, and showed perfect white teeth.

"I'm heading for a chilled vodka martini and bed," she said.

TWENTY-SIX

ONCE Rhona left, Hollis wanted to tiptoe off to bed, but knowing that Agnes Johnson had not rattled out to watch the events behind the building, she felt uneasy. It wasn't her job, but that didn't prevent her from feeling responsible. In the office she flipped open Agnes's file and phoned.

Almost four in the morning. Why would there be a busy signal? She grabbed the master key, trundled through the empty lobby and up to Agnes's apartment. When she pushed the buzzer nothing happened. Reluctantly, she unlocked the door, but when she pushed the door refused to budge. Was someone on the other side holding it closed, or had Agnes fallen against it?

"Agnes, can you hear me?" she said.

No response. She used both hands and, inch by inch, moving something heavy on the other side, managed to open the door wide enough to peer inside. She saw thin sticklike legs and worn blue slippers.

Oh God, she hoped Agnes wasn't dead. She wished she'd come earlier. If only she'd brought her cell phone with her. Speed could be important. Crouched down, she reached through the opening and shoved Agnes far enough away to enable her to slip through the partially open door.

Agnes sprawled on the floor clutching the phone receiver.

Hollis knelt beside her, felt for a pulse, found a faint one, removed the receiver from Agnes's limp hand, and phoned for help. Then, sure that Agnes was breathing, she hurried to the living room, retrieved the cozy knitted afghan from the back of the sofa and brought it back to cover her friend. Feeling helpless and wishing she could do something more, she held Agnes's hand and wondered if the woman had had a heart attack or a stroke, the common killers of elderly women.

Again the street filled with emergency vehicles, but this time they didn't tarry. The paramedics, refusing to answer Hollis's questions, loaded Agnes on a stretcher and rushed her off to the hospital. As Hollis watched the ambulance, siren braying, pull away from the building, she prayed that that Agnes arrived in time to be helped.

What a night! Before she crawled into bed beside Willem, who snored gently, she set the alarm. Enveloped in the warm sheets and longing to sink into oblivion, her tired mind refused to stop, and the events of the evening played over and over while she tossed and turned.

Next morning Hollis rolled over, clicked the alarm off, and saw that Willem was gone. No doubt he'd slipped out early to go home and prepare for his class. It had been good of him to stay. She stretched and both dogs leaped to their feet, rushed to her side, and began to lick whatever part of her they could find.

She pushed them away and jumped out of bed. Her smart dogs might want to greet her, but more likely they knew they'd found a surefire way to get her moving. Out of bed, she planned her day. Once the girls left, she must contact Norman, phone Brownelly, and then visit the hospital to check on Agnes and Ginny's boyfriend. In the kitchen she opted for the convenience of smoothies and threw yogurt, orange juice, and bananas into the blender. Two tall glasses and toast awaited the girls when they emerged. Dark circles under their eyes provided mute testimony that they'd spent half the night in the yard watching high drama.

"Tuna or salmon? Lunch at school again today."

"Salmon," they said in unison. Jay did not accuse Hollis of neglect but accepted that this was how it was going to be.

Back from the invigorating walk to school, Hollis checked for messages on the land line. She'd been obsessively pulling her BlackBerry out of her pocket since early morning. No one had contacted her on either one.

TWENTY-SEVEN

RHONA needed double-strength high test caffeine to jump-start her the next morning. Sleep deprivation, an occupational hazard, required extreme measures. She'd applied concealer under her eyes to partially hide the dark circles and makeup to cover her pallor but could do nothing to clear her bloodshot eyes or remedy her bone weariness. When she reached the office at eight Ian sat at his desk. Rhona had read that metrosexuals used makeup to enhance their appearance, but the grey cast to Ian's fair skin and the circles under his eyes had received no cosmetic help.

"What's up?" she asked.

"Cartwright abandoned his car in the commuter lot at Finch and Yonge. I had it towed and I've given the forensic team a heads up to make it a priority. "

"Put out a press release on Cartwright. Pull up his mug shot from the files. Run it and ask anyone knowing his whereabouts to contact the police."

"And the usual warning that he may be armed and dangerous?" Ian asked.

"Of course. We may get lucky but I imagine he's gone to ground. The Black Hawks must have a hundred ways to escape detection."

Rhona filled her mug at the coffee machine. After a long swig she plunked into a chair. "At least we have the victim's ID."

"We ran her prints and her name once we knew it. Nothing there."

"Hollis Grant refuses to tell us how she contacted her tenant Mary Montour, but if Veronica Horn lived with her and Mary ran away because she was afraid, we definitely have to interview her. I'll insist on a contact number. I also have to talk to Agnes Johnson."

"She's the one who gave us a detailed description of Sabrina Trepanier and a man coming in on Monday evening."

"Right, and, according to Hollis, she remembered something else she thinks we should know." She finished her coffee. "What else?"

"Veronica's autopsy results. More follow-ups on the johns. I'm talking to the guns and gangs crew about Cartwright's position with the bikers."

Rhona checked her watch. "Hollis should have delivered those kids to school by the time I get there. I'm off."

Buzzed in by Hollis, who was waiting in her office, Rhona didn't sit down. She stood in the doorway.

"I must contact Mary Montour immediately. Give me a number to reach her."

Hollis, about to sit down, stopped. "I can't because I don't have it. A friend talked to her."

"Give me his or her number. We have to get moving."

Hollis regarded Rhona as if she was an annoying fly. "I'm sorry. I will contact him right now while you wait, but I'm not giving you his number."

Rhona stepped into the office. "I don't understand the secrecy."

"To be frank, neither do I, but he insisted on it and I respect his right to do that." Hollis yanked her cell phone from her hoodie's pocket, turned away from Rhona, and punched in the message.

I have a police officer here who needs to know Mary's phone number. It's urgent. Please contact her and get back to me quickly.

She sat back and waited.

Rhona didn't smile or thank Hollis. "I'll take a minute and talk to Agnes Johnson. What apartment is she in?"

Hollis shook her head.

"Why not?"

"When she didn't come down to see what was happening, I knew something was wrong, and I found her on the floor of her apartment."

"Dead?"

"No. I think she had a stroke or maybe it was a heart attack. She was unconscious. I called this morning. She's alive. I hope she makes it. I plan to visit later."

Rhona perched on the visitor's hard chair. "Tell me what she told you."

"Early in the morning she noticed a man in lurking in the shadows with a bundle on the ground in front of him. He stayed outside until the man delivering the morning paper left. Then he gathered up the bundle, pushed it under his jacket, and hustled into the building. When he came into the light, she saw that he wore dark clothes and had pulled a dark beret down over his hair"

"Why didn't she tell us this right away?"

"She forgot. She woke up because she had a migraine, took medication, and sat in the window while she waited for it to work."

"Did she recognize the man?"

"Not then, but that's why it all came back to her. Yesterday she thought a man in the elevator wearing a black cap was him."

"Too bad she didn't remember sooner, but later is better than never. Run yesterday's security footage for me."

Hollis did as she was told. At three fifteen, Agnes entered the elevator from the fourth floor, and on the third a man wearing a black hat got on. They watched as Agnes spoke and then waggled a finger at the man before both exited.

"Who is it?" Rhona demanded.

"My god," Hollis said as she digested what she'd seen.

"Run today's tape from early this morning. I want to know if he's gone out," Rhona ordered.

Tim O'Toole was in his apartment.

"Did he do it?" Hollis asked.

"Too soon to know for sure, but his actions put him in the frame," Rhona said before she sent Hollis out of the office.

"Ian, we have a suspect who remains in his apartment. Get a search warrant and brief Frank. I'll instruct them to approach quietly — no sirens. I'll make sure he stays where he is."

Rhona hung up and allowed herself a moment of relaxation before the chaos to come.

Hollis knocked on the door frame.

Rhona kept one eye on the camera. She didn't want the perp to escape.

"My friend called. Mary Montour left the reserve and he doesn't have her cell phone number."

"Let's hope she's on her way back," Rhona said and directed her attention back to the screen.

Hollis chose not to confide Norman's refusal to answer her question about Brownelly. Whatever his connection, he wouldn't share it. He suggested that she see him as soon as she could.

"Will you need anything else?" Hollis said.

Rhona shook her head.

Hollis backed out of the room. Whatever Norman revealed would be important. She checked the time. If she moved smartly she could combine a visit to him with a stop at St. Mike's and be back to pick up the girls.

Again she exercised care. She took the Yonge subway to Bloor Station and the Bloor line to St. George Station, where she jumped on the southbound train just as the doors were closing. On each leg of the trip she positioned herself at the end of the car and surveyed the other passengers. While some men and women from the first train transferred to the second, none from the first embarked on the third. When she reached Union Station she detoured upstairs, where the magnificence of the soaring building always impressed her. Then she sauntered back downstairs, grabbed a coffee at Tim Hortons, and moved through the connecting passage to the rail link to Queen's Quay. The whole process took more time than she'd anticipated, but she had to keep Norman safe.

Inside his apartment, she hugged him and mourned the loss of the young man he'd once been.

"Come. I made coffee and bought baklava from the grocery store next door."

Hollis felt her eyes widen. This man didn't leave the building.

Norman smiled. "You want to know how come I went out, when I told you that I never do."

"My face always gives me away," Hollis said.

"There's a connection between the two buildings through the garage. I don't go out. When I'm really paranoid, they leave my groceries downstairs."

Hollis helped herself to food and drink and waited for Norman to begin.

"Long story," he said and wriggled as if unsure about his position or where to begin.

"Straight narrative is best," Hollis said.

"I used to paint the countryside." He stopped.

"You claimed that if it was good enough for the Group of Seven it was good enough for you," Hollis said, smiling at the recollection.

"Sometimes, if it was mild and I didn't have money for a motel, I holed up in a barn or a deserted building. I always carried a bedroll and food," Norman said.

Silence stretched. Hollis decided to fill in the blanks and see if she was right. "You camped and woke up to find yourself in the middle of something bad?" she offered.

Norman's eyes widened and he straightened up. "How did you know? Who told you?"

"Norman, don't be paranoid. Where else would your story have been going?"

"Okay. I am paranoid. You're right. I watched terrible things happen. Because I'm a good and stupid person, I went to the police and told them what I'd seen."

"Stupid?"

"If I'd thought it through, I would have known that those men would come after me if they figured out who'd squealed. I testified *in camera*. The police wanted me to move somewhere and take on a new identity, but how can an established painter do that?"

"Do you want to tell me what you saw, or do you want to leave it?" Hollis asked, wondering if she wanted to know.

"I saw five men from a rival biker gang murdered. I heard every word they said and saw every horrible moment."

Hollis wished she hadn't asked.

"What connection does Calum Brownelly have with this story?"

"He was there, and early in the investigation the police called him 'a person of interest.'"

She didn't want to ask the question, but she had to. "Was he one of the murderers?"

As she waited for Norman's answer, she thought that this was far worse than anything she could have imagined. No wonder Norman had worried about her and Jay's safety. With the biker wars going on, kidnapping Jay would have given Hell's Angels a trump card. Now she knew why he'd insisted she walk the child to school.

Norman shook his head. "No, but he was there."

My God. Rhona had to know everything the moment she returned from St. Mike's.

TWENTY-EIGHT

HOLLIS cautiously retraced her steps but alighted from the subway at Queen and made her way to the hospital. First she'd check on Ginny and her ex-boyfriend. An inquiry at the desk told her Larry Baptiste remained in Emerg. She swung out of the building and picked her way through the smokers in hospital gowns who dragged their IV poles or sat in wheelchairs sucking down the smoke they craved. She walked north and turned into the ambulance entrance to the emergency ward.

For once a triage nurse was free and directed her through swinging doors and along a corridor to a four-bed holding area, where a police officer sat head down, nodding gently. Instead of waking him, she quietly peeked into each curtain-enclosed space. In the far corner she pulled back the curtain to see Ginny with Larry Baptiste's hand enfolded in hers, slumped forward with her head resting on the bed. She was asleep. Hollis was about to let the curtain fall and tiptoe away when Ginny opened her eyes, stared unseeing, and then recognized Hollis.

"How is he?" Hollis asked.

"Unconsciousness still."

"Take a break and I'll buy you breakfast downstairs," Hollis offered.

Ginny stroked the young man's hand. "I'll be right back, Larry," she said and stood up.

Hollis avoided the always packed coffee shop on the main floor and led Ginny through the maze of corridors to the entrance on Queen Street and a smaller, less popular Starbucks. They grabbed the corner booth next to the window. Ginny ordered carrot cake and a large latte.

"Have you talked to his doctor?" Hollis asked.

"I'm not a relative. I shouldn't even be there. No one tells you anything unless you're a relative." Ginny sagged forward and the tiny table rocked and threatened to spill their coffee.

Hollis steadied it. "Why do you think he climbed the scaffolding?"

"I know he wasn't going to kill me, and I'm sure he didn't kill Sabrina. Probably didn't think I'd let him in the building if he buzzed or in my apartment if he got in the building."

"Why would he think that you wouldn't let him in?"

Ginny shook her head. "I've been so stupid. You can't imagine how stupid." She considered her cup as if something important hid deep in the depths.

Hollis waited. As a community college teacher, she'd developed patience and learned to wait. Students, anxious to reveal information, often followed circuitous torturous routes to reach the subject they really needed to talk about.

Ginny picked cake crumbs from the paper napkin. "I thought I'd marry Larry and end up on the reserve with tons of kids and no life. We started to date in grade eight and planned to get married but I felt trapped, like I'd never have a life." She took a mouthful and swallowed. "Larry is a good guy. He works, doesn't drink, and loved me. I ruined everything." Tears trickled down her cheeks.

"What did you do?" Hollis said and wondered if she should have waited.

Ginny sighed. "It's so awful, I don't even want to tell you."

This time Hollis said nothing.

"We had a place to be alone in a building behind his parents' house. He works as a mechanic in Battleford and he fixed up the shed as a garage so he could also work on the reserve and make more money. He was saving up so we could get married and start off with nice stuff, and I knew where he hid the money he made on the reserve before he took it to the bank." She took a ragged breath. "One night when everyone had gone to bed I took a bag of my stuff over to the shed, stole the money and his truck." She stared at a spot on the floor waiting for Hollis to say something.

Hollis didn't comment.

"It was a real old junker, so I didn't get much past Battleford before it started to smoke. I chugged into a garage and asked the guy running the place if I could leave it there until I got back from Winnipeg. I didn't stop in the Peg. I hopped on a bus to Toronto. Jigs, a guy who seemed really nice, talked to me in the bus depot and offered to help me get established. That's how I ended up on the street, until Fatima rescued me but I already told you all that didn't I?"

"You did. I understand why Larry would think you wouldn't let him in."

"I would have," Ginny wailed. "Since Sabrina's murder I've been figuring out how to go home. I never stopped loving Larry, but he must hate me for what I did and what I'm doing."

"How did he find you?"

"After the murder I phoned my sister. I had to know how my family felt about me before I made plans to go home. When she said it would be okay, I asked her to send me a good luck charm I left at home." She shook her head. "I know it's crazy, but I figured it might keep me safe until I got back."

"But how did that connect to Larry?"

"I didn't know it, but Larry called my sister every couple of days asking if they'd heard from me. After my phone call, my sister told him where I was."

Ginny squeezed the paper cup so tight that coffee spurted upwards. "Maybe if he risked his life to climb that scaffolding in the dark, maybe he still loves me? If only he'd knocked on the window and told me it was him."

"Probably afraid you'd scream and call the police."

Ginny sighed. "Stupid me, that's exactly what I would have done."

They finished and walked around the building and back into Emerg. When they reached Larry Baptiste's bed, he was gone.

Hollis hadn't noticed if the cop was still sitting in the hall. She hurried back. He wasn't there. When a nurse trotted toward her, Hollis stopped her.

"Do you know where Larry Baptiste, the man in the coma, has gone?" she asked, praying that the nurse wouldn't say he'd died and been taken to the morgue.

"He's gone for more X-rays. He came around and they want to assess the damage."

"They'll send him back here?"

"Depending on what they find, we may admit him to the neurological ward."

"Where can we find out?"

The nurse, who'd been edging around Hollis, shook her head. "Wait. They'll bring him here before he goes anywhere."

Hollis went back and reported her conversation to Ginny.

"We shouldn't have left. If he's conscious, I could have told him how sorry I am."

"Ginny, you can do that, but don't be surprised if he doesn't take in what you're saying. If he's conscious he'll be confused. He took a terrible blow. We all heard his head hit the board. He'll be lucky if he regains his senses and is his old self."

Ginny stood rubbing the sheet between her fingers and shaking her head. "I should have waited, should have been here." She collapsed on the bed and gathered the pillow to her face. "It smells like him," she said, her voice muffled by the fabric.

Hollis didn't want to leave Ginny, but she had other issues to deal with. She'd turned her cell phone off in the hospital. What if Brownelly had returned her call?

"Ginny, I have to check my phone. I'm going outside but I'll be back."

The figure on the bed didn't move, didn't indicate she'd heard, but Hollis felt pretty sure she had.

Outside she shivered. A cold May day with a nippy wind and she'd left her jacket inside.

She had a message. "Ms. Grant. I phoned but you didn't answer. I will meet you at Druxy's in the Eaton Centre food court at twelve thirty."

Hollis flipped her wrist. Nearly eleven. Two blocks from St. Mike's to the Eaton Centre. Should she meet him, now that she knew what he did? Surely nothing would happen in the shopping centre with the hordes of people. She wasn't sure that was true, but she'd have to risk it because she wanted more answers.

She'd keep Ginny company for fifteen minutes and then find Agnes Johnson. *I'll be there,* she texted.

When she entered the corridor, an orderly pushing Larry on a stretcher preceded her. A nurse accompanied them and the police officer trailed behind. Hollis joined the procession but along with the officer stayed in the hall out of the way, knowing how little space there was for the orderly and nurse to skillfully transfer Larry from the stretcher back to the bed.

"Larry! Larry, you're awake."

Ginny's joy-filled voice carried to the hall. The officer and Hollis looked at one another and moved into the room.

Ginny was inches away from Larry's face, holding his hand.

"Hey, get back," the officer ordered. He reached to pull Ginny away.

"No, let her stay," Larry said in a voice so low that Hollis strained to hear. "She's my girl," he added.

"How can you forgive me? I took your money and your truck," Ginny whispered.

"I know why you did it. I rushed you. I scared you. I'm sorry."

"But ..."

His voice grew stronger. "No buts. It was a beater, not worth anything, and the guy you left it with found ID in the glove compartment and called me. I got it back. You only took the money I'd been paid for repairs I did on the reserve. It wasn't much. The rest is in a bank in Battleford. Ginny, I love you. It's okay." He shut his eyes. "I'm tired."

Hollis leaned over. "Ginny, I'm going now. Take care of him."

TWENTY-NINE

THE tactical squad members, old hands at arriving stealthily, drifted into the lobby. Rhona assured them that the perp remained in his apartment. Although Hollis had given her the master key, she wouldn't be the one to open the door. Once they'd secured the scene, she'd make the arrest and take him downtown for questioning while detectives searched the apartment. If they found what Rhona suspected they would, the case would be all but over.

When the squad knocked, announced its presence, and demanded entry, no one answered. The leader barked a second command to open, and when nothing happened, the squad, guns drawn, entered the apartment. A careful search confirmed it was empty.

Tim O'Toole, the prime suspect in a terrible murder, was gone.

How could that have happened? Rhona had checked the tapes from shortly after Larry Baptiste had been removed, and the man had neither entered nor left. He must have disappeared some time during the chaos, but what had alerted him? In her mind she ran the shots of Agnes Johnson standing with him in the elevator. Agnes had spoken to him and waggled her finger at him. Whatever she'd said it must have been enough to alert him that he needed to move on. Without hearing from the hospital, they'd assumed Agnes had had a heart attack or a stroke, but it now seemed more likely that O'Toole had assaulted her.

She phoned St. Mike's, spoke to the nurse in charge of Agnes Johnson's floor, and relayed her suspicions.

"That could be true. She hasn't responded like a stroke patient. We attributed it to the drug that was administered when she came in, but your explanation makes more sense."

"Is she well enough to talk to me"

"She certainly is."

First, the apartment. To help find Tim O'Toole, they'd uncover the secrets hidden in his apartment. The tactical squad left and Rhona, along with Ian and several of the forensic investigating team, began her work.

They each took a room. Rhona went to the bedroom. In the closet she checked hanger by hanger but found no blood-stained clothing. There was no sign of a laundry basket, no hamper for dirty clothes. She bent to look under the bed and saw two long plastic storage boxes, so she pulled them out.

When she snapped the first one open, she sat back and stared. Women's underwear of every conceivable kind filled the box. Teddies, bikini briefs, thongs, black lace bras, utilitarian white cotton jockey underwear. A peeping tom, an underwear thief. Obsessions that could lead to more serious crimes. Her stomach flipped and her mouth was dry as she contemplated what she might find in the next box.

Opening the lid released the stale, metallic smell of blood. Three Winners plastic bags filled the long container. Two bulging ones had large exclamation marks painted in red over the S in the logo.

Winner!

The third empty one lacked the punctuation. What did it mean?

In the first bag Rhona found blue jeans, a black hoodie, and black gloves, all stained and stiffened with dried blood. A red leather wallet lay beside the clothes. Before she examined the second bag, she flipped the wallet open. Nothing. No identification.

She opened the second bag and found a black T-shirt, black denim jacket, and black jeans similarly saturated with blood. Neatly tucked beside the black clothes, a discoloured pink handbag told her Sabrina's blood had stained the clothes. The third bag was waiting for its exclamation mark and the blood-stained clothes from a third stabbing.

Two questions — why was Tim O'Toole killing women, and who was next on his list? Thank God for Agnes Johnson and her nosiness but not for her intervention.

She called the team to the bedroom and pointed to the box and three bags.

"Two of these contain the perp's blood-stained clothing. There is an unsolved murder that relates to the wallet and the contents of the first bag. Unfortunately, the wallet is empty. The pink purse in the second bag belonged to Sabrina Trepanier. I'm sure we'll find that the blood is hers." She held up the third bag. "As you see, this is empty. He intends to kill again. We have to find him before he does." She snapped the lid back on the box. "Go through everything and create a picture of the man. If you can find a photo, that would be great, otherwise we'll use the one on the security tape for the police and for the media. We must find him before he attacks his third victim."

"When do you think he left?" Ian asked.

"We saw a shot of him in the elevator with Agnes Johnson. She was talking and appeared to admonish him. I suspect he left then or when the building filled with interested tenants and the response team last night. I'm on my way to talk to Agnes Johnson. I think I'll find out that she didn't have a stroke but was attacked by Tim O'Toole. Keep me informed about what you find."

THIRTY

AGNES Johnson was parked in the hospital corridor, slumped in a chair designed to keep geriatric patients from wandering. A tray fastened like a child's high chair prevented the person in the chair from escaping. Hollis was horrified. If ever she'd known an elderly person with all her wits about her, it was Agnes Johnson. But maybe the stroke had changed all that. Her elderly tenant slumped to one side, snoring loudly. Hollis tiptoed past. She waited at the nursing station where nurses in cheerful coloured uniforms did paperwork, spoke on the phone, and sorted files. Finally, a young woman looked up.

"Yes," she said and her voice conveyed the impression that this had better be good, because she was a busy nurse with no time to waste.

"I'm here to see Agnes Johnson. Is she ready to go home?"

"Well, *she* certainly thinks she is. Tried to do it and fell, so we popped her in the Geri chair. We're waiting for the doctor."

"Did she have a stroke?"

The woman neatened the pile of paper she held in her hand. "Are you a relative?"

"No. I'm her landlady."

"Sorry," the nurse said without a hint of sorrow in her voice.

"Hollis, is that you?" Agnes yelled.

Hollis hurried back to a very agitated Agnes. "Look what they've put me in. There's nothing wrong with me." She reached her veined, gnarled hand to pat her head. "A lump and that's it. The bugger hit me with something heavy. Smart guy — no blood, but I guess I was fortunate, 'cause when I answered the door, he pushed his way in and said I was lucky he didn't have time to cut me up, 'cause that's what he liked doing. Then he smashed me. When I came to in the ambulance I was confused and didn't remember what had happened." She shrugged. "I might have had another TIA."

"A what?'"

"Transient ischemic attack, a mini-stroke, because everything was blurry and I couldn't talk very well. I've had them before. Anyway, the paramedics must have figured I'd had a stroke and that's how I ended up in this bloody thing."

"Who hit you?" Hollis said, squatting to face Agnes.

"Who do you think? Tim O'Toole. Did you tell the police?"

Hollis patted Agnes's hand. "I did and they're dealing with him." Since she'd left before anything happened, she wasn't absolutely sure this was true.

Agnes frowned. "I've always barged in and said things I shouldn't have. When I rode down in the elevator with him, I told him I'd seen him hiding on Monday night and sneaking in with whatever he was carrying. I told him he should smarten up and get a life and not be out at night doing god knows what."

"What did he say?"

"Called me a nosy old bitch and told me I should mind my own business. Then I said that I was sure the police would like to hear what he'd been doing."

Hollis shook her head. A vulnerable woman on a walker, and she'd said that.

"Last night when I heard the sirens and watched the emergency team roar into the building, I was at the door, ready to come down to see what was happening, when he knocked and barrelled in. Next thing I knew I came to on the floor and crawled to the phone, grabbed it, and passed out again." She touched the back of her head. "Except for this bump and a headache, I'm fine. I want to go home."

Hollis stayed hunched down on her heels. It was painful, but she didn't want to tower over Agnes. "Agnes, I have to go." Hollis stood up, fished her card from her shoulder bag, squatted, and held it out to Agnes. "If it will help, say I'm your next of kin and ask the doctor to call me. As soon as you have permission to leave, I'll bring your walker. Detective Rhona Simpson will come to talk to you once she knows what happened."

"Since I don't have any family, I'll claim you as my niece." She smiled and Hollis noted that she had her own teeth. "It would be nice to have you, your daughter, and your dogs as family."

"From now on that's who we are," Hollis said and patted Agnes's shoulder.

As Hollis headed to the elevator, she met Rhona.

"I have news for you," Hollis said.

"Hearing those words from you is enough to frighten me," Rhona said, widening her eyes and raising her eyebrows. "Tell me."

"I assume you know Ginny Wuttenee's background?" She didn't wait for Rhona to answer but plowed on. "She and Larry Baptiste have reconciled. He's not pressing charges because he got his truck back and would have loaned her the money. As soon as he's better and you say it's okay, they're heading back to Red Pheasant and ..."

"There's more?"

"Tim O'Toole attacked Ms. Johnson. She's parked out in the hall in a Geri chair, but there's nothing wrong with her other than she hates being in it and is driving the nurses crazy. She'll tell you all about it."

"That's it?"

Hollis nodded. "I have a question for you?"

Rhona shuffled as if preparing to launch. "Try me."

"Was Veronica the murdered woman that you found?"

"She was."

"Do you know who killed her?"

Rhona eyed Hollis.

"I know that look. You're going to tell me you're not at liberty to say."

"Right."

Hollis stuck out her hand and Rhona took it. "Don't you think we make a great team?" Hollis said, giving her best wicked grin and shaking the detective's hand.

"You're too much. Go home and walk those beasts," Rhona said, withdrawing her hand and moving past Hollis.

Instead of following Rhona's instructions, Hollis headed for the Eaton Centre, wondering about Brownelly and why he'd agreed to meet her. She pushed through the midday throng clogging Queen Street and entered the Eaton Centre, stopping briefly to covet the spring collection in the Town Shoes window before she propelled through the revolving doors to the first floor. She curved right toward the escalators. On her way down she admired the wonderful mix of people, letting her eyes absorb the variety. As she surveyed the crowd below in the food court, her gaze locked with Cartwright's.

Cartwright.

Why was he here? Was it because of Brownelly? The fury in Cartwright's eyes frightened her and she averted her gaze. When she looked again he was gone. Maybe she'd imagined him?

Brownelly sat with his back to the wall deep inside the eating area. He didn't rise as she approached. Instead he moved the tray, which held a hamburger, fries, and drink closer to him and popped a French fry in his mouth. When she sat down, he didn't offer to get her anything. Boor.

"You keep bugging me. What is it you want to know?" he said while chewing a giant mouthful of hamburger with his mouth open. A piece of shredded lettuce clung to his chin. Hollis felt no compulsion to tell him and even less to reach across and remove it.

"More background. Why did you give Jay up? How old was she? Why haven't you made a home for her? What do you do that you're gone for long periods? Why does the CAS want you to see your daughter at their offices?" She sat back and waited.

He took another gigantic bite and talked around it. "Jay was three when her mother died." He swallowed. "Her mother was murdered."

Hollis hadn't expected anything like this. She didn't know what to say.

"Surprised! It was a gang shootout and she was in the wrong place."

If he'd been in a gang then he could have been the target. In effect, he would have been responsible. What could she say? It only made it worse if they'd been after him.

"That's terrible."

"You have no idea."

Hollis nodded. "No. I don't." She wanted more answers but it would be better to allow him to proceed at his own speed.

"Neither my wife nor I had relatives in Canada, and I wasn't sending a three-year-old to the U.K. to a distant cousin. I asked the Children's Aid to find a good foster home for her, and they did."

"You didn't consider a housekeeper, a nanny?"

Brownelly tipped his head to one side. "No. To understand why, you'd have to know a lot more about my life than

I'm prepared to tell you. Let's just say it wasn't an option. One of these days I hope to provide a home for Jay, but not right now."

She did know a lot more about his life. She knew why it wasn't an option. "I'm going to speak out of turn. She's eleven. You've missed more than half her childhood. You need to make a home for her. It's not my business, but someday you'll be sorry if you don't act now."

The man stood up. "It is none of your business. I love Jay. Look after my baby and keep her safe."

THIRTY-ONE

WHEN Rhona learned what Agnes Johnson had said to Tim O'Toole, she surmised that the man had escaped during the chaos the previous night. Now her task was twofold, preferably to find and arrest him, but if that didn't happen to figure out who his next victim might be. She hated to admit it even to herself, but Hollis Grant might help. Hollis had told Rhona that she'd interviewed street prostitutes when she was looking for Mary Montour. It was a long shot, but Hollis might have discovered a woman who had had a run-in with Tim O'Toole. Back to 68 Delisle.

Early afternoon and the building was quiet. She buzzed Hollis.

"It's Rhona Simpson. I have questions for you."

Hollis invited her into the apartment, where the two dogs greeted her. The Golden Retriever presented her with a stuffed bear that needed to go in the washing machine, while the other dog nosed her hand looking for patting. Rhona wasn't a big fan of dogs, a fact that Hollis must have remembered.

"Dogs. Go and lie down."

Amazingly, they did. Rhona couldn't imagine a cat doing that or even acknowledging that it had been given an order.

"I need to bring you up to speed on what's been happening and then you'll know if you can help."

* * *

Hollis felt her eyebrows lift and her eyes open wider. Since when had Rhona requested her help? Always a first time. She folded her feet under her on the couch and settled back.

"First, Barney Cartwright escaped before we could charge him with Veronica's murder."

Hollis swung her feet to the floor and straightened up. "I saw him less than an hour ago in the food court in the Eaton Centre. He gave me the evil eye, and the next time I looked he was gone."

Rhona flipped open her phone and relayed the information with a caution to be careful, since they had to assume he was armed and dangerous."

"That was a bonus I wasn't expecting. What were you doing in the food court?" Rhona grimaced. "Stupid question. What does anyone do in a food court?"

"I met my foster daughter's father. I wanted to talk about her and about him, but he didn't give me much satisfaction. He's a mysterious man who appears and disappears, and I wanted to know more about him. He wasn't into sharing."

Rhona showed no interest in Jay's father. "I talked to Agnes Johnson. Tim O'Toole attacked her. I don't know if he intended to kill her or warn her off, but he did it because he thought she knew more than she did and he wanted to shut her up. Women of that generation are tough and he didn't succeed."

"What did he think she knew?"

"That he murdered Sabrina Trepanier."

"What!" Hollis leaned forward. "You're kidding. He's such a nothing kind of guy."

"We have evidence he's killed before and may kill again. That's where you come in."

"Me. I hardly knew him."

Rhona shook her head. "Wrong track. We think he's killed women, prostitutes, who have refused and rejected him. Fatima told us that Sabrina had been quite nasty when he propositioned her. I know that you did your research on Mary and what she was up to. Did you talk to her fellow workers or any of the women on the street about who might have frightened or threatened them?"

"Before I tell you, I want to know if the police knew what she was doing before I told you?"

"No."

"It seems like such a thankless, never-ending challenge. I can't imagine how she continued year after year with so many failures."

"Half full, half empty. She must have seen it as half full. Never mind what she was doing. Did you talk to anyone who might give us some clues about Tim O'Toole."

Hollis reviewed the conversations that she'd had. "I think so. A young Aboriginal prostitute I talked to one morning while she was having breakfast gave me some information. Initially, hostile didn't begin to describe her attitude. She ranted at me but calmed down and while we were talking, she did say that she chose who she wanted to go with. I must have looked as if I doubted her, since she gave me chapter and verse about the most recent man she'd refused. Thinking about her description, which wasn't much, it could have been Tim."

"Would you recognize her again?"

Hollis nodded.

Rhona checked her watch. "We should go see. She's probably home at this time of day but maybe we can find out where she lives."

Hollis fidgeted and didn't respond.

"You don't seem enthusiastic?"

"I'm not. I'll volunteer to go, but I don't think we should go together."

Rhona smiled. "Tactful, aren't you? Okay, you go. Don't do anything rash. If you see Tim O'Toole, report to us immediately but *do not*, I repeat, *do not* approach him."

Before she set out on her mission, Hollis made sure the dogs were okay and that there were no priority calls from tenants. She slipped on her denim jacket, shouldered her bag, and left checking that no one who seemed threatening hovered near the building. She waited until three high school girls giggled their way toward Yonge Street before she left the portico, fell in behind them, and turned into the subway entrance. On the platform she followed her routine and stood with her back against the wall, well away from everyone. On Jarvis Street she sauntered along, keeping an eye out for her quarry.

Inside the Golden Goose restaurant, she greeted Bridget, remembering that both Bridget and her coworker had asked her to let them know if she heard from Mary. She felt a pang of guilt. Why hadn't she remembered to do that? Sometimes you got so involved in what you wanted that you forgot your common decency responsibilities to others.

"Did you find Mary?" Bridget asked, positioning herself so that her ever-present boss couldn't see her talking.

"I did. I apologize for not telling you that she's okay. Now I need the name and where I can find a pretty Aboriginal girl I spoke to when I was here. You'd left with your husband, but I thought you might know her."

"More than one come in here. Can you describe her?"

"Long, dark hair with neon red streaks, small scar on her forehead over her eyebrow. I can't remember which one, but I noticed what good skin she had other than the scar. She was hostile."

"That makes it easier. Her first name's Darlene — don't know her last name."

Bridget bent forward and wiped the table.

Hollis didn't have much hope that Bridget could answer her next question, but it was worth a try. "Where can I find her?"

"I'll get you coffee," Bridget said.

"No thanks. It's urgent that I find her."

"Urgent. That doesn't sound good. She was in earlier and she's sick. Something viral, probably. She was wheezing and coughing. One of the other girls told her to go home to bed and she'd pick up some medication and bring it to her place." The coffee in the pot in Bridget's hand sloshed from side to side. "I don't know where she lives, but I know where her friend lives, because she was complaining about it the other day. It's infested with bedbugs and she was looking for a new place and wondering how to make sure she didn't take the bugs with her. It's a building on Shuter. I'll write down her name and the address." She pulled out her order pad and scribbled the information.

Hollis thanked her and walked over to Shuter Street, where she found the building, buzzed the apartment, and explained why she was there.

Standing inside the door, she noticed how tidy the place was and acknowledged that when she'd been told about the bedbugs, she'd expected a dump. She hoped she wouldn't be invited in and told herself that when she got home she should strip off her clothes and stuff them into a garbage bag ready for the laundry.

"Tell me again who you are and exactly why you want to find Darlene?" the young woman with bleached, tightly curled hair asked. Without makeup, she appeared alarmingly young, too thin, and exhausted. Hollis wondered if she was supporting an addiction. The girl didn't invite Hollis to sit down, so Hollis didn't have to invent a reason for remaining at the door.

"She may be in danger. A call girl was murdered in the apartment building where I work. The police officer in charge of the case knew I'd talked to women in the Golden Goose when I searched for Mary Montour. Darlene told me something the detective thought might make her a target and asked me to find her, because she may be in danger."

The girl held up a hand as if to stop the torrent of words. "Whoa. Start at the beginning — what you're saying doesn't make sense. Who's Mary Montour?"

"Mary, the Aboriginal waitress at the Golden Goose. She disappeared a few days ago and left her eleven-year-old niece behind. I'm looking after the child and I started tracking Mary to see where she might be. I talked to Bridget, Sandy, and Darlene. Mary is okay. But this doesn't have anything to do with Mary. The murdered woman had turned down a possible client and we think he killed her because of that. Darlene told me she didn't go with men she didn't want to go with and gave me a vague description of a man she'd refused. I think it might have been the man the police think killed the woman in my building, and I want to find Darlene and warn her."

"Why aren't the cops doing this?"

"Because the detective knew I'd been asking about Mary and had spoken to Darlene and believed I might have a better chance of finding her in time."

"*In time*. That's scary. She lives near here. I'll write down the address. There isn't any security, so go up and knock on the door. Darlene may not answer, because I bought her a ton of heavy duty stuff for whatever she's got."

Hollis grabbed the paper and headed for the stairs. She hoped she'd be in time.

THIRTY-TWO

HOLLIS found the seedy low-rise without difficulty. She pushed into the small lobby where the reek of a thousand cheap meals, unwashed diapers, and cat urine assailed her. She fumbled in her shoulder bag for a scarf to put over her nose but came up empty. The lobby was awash in discarded flyers and envelopes. The mailboxes, some of them pried open, told her C. Ross lived in 312. There was no buzzer, no inner door to protect the tenants from unwanted visitors, and no elevator. A glance upward in the unlit stairwell revealed empty sockets where light bulbs had once been. At night when she walked the dogs, she always pocketed a flashlight to enable her to pick up after them. She scrabbled in her bag before she remembered she'd left it at home hanging up with the leashes by the door. How she wished she had it now. In her purse her hand touched her cell phone and she hauled it out.

It was turned off.

How could she have been so careless? She allowed a minute or two for it to pick up messages. A text message from Rhona asked her to call.

She tapped in the number and was instructed to leave a message.

"I've found Darlene. I'll call again when I've warned her." She picked her way upwards.

On the third floor a dirty window at the end of the corridor allowed her to see the numbers on the doors. Her target, 312, was at the end.

She knocked but there was no answer, which was odd, as the girl who'd given the lead said Darlene had gone home to bed. A second flurry of banging also elicited no response. Maybe the girl was asleep or had gulped down so many pills that she'd passed out. Hollis tried the door and found it unlocked. To enter or not? Darlene might need help if she'd taken too much medication. Ill or not, she needed to be warned about Tim O'Toole.

Hollis pushed the door open and braked as her eyes registered what her mind was unwilling to believe.

Tim O'Toole stood facing her with one arm clutching Darlene and the second holding a knife to her throat. A thin line of blood trickled down her neck. Darlene's ashen face told the tale, as did the smell of urine and fear.

"My god," Hollis said. Her stomach lurched and her mouth went dry.

"Close the door and lock it. Don't make a sudden move or I'll slit her throat."

Hollis reached behind her, grabbed the metal knob, and clicked her fingers against it to make a sound she hoped would convince O'Toole that she'd locked it.

At that moment Darlene coughed. A harsh hacking noise filled the room as she sagged back against Tim. "I'm sick," she moaned.

"Not for long," Tim said and produced what must have been intended as a laugh but came out as a croak. "Nosy landlady. Couldn't leave well enough alone. Had to meddle. Too bad. Your daughter and your dogs will miss you."

Why hadn't she waited to actually talk to Rhona? What did this insane man plan to do? Surely he wouldn't murder both of them in a downtown apartment building in the middle of the day. What was she thinking? What did the time of day have to do with it? Should she scream? In this neighbourhood screams were not uncommon and were probably ignored. A scream would enrage Tim O'Toole. No. She'd try to play it cool, try to talk him down, try to buy time hoping that Rhona would figure out where she was, although that wasn't likely.

She was on her own.

"I'm going to enjoy this," O'Toole said. "Usually I wait until my ladies are asleep. It's the gurgle, the spurting blood that I enjoy, but now I can do it bit by bit. This could take a long time. It can take hours for a person to bleed out."

"The police know it's you," Hollis said and regretted the wimpy statement almost immediately.

"Maybe so, but they have to catch me." He frog-walked Darlene across the room to the kitchen table in front of an open window. He pushed her down on one of two chrome-and-red-plastic kitchen chairs oozing kapok stuffing. "Maybe decorations would be fun," he said. "Tattoos? Now what would be appropriate for these two?"

Decorations? Tattoos? He was mad. She shifted from one foot to the other and wondered if it would be worth it to bolt.

"If you run, she's dead," O'Toole said in a level voice. He kept the knife at Darlene's throat and pulled two pieces of yellow plastic rope from his jacket pocket. "You," he nodded at Hollis, "come over here and tie Miss High and Mighty Too Good to Have Sex With Me to the chair. I know knots and I'll tell you how."

Could she knock him over and get them out? What if she refused to move? He couldn't grab her because he was holding Darlene. But Darlene wouldn't be any help. Hollis mentally measured the distance.

As if he'd read her thoughts, O'Toole said, "Move or I kill her." His lips curled. "I'll enjoy it."

"Please do what he says," Darlene begged and coughed.

"Bitch, put your hands behind you and behind the chair," he ordered.

Darlene lifted her shaking hands but seemed unable to make them move.

O'Toole gave her a jab with the tip of the knife. "Hurry up." The blood trickling down her neck flowed faster.

Still holding the knife to her throat, once her hands were positioned, he moved to the side. "Bitch landlady, wind the rope around her hands and around the chair then tie a simple knot, left over right, right over left, and under."

Hollis gauged whether she could shove him aside but dismissed the thought. She couldn't risk Darlene's life. She obeyed.

"Bitch, now it's your turn. Pull that chair," he pointed to a second chair, "over here and back it up against the first one."

Hollis's cell phone rang. She looked at O'Toole.

"A little excitement. Go ahead. Let's see what kind of an actress you are. Say you're busy and you'll call them back," O'Toole instructed.

God, she hoped it was Rhona. And that she could think fast enough to find the right words to alert her. There wasn't much time. Her knees felt like they might give way and her mouth was so dry she didn't know if words would come out.

It was Rhona. Tears blurred her vision. Maybe they had a chance. She listened and responded. "No. Not now. I left it at the Golden Goose restaurant." Could she risk leaving it on, hoping Rhona would hear the conversation?

"Turn it off," O'Toole ordered.

She clicked it off, praying Rhona had heard him and would get what she'd tried to communicate.

O'Toole left Darlene for a moment and lurched toward Hollis, wielding the knife. "What did you leave at the restaurant?" he demanded.

Think fast. Something plausible and non-threatening. "That was my daughter. I borrowed her iPod the other day and left it in a bag at the restaurant." She tried a smile. "You know how kids are. They love their gadgets."

O'Toole stared at her. "Toss the phone on the table. No more calls. We have decorating to do." He stepped back, moved the knife an inch or two away from Darlene's neck, and ran his finger gently along the blade. "Nice and sharp. Good for a tattoo. Bitches, choose what you want me to make."

A sadistic, chilling laugh.

Damn him. I'll play his fucking game, Hollis thought. "Takes an artist to make a tattoo," she said. "Takes more than an amateur's couple of cuts."

He sneered. "How 'bout X's and O's. Don't need to be an artist for that, it's pretty simple. Hold out your arm."

Hollis gritted her teeth and extended it.

"You can play too. Won't that be fun?"

Hollis said nothing.

O'Toole incised a line on her hand. Blood welled.

"No. Your hand has too many veins, too bumpy. Your wrist would be better. I can always slit it if I get bored. Turn your arm over."

When Hollis did as she was told, blood dripped on the floor.

Two parallel lines and two vertical.

It hurt like hell.

O'Toole smiled.

Hollis shivered. It was technically a smile, because his lips curved upward, but it was a predator's victorious acknowledgement that he had his victims and like a cat intended to amuse himself with them, watch their terror and pain until he'd satisfied himself.

O'Toole stepped away from Hollis and pointed to her hand. "Not flowing fast enough to kill you. I think I'll have a smoke and watch you two. You stand over there beside Darlene. I'll run through the options of how to kill you, and I'll let you choose which one you prefer. Maybe you'll each choose a different one — that would be fun."

After Hollis moved and still holding the knife at Darlene's throat, he slid a pack of cigarettes from his shirt pocket, pulled out a lighter, and lit up.

Hollis hated cigarettes, but right now she welcomed anything that slowed him down and would give the police a chance to find them if Rhona had picked up and understood her message.

He used his free hand to blow smoke in Darlene's face as he leaned forward and again jabbed her neck. He chuckled as blood welled and dribbled down.

Darlene coughed before she sobbed. "Please let us go. We won't tell anyone."

Hollis recognized the futility of pleading. A sadist loved to watch his victims, and there was no doubt that they were in the clutches of a sadist. Their only hope was to distract him. She would call on every acting skill she possessed to feed his need to enjoy their pain the pain and terror she felt.

Not that it would be hard. The fine line would be keeping him on the hook without antagonizing him to the point where he got fed up and killed them.

"You won't tell anyone," O'Toole said. "Isn't that rich? You'd run screaming to the cops the second you had a chance." He shook his head. "Where were you when they were handing out brains? You probably thought they said 'trains' and decided you'd rather fly. I'm not stupid, so don't insult my intelligence."

He sucked on his cigarette and blew a perfect smoke ring.

"How did you do that?" Hollis asked, although she didn't give a crap. Anything to keep him occupied.

"Why? You thinking of taking up smoking?"

"I used to smoke. Everybody used to smoke, but I could never make one of those," Hollis said.

"Now the fucking do-gooders won't let you smoke anywhere," O'Toole said, taking another deep drag. He considered Hollis. "You used to smoke, did you?"

She nodded.

"Well how about you do it again and I'll teach you how to blow smoke rings. Acquire a new skill before you die."

Shit. She'd throw up. The truth was she'd never smoked and hate the smell of it.

"But how do I do that?" He leaned forward and passed her the lit cigarette. "Remember? You suck in the smoke and exhale."

Hollis did as she was told. It was vile. Beyond vile. She gagged.

O'Toole watched her. "Makes you feel sick, doesn't it? Good. Now hold a mouthful and then curl your tongue, make a perfect circle with your mouth, and exhale."

After several unsuccessful attempts, Hollis felt woozy and uncentred, as if her legs might give way. "Could I sit down before I fall down?" she asked.

"I'd rather see you fall down," O'Toole said. "You keep standing and keep smoking."

Hollis's cigarette had burned down to her fingers.

"Keep holding it. A little taste of the pain to come," he said.

Shit, enough was enough. Hollis dropped it. If she didn't step on it, it might start a fire. Would the fire department get there in time to save them? Not likely and even more unlikely the O'Toole would let it happen. She stomped on the butt.

"Tut, tut, you're not being an obedient girl. Disobedient girls must be punished," O'Toole said and slapped her face.

Hollis recoiled. Her face burned.

"More, much more if you don't do what I tell you," O'Toole said as he lit another cigarette and passed it to Hollis.

She resolved to take small puffs to make it last longer.

Ten cigarettes later, Hollis, overcome with nausea, sank to the floor, landing in a puddle of her own blood, which had dripped steadily as she underwent torture by smoke.

While O'Toole had been toying with Hollis, he'd ignored Darlene, who slumped on her chair. Her coughing accelerated as Hollis filled the room with smoke.

O'Toole booted Hollis. "Get up, bitch. I'm not finished," he said.

Hollis rolled on her hands and knees and attempted to rise.

O'Toole kicked her hands and she collapsed again. "Stand up," he ordered.

Darlene coughed, choked, coughed again, and spewed vomit.

"Shit." O'Toole said. "Enough of these games. Time for the real stuff."

THIRTY-THREE

BACK in the department Rhona questioned whether she should have entrusted the search for Tim O'Toole's possible next victim to Hollis. Before she formulated an answer, her phone buzzed. It was Ian, who'd remained at the O'Toole apartment.

"He was a spy tech nut," Ian said.

"What did you find?"

"Long distance scopes, night vision goggles, lock picks, a variety of bugs. Surprisingly, given his fascination with these things, his computer didn't require a password and we accessed it immediately."

"Keep going."

"We found a computer program that tracks any bug he's planted. An officer with us activated a search and," he paused.

"Never mind the high drama," Rhona said.

"Sorry, not intentional. An officer just showed me two ingenious devices. I've seen the outlet adapter listening device before but not the calculator. Anyway, what I was about to say was that somehow O'Toole managed to attach a bug to the pink coat we found at the murder scene. He'd been tracking Sabrina."

"That's how he knew she was sleeping in Ginny's apartment. Sabrina *was* the intended victim." Rhona thought of Hollis following up leads to find the Aboriginal woman who might have given Tim O'Toole a hard time. Hollis could be in trouble if O'Toole had bugged the woman. An adrenalin rush.

She'd made a serious mistake. She shouldn't have asked Hollis to find the prostitute. "Any other active ones?"

"One at a location we identified as the Goodwill store on Richmond Street. I've sent an officer there to find it."

"If it's a Goodwill shopper we'll pick her up. He's out there somewhere. Now that we know how he pinpoints his target, we have to get to her first. Anything else?"

"Collection of knives. Seventeen very sharp ones, and he has an electric knife sharpener."

"Bring everything in for forensics. We should find traces of the two victims' blood. I'll check for a missing or murdered prostitute. He targeted the ones who turned him down."

Rhona punched in Hollis's cell phone number. It went to message immediately. Did that mean Hollis had turned it off or that she was in trouble? Surely, because of her daughter, Hollis always kept it on, and if it was turned off, Hollis needed help. How could Rhona find her? Stupidly, she hadn't asked the name of the restaurant on Jarvis Street, but when Hollis mentioned its name, she'd had a fleeting thought. What had it been? She wanted to reach up in her subconscious and retrieve the information. A fairy story, it had related to a fairy story, and had something to do with food. She wanted to scream.

What had it been called?

Maybe one of the beat cops could tell her, but how would she phrase the question? A wild goose chase. Wild goose? Golden Goose — that was it, the goose that laid the golden egg. She picked up the phone and set the machinery in motion to have an officer check to see if Hollis had been there and if anyone knew where she'd gone.

While she waited she ignored the uneasy feeling in her stomach and returned to her search for the possible first victim. She fed information into her computer and waited for the cross-referencing to find a victim. In short order she read that a young drug addict from the burbs who'd hustled on Jarvis Street to pay for a drug habit had disappeared the previous month. They'd start with this woman. If her DNA matched the blood in the Winners bag, finding the body would be the next problem. She thought of the Russell Williams case, in which the perp had given precise directions to find his victim. Maybe they'd have that kind of luck when they tracked down Tim O'Toole.

Her phone buzzed again.

"The bug is attached to a woman's jacket donated to Goodwill."

Not a useful lead. Why hadn't Hollis turned on her cell phone? Rhona punched in the numbers again. Four rings.

"Yes."

"Hollis, are you okay?"

"No. Not now. I left it at the Golden Goose restaurant."

Rhona heard a man's voice tell Hollis to hang up.

He had her.

Were they in the restaurant or was Hollis telling her that someone at the restaurant knew where she was? She called for a car, grabbed her bulletproof vest from her locker, and had the siren screaming as they headed to Jarvis Street.

Officers, guns drawn, went in first. Everyone inside froze. The police moved through the restaurant into the kitchen and returned.

"Not here," one said to Rhona, who'd waited outside. Inside, Rhona stopped just inside the door and addressed the patrons who sat in stunned silence. "I'm looking for Hollis Grant, who came here looking for another woman."

A waitress stepped forward. "I'm Bridget. Hollis came here less than an hour ago and asked about a woman named Darlene. Because I didn't know where Darlene lived, I sent her to a friend of hers on Shuter Street, because I was sure she did know." Her lips curved into a nervous smile. "I have the address." She pulled her order pad from her pocket and scribbled on it.

"Thanks," Rhona said over her shoulder on her way out the door. She directed the waiting officers.

They approached the apartment carefully, believing Tim O'Toole might have caught Hollis there, but they were out of luck. Darlene's friend's eyes widened as the police swept through her apartment. When she saw Rhona, the only woman officer in the group, she gravitated to her.

"What are you looking for?"

"Your friend Darlene and it's urgent. Give me her address." Rhona handed her notebook and pen to the young woman, who wrote the address in large, loopy script.

The tactical squad regrouped outside the building.

"If he's holding the women, we proceed with caution," Rhona said. "It's a third-floor apartment. What's the best way to get them out?"

"We'll locate the apartment and the fire escapes. We'll have officers outside as well as in and on the fire escape in case the perp makes a run for it. We go in quietly. Knock on the door. Tell him we're there and see what happens."

"Guessing that when he sees there's no way out he'll give up?" Rhona asked.

"That's the hope. Let's go."

Rhona had seen Hollis in tough situations before but none quite as bad as this.

THIRTY-FOUR

A prolonged, gagging cough and the unmistakable sound of vomiting.

No time to wait.

"Police. Open the door." Guns drawn, the officers tried the door, found it unlocked, and rushed inside.

Hollis, not yet tied up, dove for the door the moment the police entered the room. They grabbed her and pushed her behind them and out the door. She moved no farther than the hall.

O'Toole stood with his knife at Darlene's throat.

The police stopped.

"One more step and she dies. Why don't you shoot me? I'll kill her as I go," O'Toole said in a mocking voice.

The squad's negotiator introduced himself and said, "Time to let her go. It's all over."

O'Toole grinned at them. "I don't think so."

Hollis, standing in the hall, saw a movement at the window behind O'Toole. An officer appeared, squatted, and rested his gun on the bottom frame of the partially open window.

The negotiator, still talking, shifted to one side.

Hollis realized he'd removed himself from the line of fire.

"Let her go," the negotiator said.

"Not now. Not ever. In fact, I'll enjoy watching all your faces when I kill her," O'Toole said and deepened the cut in Darlene's neck.

The officer at the window fired.

Chaos.

O'Toole, his arm pumping blood, dropped the knife. Officers subdued and cuffed him, untied Darlene, and called for an ambulance.

"I took too many drugs," Darlene murmured and passed out.

A second officer turned to Hollis. "You okay?"

Hollis nodded. Her arms and legs felt like jelly. She leaned against the wall and tried to control her trembling.

Rhona appeared. "You sure you're okay?" she said.

Hollis held out her arms without saying anything.

Rhona saw the bloody lines. "What the hell?" she said.

"X's and O's. His sadistic idea of a joke," Hollis said and burst into tears. She choked and repeated, "A joke, some joke."

Rhona handed her a tissue and patted her back. Hollis, tears dribbling down her cheeks, her lips trembling, looked up at her.

"It's okay. Don't talk. Try taking deep breaths," Rhona said.

Hollis pulled in a lungful of air and released it slowly. Two repeats and she felt more in control. "I had something to tell you," she said to Rhona, who'd been watching her with concern.

"Go ahead."

"Did you know he wanted to kill Darlene because she'd refused to have sex? He called her miss high and mighty who wouldn't have sex with him."

"That fits. Ms. Nesrallah told us that Sabrina rebuffed a man in the building."

Hollis checked her watch. "I'm going to be late getting the girls."

Rhona picked up Hollis's arm. "This needs to be treated."

"No. It's stopped bleeding. Leave it. I have to get the girls," Hollis said.

"I think you should be treated," Rhona said.

"No. I'll do something about them at home, but they're really not deep. I'll be fine."

"Okay if you're sure. We'll get you there," Rhona said and commandeered an officer with instructions to drive Hollis.

Hollis phoned the school before she jumped into the police car. Speeding north on Jarvis Street, she turned on her cell phone and picked up a message.

"I heard on the news that the police are asking anyone who has seen Cartwright to turn him in. If he's on the lam, I figure it's safe for me to come back to the apartment, because he won't go there. See you soon. Thank you for taking care of Crystal."

Good news doubled. O'Toole captured. Mary Montour returning. All they needed now was Cartwright's arrest. Willem needed to be in on the good news. He was in class but she sent him a message and asked him to come to the apartment as soon as he could.

At the school, before she rushed inside, she made sure the cuts O'Toole had made were covered by her clothing.

Jay and Crystal waited patiently.

"Where are the dogs?" Jay asked.

"I didn't have time to go home and get them. I have great news for you."

The girls waited expectantly.

"Crystal's aunt is on her way to Toronto. Sabrina's murderer is in jail." She didn't say that she'd been in a terrifying situation and felt like she might never stop the internal quaking.

"I'm glad she's okay, glad she's coming home," Crystal said, but her voice didn't sound happy.

"I'm going to miss sharing my room with you," Jay said.

Crystal muttered, "Me too," as she stomped along with a frown etching her brow.

In the apartment lobby, Mary, who was perched on one of the three couches, jumped to her feet, raced toward them, and wrapped her arms around Crystal. "I'm so glad to see you, to know you're okay."

Crystal pulled away and hugged herself. "Why did you leave me behind?" she said accusingly.

"I had to move fast. Veronica's ex-boyfriend, Barney Cartwright, was hunting her. She planned to run away first thing on Tuesday. The night before she gave me an envelope and asked me to send it to the police if anything happened to her. I urged her to go right to the police, not to wait, but she was nervous. She said Cartwright could arrange to have her killed anywhere, anytime, and she planned to change her identity so he couldn't find her. Tuesday morning just before I left for work, Bridget phoned from the restaurant to warn me that a man who sounded like it was Cartwright had been looking for me. I guess he figured that Veronica would tell me her plans and intended to kill me too. Cartwright was, *is*, dangerous. I got out as fast as I could."

Hollis considered Mary's words. Had Mary even tried to warn Veronica, or had she simply jumped in her car and left?

Perhaps the question had been etched on her face.

"Veronica wasn't there when I left. She hadn't told me she was going anywhere, and I didn't want to wait. For all I knew Cartwright might already have got her. I couldn't risk staying. I had you to think about you," she said to Crystal.

"That would be a first," Crystal mumbled.

Mary bent down until her gaze locked with Crystal's. "I *never* wanted to involve you in what I do, but maybe now is the time to tell you."

Crystal said nothing but didn't pull away.

"I try to rescue our women who are on drugs. I do it because of my sister, your mother. Drugs destroyed her." She grabbed Crystal's hands. "If I can save *one* woman from your mother's fate, from dying from an overdose of bad drugs, I'll feel that maybe your mother didn't die in vain."

Crystal's expression didn't change, but some of the tension seemed to leave her body. "Why didn't you tell me? Maybe I could have helped?"

Mary sighed. "Maybe I should have, but you'd had such a rough time, I wanted you to have a normal childhood and not worry about things."

"I thought you didn't like me, that you only took me because Grandma was so sick."

Mary shook her head and sighed again. "Telling the whole truth is always the best way. I knew that. I'm sorry. I was trying to do the right thing for you. I love you just like I loved your mother, and I only want the best for you."

Crystal sobbed and threw herself into Mary's arms. Over her head Mary gave Hollis a rueful smile. "Sometimes you do the wrong things for the right reasons," she said and rocked Crystal back and forth.

"Where are the papers that Veronica gave to you?" Hollis asked.

"Safe," Mary said.

"You need to tell the police your story and turn them over, and you should do it sooner rather than later. You never know. There could be something in there that would help them track Cartwright." Hollis reached in her pocket. "Let me call Detective Simpson."

Mary nodded.

Hollis punched in the number. "Hollis Grant here. Mary Montour is with me at the apartment building and she has information about Barney Cartwright that you need to see immediately." She snapped the phone off. "She's coming right away. I'd stay with you but I have to walk the dogs. Stay here.

Lock the door until the police arrive. Later, have dinner with us," Hollis said as she moved to collect the leashes.

Two good outcomes but too soon to lower her guard. Cartwright was out there. She wouldn't walk to the nearby park where the dogs could run free, because not many people used it at this time of day. Instead they'd trot north on Yonge Street past Mount Pleasant cemetery, where plenty of people would be around. No point having something bad happen at this stage.

After an uneventful walk she found Jay and Crystal watching TV with the volume turned down. Mary was napping on the sofa. Hollis examined the fridge to see what she could rustle up for dinner. When her cell phone rang, she expected to hear Norman or Willem asking what was happening.

"Ms. Grant, it's Calum Brownelly."

His voice sounded funny.

"What can I do for you?"

"I have to see you. It's important."

"Where are you?"

"At the liquor store south of you on Yonge Street. It's important. Jay will be okay for a few minutes."

He didn't sound as if he believed a word he was saying, but he was Jay's father. She wouldn't tell the child whom she was meeting or she'd want to go with her.

"Why don't you come here?"

A pause. "It would be better to talk to you without Jay hearing."

What on earth could he have to say? "This better be important. My neighbour is here and she'll hold the fort while I'm gone."

She'd park, talk to him, and then pick up a prepared supper at Best Foods plus a bottle of wine to celebrate Mary's return and her reconciliation with Crystal.

"I'm buying something for supper. Mary's here if you need anything. I'll be right back," she said to the girls and made for the garage.

The van door was unlocked but she often forgot to lock it, feeling perfectly safe in the parking garage. She jumped behind the wheel, bent to slide the key in the ignition, and felt something hard poke her neck.

"Don't move," a voice instructed.

THIRTY-FIVE

BACK at the station, Rhona, still on a high after Tim O'Toole's arrest, walked into homicide, where detectives came and went, phones rang, and a multitude of conversations distracted anyone used to working in silence. Ian sat at his desk writing busily. He looked up when other detectives greeted Rhona.

"Great job. You got O'Toole," he said.

Rhona briefed him.

"Well done. Too bad somebody didn't twig before the women died." Ian indicated the forms in front of him. "I'm recording the details. Do we know why he killed women?"

"Hollis said he called Darlene Ross 'the bitch who thought she was too high and mighty to have sex with him.' And Fatima said Sabrina refused a man who lived in the building. I'm assuming it was O'Toole."

"We'll try to lead him to tell us where to find the other body."

"And there may be others. He is a serial killer."

"He is, but maybe he stopped at two. If there were others he would have kept souvenirs."

"You have to wonder what it is in the background of men like him that sets them on this course." Rhona lifted the pile of paper from her in basket. "Thank god we stopped him. One down, one to go."

"True. Any word on Cartwright?"

"Hollis saw him in the Eaton Centre when she met her foster daughter's father during the lunch hour. I wonder what he was doing there?"

"Probably meeting a Black Hawks contact," Ian said.

"Not only have we alerted the public to watch for him, we've also had watches at the airport, bus terminal, the train station, and the taxi companies. Since we've impounded his car, if he's going to make a run for it, he has to choose some other way."

"The bikers look after their own."

"I don't know the undercover agent's identity, but we have a snout deep in the gang. He'll tell us where Cartwright is. It's only a matter of time. Why do you suppose he killed her? Tough way to get rid of a girlfriend. Maybe he was like O'Toole and couldn't take rejection. Testosterone again."

Ian huffed. "Not necessarily. You can't always blame men's crimes on that. Way too big of a generalization. He pulled his report closer. "Now we have to make sure we've covered all our bases."

"Not much worry in these two."

"Better documented cases than these have gone south because we haven't done our job."

Rhona's phone buzzed. She listened for a moment. "We're on our way."

"Where?" Ian asked.

"Back to the apartment building. Mary Montour has arrived and has papers to give us that relate to Barney Cartwright. Hollis says it's urgent."

Ian drove and Rhona thought about Mary Montour, who'd taken on the task of saving Aboriginal women from the street, from their demons, from the long-term generational effects of the residential schools. What a challenge.

Why hadn't Rhona done something like that?

At least they'd saved Darlene Ross. The Women of the Spirit couldn't fault them on their perseverance and dedication. She knew she'd never again deny her heritage. Sometime soon she'd commit herself to mentoring in the Toronto Aboriginal community, and she'd do it with pride. The report had shaken her and she didn't intend to slip back into complacency and denial.

Her phone rang. She clicked it on and listened.

"Get the registration info. Put out an APB."

"What's happening?" Ian asked intent on edging past a double parked truck.

"Cartwright has kidnapped Hollis."

"How do you know?"

"Cartwright forced Calum Brownelly, her foster child's father, to call Hollis and arrange a meeting."

"Why would he do that?"

"Because Cartwright threatened to hurt the child."

"We have to stop him."

Could they get to Cartwright in time?

THIRTY-SIX

NOT twice in one day. This was too much. Rage, pure rage spurted through Hollis's arteries.

"I came back for some papers. Now you're going to drive me somewhere safe."

Oh, no. Had he found the documents that Mary had hidden? Veronica would have died in vain if that had happened. And he wasn't going to have her drive him somewhere and then allow her to drive away. No. He planned to polish her off like poor Veronica. Not a chance. She'd drive out of here and then deal with the situation.

She drove to Yonge Street. "Hard to turn north. I'll go south."

Her calm voice contrasted with her interior shaking, which had reached earthquake proportions.

"Cherry Beach. There's a boat waiting for me," he said.

Sure, and it had been there for Veronica too.

Where were the police cars when you needed them? South past the intersection at Bloor and through the lights at Wellesley and at Dundas.

She saw her opportunity.

The lights at the intersection of King and Yonge were out, and a police officer directed traffic while the hydro crew worked to repair the traffic light. She'd take care not to hit the police officer, but she'd disobey his signal and slowly crash into whatever came the other way. She undid her safety belt but held it in position, hoping she wouldn't be trapped if the air bag blew up.

Wonder of wonders, the King streetcar entered the intersection and she braked enough to make the impact noisy but non-life threatening. The front of the streetcar hit the passenger side of the van. The air bags blew up.

"Jesus," Cartwright shouted.

She scrambled out of the car.

A shot whistled past her ear, close enough that she felt the rush of air.

She doubled over and ran toward the officer. "Barney Cartwright is the van. He has a gun. He's dangerous," she shouted as she made for the crowd on the curb. The officer called for backup and ordered Cartwright out of the van.

A hydro worker rushed to Hollis, who stood on the curb.

"Are you okay?" he asked.

Hollis reached up and was relieved not to find sticky blood. Her knees wobbled and her breath came in gasps.

"I'm fine."

Cartwright didn't fire again. Instead he raised his arms in a gesture of surrender and waited.

Sirens shrieked and police descended on the intersection. Traffic backed up. A curious crowd collected.

Cartwright disappeared into a police car and the officers found her. After arranging to have her van towed to the Mazda dealership, the police drove her home.

In the car she had time to regulate her breathing, to achieve a degree of calmness. And to wonder why Brownelly had co-operated with Cartwright. Why had he agreed to lure her to the garage?

THIRTY-SEVEN

HOLLIS opened her door and found a crowd in the living room. Detectives Simpson and Gilchrist, Mary, Crystal, Jay, and the two dogs filled the space.

Hollis walked in, collapsed in a chair and, despite her resolve to remain calm, burst into tears.

"What happened? What's wrong?" several voices asked?

"Barney Cartwright kidnapped her. She crashed the van to save herself and allow the police to capture Cartwright. He's now in custody," Rhona said.

Hollis took deep, ragged breaths until she regained her composure. Rhona walked over and patted Hollis's shoulder. "Your quick thinking and courage not only saved you and led to Cartwright's capture, they probably saved other people's lives." She smiled. "I would like to recommend you for an official commendation."

Hollis couldn't believe what she was hearing but it was good news and she thanked Rhona before turning to Mary and Crystal. "You're safe. Did you get to the papers before Cartwright got to them?"

Mary held out her hand to Hollis, who stood up. Mary reached for her other hand. "Thanks to you, I did. The police opened the envelope. Veronica wrote down information about the Black Hawks and the money laundering that Cartwright revealed when he was drunk." She shook her head. "I suspect Veronica planned to blackmail him. She must have told him that she had the information or he wouldn't have come after her. Poor Veronica. To think she could play games with a man like Cartwright."

A knock on the door diverted them from thoughts of Cartwright and Veronica. Hollis freed her hands from Mary's grasp and answered.

Without an invitation Calum Brownelly stepped into the room.

The crowd stared. Rhona stepped forward, a partial smile on her face. Then as quickly as it had come it was gone. But not before Hollis had seen it. Rhona Simpson *knew* Brownelly but wasn't supposed to let others know that she did. What did this mean?

"Daddy. Why are you here?" Jay said and ran to her father, who held her tight.

Hollis stood tall. He had a nerve coming here after what he'd done. If she hadn't thought quickly, she'd be dead.

"Why did you lure me into the car with that thug?" she asked.

Rhona stepped forward as if to intervene but Hollis held up a hand to stop her or anyone else. She wanted answers.

"I am *so* sorry. I can't tell you *how* sorry," he said, his raspy voice even more gravelly than before. "I did call the police as soon as I hung up."

"He did," Gilchrist said.

Hollis examined him. His eyes, his lips, his shoulders, everything drooped. He presented the perfect image of contrition.

"Truly. I am," he said, staring at her over Jay's head.

"You belong to his gang. How did he get you to do it?" she asked?

Brownelly glanced at the assembled crowd. No doubt he hadn't expected to tell his story to the multitude. "You're right. I've known Barney Cartwright for years. He thinks of me as a …" he hesitated.

"As what?"

"Not a friend, a trusted colleague."

"A colleague! He's a murderer, a villain. What does that make you?"

"I'm sorry."

Hollis waited. There had to be more to the story.

"The phone call happened because he met me when I was on my way to see you and Jay." Here he hugged his daughter close. "As I came up the drive, Barney appeared. He stopped me and said he had something to do in the building, but in ten minutes he wanted me to phone you and say I was at the liquor store and had to talk to you."

"Did you ask him why he wanted you to do this?"

"I did and I asked why he didn't simply go in and see you. He said you'd call the police, but he'd be able to talk to you in the liquor store parking lot. I said I couldn't understand why it was necessary." His arms tightened around his daughter. "He threatened to hurt Jay if I asked any more questions or didn't persuade you. He added that nothing would happen but he had to talk to you."

Hollis knew her face must reflect her increasing incredulity. "You believed him? What a cock and bull story."

Brownelly made a rueful face. "I know, but for reasons I can't reveal, I had to play along and pray that when I called the police, they'd find you before he did any harm. If I hadn't made up my mind before I arrived, having Barney make me do that and threaten my daughter would have convinced me."

Hollis leaned forward. "Convinced you of what?"

"That what you said was true. I need to make a home for Jay. I've resigned from my job. I'm taking Jay to Calgary. I have skills I can use and we'll be a family."

Jay reached up and flung her arms around her father's neck. "Dad. Really? Really? Dad I'll be the best daughter ever." She let go and whirled around the room. Her face reflected a joy Hollis had rarely seen. Her cheeks flushed, her eyes sparkled and her smile spread from ear to ear.

Hollis put the pieces together. Rhona knew Brownelly. That must mean that he was *not* a criminal, but Norman had worried about her safety because she knew Brownelly. The Black Hawks intended to kill Norman because he'd testified against them. Norman thought Brownelly belonged to the Black Hawks, but that couldn't be true, because of Rhona's reaction. The only possible conclusion was that Brownelly had worked as an undercover officer.

"That's wonderful news," Hollis said.

In fact, every person in the room smiled.

A knock at the door. Hollis, still smiling, opened it and found Willem.

"I just got your message. I was worrying about you and here I am." He looked past her at the crowd in the living room. "What's happening?"

Hollis pulled him inside. "I have so much to tell you. The murderers have been arrested. Jay's father is here, and he's moving to Calgary with her."

Brownelly addressed the group. "We'll going out to celebrate. It's on me. Let's head for the Old Spaghetti Factory."

Willem pulled Hollis close. He looked at the assembled crowd. "Maybe very soon Hollis and I will have some news for all of us to celebrate," he said and kissed her.

MORE HOLLIS GRANT MYSTERIES

Cut to the Chase
978-1894917896
$16.95

Danson Lafleur's been on a crusade to investigate deported criminals who return undetected to Canada, and now he's missing. Can he be the unidentified man in the morgue? Danson's desperate sister pleads with artist and amateur sleuth Hollis Grant to search for her brother, since the police don't appear to be taking his disappearance seriously. Leads seem to connect Danson and Gregory, his mystery flat-mate, to drugs. But who is Gregory, and what is his connection to the Russian mob? As Hollis investigates, she clashes with homicide detective Rhona Simpson, a woman annoyed by amateur sleuths in general and Hollis Grant in particular. Rhona, adjusting to a new, attractive, enigmatic partner, wants Hollis off the case. Toronto in November is as cold as Danson's trail. Will Hollis connect the dots before the body count rises?

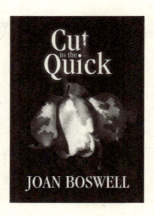

Cut to the Quick
978-1894917476
$14.95

Hollis Grant is in Toronto, hoping for a quiet summer of study. She hopes to spend some time taking a course in painting from her best friend's husband, Curt Hartman. But the murder of her friend's stepson ends those plans as the friend teeters on the edge of hysteria. She needs support and begs Hollis to move in. Hollis discovers that all is not as it seems. Was the stepson the real target or is it his father, famous artist and Hollis's instructor, Curt Hartman? It appears that both father and son have led clandestine lives. Would someone kill them because of their secrets? Hollis poses those questions to Rhona Simpson, the Toronto homicide detective. It soon becomes clear that the crime is the work of a cold-blooded murderer who intends to strike again. Terror mounts at the Hartmans'. Arson, a bomb, a sabotaged sailboat — the killer is closing in. Who will be the next victim?

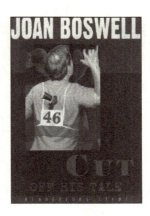

Cut Off His Tale
978-1894917186
$12.95

The starter's gun explodes, and Hollis Grant excitedly begins her very first marathon, only to stumble almost immediately over the body of the Reverend Paul Robertson, her soon-to-be ex-husband. When the crush passes and the medics arrive, it becomes clear that he has not collapsed from the rigours of the race but has been brutally stabbed. Hollis's challenge is to find out who would hate the Reverend enough to stick a knife in his back. Could it be a parishioner at his church who dislikes his activist stance toward gay marriage? Or one troubled soul among the many who have sought his psychological counselling and then found themselves laid bare in the Reverend's latest book? As Hollis and Detective Rhona Simpson probe the secretive life of Paul Robertson, they discover multiple motives. As the murderer comes after Hollis herself, the solution to his murder takes on the urgency of life and death.

Visit us at
Dundurn.com
Definingcanada.ca
@dundurnpress
Facebook.com/dundurnpress